The bird's eye swiveled: lavender. The precise hue of her favorite flower.

I'm sorry, it seemed to say.

Before Kara could swat it away—before she even knew what was happening—the bird swooped onto her neck. Kara heard a *snap* and watched the bird disappear into the Thickety, her necklace held fast in its talons.

"No!" Kara exclaimed, grasping the spot on her chest where the locket had rested for the last seven years.

It was all she had left of her mother.

And it had been stolen.

Without thinking, Kara crawled through the hole in the Thickety, determined to get it back again.

THE THICKETY

A Path Begins

J. A. WHITE

Illustrations by
ANDREA OFFERMANN

 KATHERINE TEGEN BOOKS
An Imprint of HarperCollins Publishers

Katherine Tegen Books
is an imprint of HarperCollins Publishers.

The Thickety: A Path Begins
Text copyright © 2014 by J. A. White
Illustrations copyright © 2014 by Andrea Offermann

Library of Congress Cataloging-in-Publication Data

White, J. A.
    The Thickety : a path begins / J.A. White. — First edition.
        pages   cm
    ISBN 978-0-06-225723-9 (pbk.)
    [1. Magic—Fiction.]   I. Title.   II. Title: Path begins.
PZ7.W58327Th   2014   2013021509
[Fic]—dc23   CIP
                                                                      AC

Typography by Amy Ryan
15 16 17 18 19   CG/RRDH   10 9 8 7 6 5 4 3 2 1
❖
First paperback edition, 2015

For my wife, Yeeshing,
who is all the proof I need
that magic exists

PROLOGUE

Kara lay in bed thinking of names. Mother and Father had yet to settle on one, even though there were only six weeks left until she became a big sister. It was clear that they needed her help. *Jonathan?* No—too common. *Nathaniel?* Not that either—she knew a Nathaniel and he picked his nose. *Samuel?* She liked it, except everyone would end up calling him Sam, and that wouldn't do at all.

I really want it to be Victoria.

Kara giggled softly. It was a pleasant thought, but she was positive the baby would be a boy. Mother had said so, and Mother was always right.

Philip? Edmund? Arthur?

Kara fell asleep.

When she opened her eyes, there were two men standing at her bedside. One was big and one was small. The darkness of the room obscured their features, giving them the appearance of living shadows.

The big one held a potato sack in his hands and shifted from foot to foot.

"Sorry, child," he said.

Grabbing Kara with one massive hand, he yanked her out of bed.

She screamed.

"Don't bother with that," the second man said. "Ain't nobody home but us."

Although Kara scratched at the big man's arms and kicked her feet wildly, she might as well have been fighting a tree for all the good it did. Burlap scratched her cheek as he stuffed her into the sack.

The cord knotted tight above her head. A new, more suffocating darkness enveloped her.

"This one's got a demon's spirit!" the big one said. "See here! She bloodied up my arm."

"It's just a scratch, Josef."

"I should get some ointment after, in case she's the same as her mother. Could be it's a spreading type of thing."

"Don't be a fool."

"Easy for you to say. She didn't scratch you."

Floorboards creaked as the small man bent next to the potato sack. Kara listened to his short, sharp breaths less than a foot from her ear.

"She ain't dead, is she?" Josef asked.

"No," the man replied. "She's listening carefully. Aren't you, little one?"

Kara, despite her best efforts, let a whimper escape her lips.

"Don't be scared," he said. Even through the thick

material of the sack, Kara could smell his breath, a mixture of boiled turnips and the clear liquor Father called moondrink. "We ain't gonna do you no harm. The head man himself sent us, and he told us that. 'Be careful,' he said, 'but don't hurt her. Not until we're sure.'"

There was a long pause, and then both men burst into laughter. Kara heard the pop of a bottle being uncorked and slurping sounds as each man drank from it.

"I want Mommy," she said.

"Good," the man replied. "Because that's where we're taking you."

They tossed her into an open wagon and sped through the night.

The road was bumpy, and the wagon's frame shook and rattled in protest, bucking Kara from one side of the flatbed to the other. Splinters and ill-hammered nails scratched bloody lines on her skin.

Finally the wagon came to a stop.

She was slung over someone's shoulder—Josef, no doubt. He had the same moondrink smell as the small man and tottered a bit as he walked. Kara did not think it was from her weight.

The two men exchanged not a word, and their sudden silence discomforted her.

"Where are we going?" Kara asked.

No response.

"Tell me where we're going!" As she spoke Kara pounded her fists against Josef's back. He tightened his grip slightly but otherwise showed no reaction.

They continued onward. Kara listened carefully to the too-quiet night. Nothing but silence, save the measured, rhythmic patter of boots against earth.

Until someone coughed.

The sound came from Kara's right. She supposed it could have been the smaller man, but Kara didn't think so. It sounded like the cough of a woman.

They were not alone.

"Help!" Kara screamed. "Please help me!"

Kara's pleas were answered by the creaking of stairs, straining beneath the huge man's weight. The night air slipped its cold fingers around Kara and squeezed tightly.

Where are we? she thought.

Kara was dumped from the potato sack and given her answer. She was on a small scaffold in the unused field north of the village, one of the only places in De'Noran where crops refused to grow. The scaffold rose about ten feet off the ground and teetered unsteadily. In the distance the black-leaved trees of the Thickety swayed toward Kara and then away, as though beckoning her.

Kara had been in this field yesterday, picking wildflowers as she waited for news of Mother. The scaffold had not been there.

They had built it in the night.

"Good evening, Kara," said a familiar voice.

Fen'de Stone bent down before her. He was tall, with a thatch of thick brown hair tied in a neat ponytail, and wore the crimson robe that befitted his position as leader of De'Noran. One eye was slightly larger than the other, though both were the same piercing blue. "Predator eyes," Kara's father called them—but only within the privacy of their home, and even then with a hushed voice.

Those unblinking eyes stared into Kara's now, as though searching for something.

"I apologize if they frightened you, dear. It would have been best to simply explain the situation and bring you here peacefully. But all of this has happened so quickly— we couldn't take any chances."

Kara felt dizzy. She should have been asleep, not shivering in the night while speaking to the leader of her village about things she did not understand.

"Where's Mother?" she asked. "Where's Father?" Surely they would be able to explain.

Fen'de Stone looked surprised. The expression rested uneasily on his face, like an ill-fitting mask.

"Why—they're here, Kara," he said. "We're all here. Didn't you notice?"

He stepped to the side.

A sea of faces stretched out across the field. The entire population of De'Noran— men, women, and children— standing as still as scarecrows. All eyes on her.

Kara saw the old wagon that had brought her here in the distance. The crowd must have parted to allow them passage to the scaffold. Her friends and neighbors had been mere inches from her captors, knowing what was happening. Allowing it.

Standing behind her now, Fen'de Stone placed one hand on her shoulder and squeezed gently.

"Even your brother is here, Kara."

"My brother?"

"That's right. He was born last night."

A brother. Just like Mother said.

But if her parents were truly here, why did they not call out for her?

Kara scanned the crowd, searching for their faces. This was not easy, for De'Noran was a large village, and though the night was dark, few people held lanterns. Nonetheless Kara was able to make out one familiar face after another. Baker Corbett, who slipped her a fresh sweet roll each time she passed his shop. Gregor Thompson, the owner of the farmland adjoining theirs, who took his coffee in Kara's kitchen most nights. And just beneath the scaffold: Grace, a girl about her own age, brilliant blue eyes glowing with excitement.

Finally she saw Father standing between two gray-cloaks. The crowd to either side of them had parted slightly, giving them space.

"Father!" Kara exclaimed. "Father! What's happening?"

Her father did not respond, but his eyes met hers. They were wet with tears.

"Father!"

In his arms he cradled a small object in a plain, brown blanket.

I have a brother, Kara thought.

"Father! Help me!"

His mouth tightened and he looked ready to step forward, but the graycloak to his left clenched his ball-staff tighter and shook his head. With slumping shoulders, Father backed down.

"I need you to see something, Kara," said Fen'de Stone.

"Can I go to Father?"

"Maybe later. Afterward. If all goes well, you can hold your brother. Would you like that, Kara?"

Kara nodded.

"He's beautiful. Pure. His name is Taff."

"Taff."

The name had not been one of the possibilities they'd discussed, the three of them squeezed into bed together, laughing. But she knew it was the perfect choice the moment she heard it.

"Taff."

Despite everything, Kara smiled. She had a brother.

"I need you to look up, child. At that tree there."

But it was such a cold night. A newborn babe

shouldn't be out here right now. He should be home, by the fire. . . .

Fen'de Stone snapped his fingers in her face.

"Look up. Now."

Kara did as she was told.

Mother's hands had been bound together and hooked over a thick branch; her feet dangled fifteen feet from the ground. She was blindfolded and gagged.

Kara screamed.

At the sound of her daughter's voice, Helena Westfall jerked against her restraints. A nervous murmur went through the crowd, the first sound they had made since Kara's arrival.

"Have no fear," Fen'de Stone told them. "She no longer poses a threat."

A gnawing emptiness, not unlike hunger, spread through Kara's stomach.

Until this moment Kara had been confused and frightened, but these emotions were now replaced by something more powerful.

Rage.

She turned on the fen'de, no longer caring that he was the most important man in the village.

"You hurt her!"

Kara flailed her fists against the man's chest. He made no move to stop her, simply watched with cold amusement.

"Your mother is a witch, Kara. A danger to De'Noran."

"Liar!"

"She has gone into the Thickety and communed with the Forest Demon."

"That's not true! Mother is good!"

"She killed two people."

"Stop it! Stop lying!"

"There were witnesses, Kara. Respected citizens of De'Noran. They saw her work black magic with their own eyes. Widow Gable. Master Blackwood."

"No! No! No!"

Fen'de Stone grabbed Kara's fists and stared into her eyes.

"Your father, girl! Your own father admits it!"

Kara slumped to the wooden floor of the scaffold. She looked up at her mother, who had once again stopped moving. Then to Father.

"Make him stop it," Kara said. "Make him stop lying."

But her father's eyes were unable to meet her own, and she knew then that Fen'de Stone spoke the truth.

The world began to spin.

"How many years have you?" asked Fen'de Stone.

Kara felt so sleepy. It was hard to understand what the words meant.

"Your age, Kara. How old are you?"

"Five."

"Five," the fen'de repeated. He sighed dramatically. "It is too late, no doubt. But the Children of the Fold are just in all things, and we shall learn if you have inherited your mother's powers. If you, Kara Westfall, are a witch as well."

It was then that Kara noticed the second tree. Smaller than her mother's but with an identical peg pounded into its bark.

"You understand, then," Fen'de Stone said, following her eyes. "That's good. Easier."

"I'm not a witch."

The fen'de smiled, and Kara realized, with a sickening feeling, that the man was having fun.

"A promising beginning," he said, clasping his hands together. "But let's find out for sure, shall we?"

Josef and the smaller man—who Kara now recognized as Bailey Riddle, the gravedigger—led the creature through the crowd. It most closely resembled a dog, with jet-black fur streaked with gray and an elongated snout. Fur hung loosely from its frame, as though the animal had been cursed with an overabundance of skin.

"Their kind has become rare, a shadow of their former selves," Fen'de Stone said. "In the Old Stories, these beasts walked proudly with the great hunters and helped them track witches to the darkest corners of the World." The leader's eyes grew distant, reimagining the former glory of his people. "We used to call them by their true names. Gant-ruaal! Thrandix! Danik Juzel! In these ignorant times, however, they are known as nightseekers."

The strange creature was having trouble navigating the stairs. Josef gave its chain a vicious tug, and the nightseeker, emitting a low-pitched squeal, dragged itself forward on folded-back paws. Despite her terror Kara felt a rush of sympathy for the thing. When it finally reached the top of the scaffold, it looked at her askance, with violet eyes that would have been pretty on a less monstrous frame.

Fen'de Stone nodded to Josef, who slowly untwisted the chain from his arm and set the creature free.

"Go," Fen'de Stone said, clicking his tongue and gesturing toward Kara. "Tell."

The nightseeker eased itself to its feet and made its

way forward. Kara tried to move, but Riddle held her in place.

"Watch this," he whispered in her ear. "It's *something*."

The nightseeker shifted forward until its long snout made contact with the scaffold, and then it extended its rear legs, revealing two large, hairless paws. Its front legs unfolded next, the cracks of shifting bones reverberating loudly through the silent night as the creature grew before her eyes. Soon it was twice its original size, three times. The makeshift scaffold groaned in protest under this surprising new weight.

The nightseeker sat back on its haunches. Its whimpers grew to a piteous whine as a translucent needle, as long as Kara's forearm, emerged from its front paw. The beast looked up and bared its teeth, revealing large, jagged incisors that had not been there a moment ago.

"I would take a step back, Bailey," Fen'de Stone said softly, "if I were you."

Kara's arms were released half a moment before the

nightseeker leaped across the scaffold and knocked her to the floor. It placed one massive paw on Kara's chest and gazed into her eyes. Warm slobber dangled from its mouth.

Kara did not realize the needle had pierced her arm until the nightseeker sat back and regarded the blood at its tip. At first Kara thought it might lick it, but instead the nightseeker plunged the needle deeply into its nostril. With a shudder of its massive body, it sucked up her blood and snorted deeply.

After a considerate pause, the nightseeker straightened, as though a decision had been made. It raised its needle paw high into the air and angled it toward Kara's right eye.

"No!" she screamed. "Please!"

The nightseeker's other paw was an impossible weight on her chest. No matter how hard she jerked and twisted, she could not move a single inch. Each breath was a struggle.

"Judgment has been delivered!" Fen'de Stone proclaimed. "It looks like we'll be ridding the world of two witches tonight! A return to glory for the Children of the Fold!"

The crowd erupted into cheers.

"No," Kara said, but her voice was quiet now. "I'm not a witch."

The needle inched closer to her eye until it was all Kara could see, a clear pinpoint in the night.

"I'm not a witch. I'm not bad."

She stared ahead, wanting to close her eyes but needing to see.

"I'm a good girl."

The crowd began to clap. A steady rhythm.

"Don't hurt me."

Looking past the needle, Kara met the violet eyes of the nightseeker.

"Don't hurt me!"

The creature shuddered and made a noise deep within

its throat. The crowd had grown far too loud for anyone to hear it, but it wasn't a growl, not exactly. There was no fury in it.

With one swift motion, the nightseeker backed off Kara's chest, the needle already retracting into its paw. By the time it had gone three steps, its body had shrunk to its original, innocuous form. Looking tired and drained, the creature tottered toward the stairs.

The crowd grew silent.

Fen'de Stone regarded Kara, his eyes narrowed to dangerous slits.

"What did you do?"

Kara shook her head. She hadn't done anything.

"A spell. You cast a spell, didn't you?"

Kara shook her head again.

"You bewitched this creature and—"

"That girl didn't do nothing!" From her position on the scaffold, Kara couldn't see the speaker, but it was a woman's voice.

"That's right!"

"That creature of yours made its choice, all right."

"She ain't no witch!"

"Let her go!"

This last voice Kara recognized. Her father.

Others joined in, murmuring their agreement. The bloodlust of the crowd had been extinguished by shame. Whereas before they had seen a demon in a child's skin, all they saw now was a little girl, shivering with fear.

Fen'de Stone raised one hand into the air, commanding their silence.

"Of course," he said. He wore a smile of relief on his face, but Kara knew that it was just for show. "It appears as though she's not a witch after all. How fortunate."

He held out a hand to Kara.

"Allow me to help you to your feet, dear. I am so sorry if we scared you—but I'm sure you understand. One can never be too careful about these things."

"My mother," she said.

"Oh yes," the fen'de replied, and his smile transformed into something far more genuine, far more terrible. "Your mother."

Afterward the crowd began to shuffle toward the village, conversations already turning back to practical matters such as livestock and fertilizer. The sun had risen in the sky, the day's work begun.

Kara's father stood at the base of the stairs. The baby in his arms wailed fiercely.

"He's hungry," Father said. There was a large, red welt on his cheek where one of the graycloaks had struck him. He refused to meet her eyes.

Kara looked at the small bundle in his arms.

"Can I hold him?" she asked.

Father nodded, passing the baby to Kara with a relieved expression on his face. He collapsed to the earth as though holding his son had been the only thing keeping him on his feet.

"I'm sorry," he mumbled. "I'm sorry. I'm sorry. I'm—"

Kara left him and started toward the village.

Gently folding back the blanket, Kara regarded the newest member of her family. She hadn't seen many babies before, but she could tell that Taff was small, even for a newborn. His eyes, barely open, were light like their father's.

"Hello, baby brother," she said. "My name is Kara."

The morning was cold, and Kara held him close, trying to pass her warmth into him.

"I have sad news, Baby Taff. You'll never get to meet Mama. But you don't have to worry. I'll always be here. I'll always protect you."

Kara took one last look across the field. Her mother's body had been removed. Workers were already dismantling the scaffold. The only sounds came from a group of giggling children tossing pinecones at Bailey Riddle, who spun round and round and screamed girlishly in mock pain.

"No one is ever going to hurt you," Kara whispered to the baby.

She stared at Bailey Riddle until he finally looked up and met her gaze. Unlike Taff, Kara had her mother's eyes, black as a forest night.

The man gasped.

"No one," she said.

Kara held her brother close the entire walk back to the village. By the time they reached their house, he had fallen asleep in her arms.

Bailey Riddle died later that night, viciously attacked by some sort of wild animal. There were no witnesses, and as Bailey was not especially well liked, he was simply buried and forgotten.

These things did happen.

BOOK ONE
SIGNS

*"A witch often hides behind
an innocent face.
That's why you must know
the signs to look for."*

—The Path
Leaf 17, Vein 26

ONE

Hand in hand, the witch's children walked down the empty road.

The girl, twelve and as thin as a willow branch, wore a simple black school dress with a white collar, patched in several places but immaculately clean. Her dark hair was coiled in a tight bun. Sometimes she allowed a few rebellious strands to hang across her forehead, but not today.

Her name was Kara. Mostly she was called other things.

Taff, her brother, was small for his age, with sandy

hair. The morning was cold, and twin blooms of red spotted his pale cheeks. Without thinking, Kara reached over and checked his temperature with the back of her hand.

In the distance a figure approached.

It was early, even for the few farmers who used this road to transport their goods to the main village. Past hills of plotted land, sunlight peeked through the sky-scratching branches of the Thickety like an uncertain visitor.

Taff squeezed his sister's hand.

The figure drew close enough for Kara to recognize the plodding gait of Davin Gray. He lived on the edge of the island but spent most of his time traveling from farm to farm, making repairs. She had once asked him to patch their roof when Father had been in a bad way. Davin Gray had laughed in her face.

Despite this, Kara knew her manners.

"Good morning, Mr. Gray," she said. She squeezed Taff's hand, who surrendered a quiet, "Morning."

Refusing to meet their eyes, the man spat on the ground and traced a path as far from the pair as the road would take him.

"Evil," he growled. "Just like the mother."

When Davin Gray had passed, the children, used to such encounters, continued their journey. Perhaps Kara held her brother a bit closer. That was all.

I don't want to do this, Kara thought as they approached the farmhouse. She started to turn around but then remembered her desperation last night upon boiling water and finding nothing—literally nothing—in the cupboard to cook. What Kara *wanted* wasn't important anymore. It was all about need.

Before she could change her mind, Kara trudged up the wooden steps, dragging Taff behind her. The farmhouse had recently been whitewashed, and an expensive Fenroot branch hung across the door so Timoth Clen would recognize the residents' devotion upon his Return.

It reminded Kara that she needed to chop some firewood before night fell.

She took a moment to straighten her dress before knocking on the door.

"Be good," she told Taff.

Taff nodded.

"Promise."

"It ain't me. They're the ones——"

"Promise."

Taff sighed deeply. "I promise, Kara."

The door opened.

Constance Lamb's face, a poorly harrowed field of scars, loomed before them. Kara looked away. *The sins of my mother are not mine to bear,* she reminded herself, but the thought provided little comfort. It never did.

"What are you doing here?" Constance asked. She wore a freshly starched housedress and a white linen bonnet. Even the clouds of flour on her apron looked neat and orderly.

"Good morning, Mrs. Lamb."

"It's barely morning at all. And I asked you a question."

"I'm here about your horse, ma'am. Mr. Lamb sent for me. He spoke to my father and told him he had a mare with a gimp foot. My father suggested I offer my assistance. I'm good with animals."

Constance inhaled, slowly and deeply, then freed the air through clenched teeth.

"Well, if there was such an arrangement, it's the first I've heard of it."

"Mr. Lamb agreed to two browns."

"Two!" Constance held a hand to her heart as though such an outlandish sum might strike her dead on the spot. But Kara felt that the price—which would buy them little more than a dozen eggs and some new socks for Taff—was more than fair.

"I'll do a good job," Kara said. "I promise. I'm good—"

"—with animals. Yes, you mentioned that."

Kara waited. There was no sense in speaking more.

The woman would either allow her to earn the seeds or she would not.

"You can find your way to the stable, I presume?" Constance finally asked.

"Yes, ma'am. What's the mare's name?"

"Shadowdancer's what we call her. Though I don't see why it matters any."

It mattered a lot, but Kara didn't bother explaining. Constance wouldn't understand, and the truth would only cause rumors and whispers.

"May as well know, that horse is crazy. Don't let my husband or any of the farmhands near her on a good day, and now that she's hurting . . ." Constance shook her head. "Broke Eric Whitney's arm when he tried to help her."

"Don't worry, Mrs. Lamb. I'll be careful."

"Be quick about it, then."

Constance began to close the door.

"Ma'am! There is one other thing."

"What now?"

Kara wasn't sure how to begin. It had been so long since she asked for another person's help that the words felt strange, a language unspoken for years. But once upon a time, Constance Lamb had been her mother's friend, and Kara hoped that still counted for something.

"It's a cold morning, and my brother has been frequently ill."

Taff tugged at his sister's hand. "I'm fine!"

"If it's at all possible, could he wait inside your house while I attend to Shadowdancer? You needn't even know he's there. Taff is as quiet——"

"I am not staying with this loony old mudswallow."

"——as a mouse."

Constance regarded the two of them, and Taff in particular, with what might have been the slightest hint of amusement.

"Wait," she said, and went back into the house.

Kara and Taff stood in silence, Kara glaring at her brother.

"What?" he asked.

Constance returned with a thick, woolen blanket and a pair of mittens.

"Take these. Leave the blanket on the bench outside the stable when you leave. The mittens are far too big for you, but you can keep them anyway. I knitted them for my husband, but he refuses to wear them. Says they're 'itchy.' Consider it a gift from a—what was it?—loony old mudswallow."

Constance Lamb shut the door in their faces before they could thank her.

It was the blanket—and not the mittens—that made Taff's skin itch, but within minutes Kara noticed that he had stopped sniffling as much. Mrs. Lamb's gifts were a threadbare sort of kindness, but a kindness nonetheless.

"Can't I come with you?" Taff asked when they had reached the stable.

"No."

"I want to see."

"It's just a horse."

"But I love horses. They're interesting."

Interesting was Taff's newest word, and he used it as frequently as possible, playing with it like a new toy.

"You know what'll happen," she said.

Saying this made Kara feel cruel, but Taff needed to accept the truth of things; he couldn't get close to an animal without gasping for breath, or getting a headache, or breaking out into a coughing fit, or all of the above. Once he had stubbornly fed the sheep, and angry red splotches had erupted all over his body.

"I brought an apple," Taff said. "To feed him."

"It's a her. And she's sick, so she would probably just spit it out."

Taff withdrew the fruit from his pocket and offered it to his sister. It was shrunken and sad, the only type of crop their fields produced these days.

"Could you give it to her anyway?" he asked softly.

"And tell her it's from me?"

Kara stroked her brother's hair, which had begun to curl around his ears. She mentally added "give Taff a haircut" to her list of chores.

"I can do that."

After making sure that Taff had his drawing pad and a piece of charcoal, Kara entered the stable. She found Shadowdancer in the last stall. The mare was as large as a draft horse, with glossy black hair and wiry muscles. A silver puddle spilled across her neck like moonlight.

"I'm here to help you," Kara said, patting the horse's flank. Shadowdancer regarded her cautiously but did not shy away. "I might be able to make the hurt go away, if you let me."

Kara needed to see the injured leg, but she couldn't just grab it—that would be a breach of trust—so she asked the horse, singing the song her mother had taught her so many years ago, the one with the words Kara didn't understand, whispering it in Shadowdancer's ear like a lullaby.

Shadowdancer raised her hoof.

Kara saw the problem instantly: a too-small puncture rimmed with red. Unless the infection was given enough room to drain, the sickness would spread up Shadowdancer's leg, and once it did the blood fever would overtake her and make recovery impossible. It was a common problem, but one that had to be fixed quickly.

Reaching into the pocket of her dress, Kara withdrew a penknife. Shadowdancer bucked and turned, but Kara sang her mother's song again, her hand straying to the wooden locket beneath her dress, and the mare's eyes glazed over. Kara dug deeply into the hoof and quickly made two new holes to either side of the main wound, then packed all three with a poultice that would draw the infection downward. The medicine was her mother's recipe, ground together from Fringe weeds—two little facts Kara would *not* be mentioning to the Lambs.

"I doubt the next few hours will be very pleasant,"

she whispered in the horse's ear. "But after that you'll be fine." She slipped Taff's apple into Shadowdancer's mouth. "That's from my brother, Taff. He's sick like you. But you're both going to be better soon." She stroked Shadowdancer's mane, and a warm feeling—the feeling that she had done something good and right—expanded throughout her body.

With newfound confidence Kara searched the barn for Jacob Lamb, intending to get her seeds before she left for school. She found the farmer feeding his pigs, a squirming mass of mud-cloaked bodies packed tightly into a pen. They snorted fiercely as he dumped a bucket of cornmeal onto the ground.

"How's my animal?" Jacob asked. He spoke slowly, but his eyes were quick and sharp.

"Shadowdancer's wound got infected. But she's going to be fine now," Kara said.

Jacob stood there. He seemed content to stand there forever.

"Sir?" Kara shifted uncomfortably. "You spoke to my father of payment?"

Kara couldn't hear his reply over the cacophony of snorting. Jacob kicked one of the pigs and called it something indecipherable.

"Pardon me?" she asked.

"By the farmhouse, there's three bushels of corn! Take a few ears!"

"Corn."

"Picked it this morning."

"You promised my father that I would be paid with seeds." She winced at how weak she sounded. "Two browns, to be exact."

"You know your father. He don't always remember things right."

"He wouldn't forget this."

Jacob shrugged. "Maybe I did say two browns. Maybe not. I don't see why it matters none." He placed a single gray seed in Kara's hand and closed her fingers around it.

"There's no reason to pay you at all. You understand that? You tell anyone I cheated you, and I'll just say you're a liar. Now who do you think they're going to believe? A fine, upstanding farmer like myself? Or the daughter of a known witch?"

Kara clenched her fist around the gray, a tenth of the agreed price. "It's not fair," she said, close to tears and hating herself for it.

"Of course it ain't," Jacob said. He chortled. "But take a few ears of corn too. I'm feeling downright charitable today." He turned his back and poured water into the swine trough, continuing with his day as though she had already left. *You shouldn't treat me this way*, Kara thought, scratching her palm with work-worn nails. She imagined the pigs seizing upon the man, snorts and screams and gnashing teeth blending together as he struggled in vain to escape. . . .

"Hey!" Jacob shouted. He shook Kara, snapping her back to reality. "What are you doing? *Stop staring at me like that!*"

"I'm sorry," she said, backing away. "I'm so sorry!" Looking past the farmer, she saw the pigs lined up at the edge of the pen, watching her with rapt attention. They had finally stopped snorting.

The children made their way back up the hill, the boy wearing his new mittens, the girl clutching a potato sack that held six ears of corn. They did not speak. This was difficult for the boy, who loved to fill the air with words. He had grown proficient at reading the various silences of his sister, however, and he recognized, from her tight lips and the white-knuckled way she clenched the sack, that this was the type of silence best left unbroken.

Neither of them noticed the bird.

It perched on a branch just above them, a single eye set into its breast. The creature regarded the girl and noted, with special interest, the wooden locket around her neck. Its eye spun like a top and flashed a panoply of colors—stone gray, ocean blue, forest green— before settling on a fiery crimson. The bird watched the children until they were gone, then extended its wings and swooped with surprising speed toward the Thickety, eager to make its report. After all these years, the girl was finally ready.

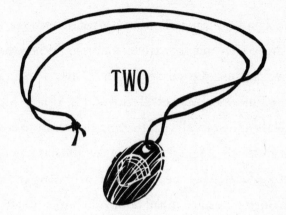

TWO

Kara was late. She walked between the perfectly spaced desks, past girls in their identical school dresses and boys in white shirts and suspenders. Eyes straight ahead. No eye contact, that was the trick. The less they noticed her, the less they would hate her. From the corner of her eye, she saw that Grace's seat was empty, and even though Kara wanted to shout with joy, she kept her face void of emotion. They didn't like it when she smiled.

Kara slid into her seat just as Master Blackwood entered the room. The old man, holding a freshly cut switch from a tamarind tree, gazed out at his young charges, waiting for silence. He did not have to wait long. When the switch leaned against the corner of the room—that was one thing. But when Master Blackwood held it in his hands, the class understood what that implied: a promise of pain. And although age might have caused the old schoolmaster to stoop over when he walked or occasionally forget his path during lessons, it had not made him any slower—or less forgiving—in his disciplinary duties.

"Work hard, want nothing," Master Blackwood intoned.

"Stay vigilant," the students replied in unison.

Master Blackwood smiled and touched the shoulder of a boy in the first row who was just a few years older than Taff. Students at the Older Schoolhouse ranged from eight to fourteen, but it was no secret that Master Blackwood favored the younger children.

"As you know, before he recorded his teachings in the Path, Timoth Clen cleansed the world of witches, sacrificing himself so we could enjoy almost two thousand years of peace." He made his way deeper into the classroom, finding them one at a time with his eyes, the switch a constant presence in his hands. "But despite what those ungrateful fools in the World might believe, that does not mean magic is dead. We, the loyal followers of the Clen's teachings, know that *for sure*." He paused in front of Kara, and she felt a bead of sweat roll down her neck. *What am I going to be blamed for now?* "And so, my pupils, you must learn to recognize the signs of a soul in danger. Not just in danger of becoming a witch, but in danger of embracing magic in its worldly forms as well, for even this is a fall from the Path. We must remain ever vigilant, so we will be prepared when Timoth Clen returns to lead our people to glory once more."

Master Blackwood left Kara's desk and continued to the front of the classroom. She sighed with relief.

"'What signs should I look for?' you ask." He held out a hand and counted them off. "A child who is not satisfied with an honest day spent toiling in the fields. A child who wants more. A child who *dreams*. For when the heart desires something, what doors do we open? What demons do we invite to take up residence in our souls?" He paused here, his old lips quivering with excitement. "Wouldn't you agree, Mr. Harris?"

Benjamin Harris, a ten-year-old boy with ruddy cheeks and an overabundance of red hair, bolted upright in his seat.

"Yes," he said. "Of course. Sir."

Master Blackwood nodded, tapping the switch lightly against his open palm. "I'm so relieved to hear that. Come to the front of the room, please."

Benjamin looked to his schoolmates for help, but suddenly they were all busy studying their desktops. Kara felt bad for him. She wouldn't have called Benjamin her friend, but he had never been cruel to her, never taken part in Grace's games.

At the front of the room now, Benjamin stared nervously at Master Blackwood.

"Shadow Festival draws near."

"Yes, sir."

"Do you like the holiday, Benjamin?"

The boy swallowed nervously, unsure what answer the teacher expected. He gave a hesitant nod.

"That's good," said Master Blackwood. "I did as well, when I was your age. What would you say is your favorite part of the Shadow Festival?" Benjamin was about to answer, but Master Blackwood held up one hand. "Let me guess. Is it Widow Miller's famous cider dumplings?"

"Why, yes, sir. That's right," said Benjamin.

"They are good, aren't they?"

Benjamin broke into a toothy grin. "I wait the whole year for 'em. My mother tries to make them, but it isn't the same. She gets so mad when I tell her Widow Miller's are better."

Master Blackwood laughed softly and draped one arm around his student. "Too bad we couldn't have one right now."

"It's funny you should say that! Just yesterday I was

telling my friends that I—"

Suddenly he stopped, covering his mouth with one hand.

"Go on, Benjamin. Tell me what you told your friends."

"I'd rather not, sir."

"Why not? *They* had no problem telling *me*. Please, share your words with the class. Of course, if you'd rather tell Fen'de Stone himself, I'm sure a visit from our great leader could be arranged. . . ."

"I said I wished I could eat a dumpling now," Benjamin said.

The room erupted into gasps and shocked whispers.

"Quiet!" exclaimed Master Blackwood. "Now, Benjamin, should a Child of the Fold ever *wish* for something?"

"No, sir."

"And why is that?"

Benjamin's lips began to tremble. He was fighting back tears, but it was a losing battle. "Because wishing can't make something happen. It's just another form of magic.

And magic is the worst sin of all. Sir."

"Good, son. That's good." Master Blackwood raised the switch high into the air. "Now hold out your hands so we can get this done with. We've already used a lot of class time."

The rest of the morning continued without incident. Arithmetic. A history lesson about Timoth Clen's first battle with the Cave Witches. Copying a passage from the Path onto their slates.

Finally students were given a short period for lunch. Carefully avoiding eye contact, Kara weaved through the small groups of children seated together on the front grass. Her stomach growled at the smells of fried turnip cakes and cinnamon bread, but she fingered the gray in her pocket, and her spirits lifted. *I have enough here to buy a small sweetmelon—past its prime, no doubt, but better than nothing at all. Won't Father be surprised when I bring home his favorite—*

Something cold splattered against her back.

Kara kept walking, ignoring the laughter behind her. She had learned that this was the best thing to do; any reaction at all would only encourage them. *It's just mud, easy enough to wash away.* "Next time it'll be a stone, Witch Girl!" someone shouted. "Just like your mother!" added another, but as the taunting began in earnest Kara slipped behind the schoolhouse, where no one would follow her.

The trail was muddy and uneven, but Kara knew this particular hill well and quickly reached the summit. The wind had grown teeth since morning, and she hugged herself as she looked down upon the island. Neatly plotted farms colored the land brown and tan and green; beyond this the ocean stretched as far as the eye could see. Just below Kara, to the south, shops and small buildings slumbered after the morning rush. A lone wagon shuddered over a rocky patch of earth as it left the village.

West, east, south. In these directions De'Noran seemed like the perfect sanctuary for the chosen followers of Timoth Clen.

Kara looked north.

There, even the sky was different, a sickly gray infected with sagging clouds. The dangerous weeds of the Fringe blanketed the northernmost edge of De'Noran, ending at mountainous trees that stood trunk to trunk like sentinels, concealing any view of the mysterious forest that covered nearly three-quarters of the island. It had many names, this place. Sometimes they called it the Dark Wood, or the Forest of Forbidden Gifts, or just Sordyr's Realm. But mostly they called it the Thickety.

"I was starting to wonder if you'd lost your way."

Kara smiled and hurried to a boulder perched precariously over the southern edge. Here, gazing out at the ocean, sat a boy. She sat down beside him, allowing her feet to dangle over nothingness.

Lucas Walker was thirteen years old, with soft brown eyes and green-tinged hair. Unlike the boys at school, in their white shirts and neatly pressed black trousers, Lucas wore the plain brown frock of a Clearer. His fingernails were dyed green from his work, and Kara could smell the Fringe smoke that clung to his skin and clothes no matter how hard he scrubbed.

"I'm sorry I'm late," Kara said.

Lucas eyed the wet patch of mud on her back. He motioned for her to turn around so he could wipe it away as best he could.

"What was old Blackwood rattling on about today?" Lucas asked. "Let me guess." He sat up straight and spoke in a nasally voice that was a more than fair approximation of the old schoolmaster. "You can see witches every-where, if you know what signs to look for. For instance, if a child has a birthday once, that's fine, but if they have one *every year*? It's magic, I tell you. Magic! Another sign to look for are children who walk with their feet! Or breathe through their noses! Oh yes—the dreaded nose-breathers! Those are the very worst of all!"

Kara started to laugh, then clapped her hand over her

mouth; such talk could get them in trouble with the gray-cloaks if they were overheard.

Lucas wiped off the last of the mud. "Better?" he asked.

Kara nodded.

"It's strange," she said, hugging her knees to her chest. "If they really thought I was a witch, you'd think they'd fear me. And if they feared me, you'd think they'd be . . ."

"Less like rabid wolves?"

She shrugged. "Different."

Lucas took a sip of his sludge-like tea, wincing slightly. All Clearers drank the tea daily to rid their systems of the noxious smoke they inhaled; it tasted terrible, but it kept them alive. "Thirsty?" Lucas asked, smiling. "It's particularly awful today." Kara stuck out her tongue. She had never been able to keep down a single sip, and Lucas enjoyed goading her about it.

Suddenly his face grew serious.

"The Fringe weeds are sprouting faster than I've ever seen," he said, pushing back his hair. "Everyone is working fourteen-hour shifts, but it seems like we never catch up. And when we do . . . the Thickety still seems a tiny bit closer. We won't be able to hold it off forever. The weeds are growing more dangerous too. You remember my friend Garren?"

Kara nodded. The young Clearer had once offered to carry a bushel of hushfruit for her. She imagined she would remember him forever.

"He stepped on a wisp of blue ivy—something none of us had ever seen before, even the old-timers—and it nearly burned through his entire shoe in seconds. We got it off just in time. Watched his boot sink into the earth and just keep falling, like it was kissed by Sordyr himself."

Kara paled, and a silence fell between them.

"Sorry," Lucas said.

Unlike most Clearers, Lucas was not the superstitious sort and spoke the name of the Forest Demon as easily as his own. But in just their few short years together, Kara's mother had imbued her with such a complete and all-consuming fear of Sordyr that it remained strong to this day.

"I have had a most interesting morning," Kara said. As she told him the particulars Lucas listened as he always did, with eyes fixed firmly on hers. If there was anyone who could help her understand what had happened, it was Lucas.

"What I imagined the pigs doing to him—it was terrible," she said. "I wanted to punish him."

"Good! I want to punish him too! He cheated you!"

"But these are thoughts no one should have. Especially a Child of the Fold."

"They're just thoughts," Lucas said. He turned to face her. "You didn't do anything wrong. No matter what they say, you're not like her. You need to remember that."

As Kara looked up to meet his eyes she saw a black shape flutter to the back of Lucas's shirt.

"Don't move," she said.

"What?"

"*Shh*," she said, rising to her feet and circling around him. "Talking is moving."

"No. Talking is telling me what's going on."

She found the squit, no larger than a thimble, positioned between Lucas's shoulder blades. Its mandibles were already extended and feeling for the best spot to begin.

"It's a squit," Kara said.

"I don't know what that is. Is it bad? It sounds bad."

"They're rare. Usually they come out only in the warmer months, unless they're mating. Then——"

"Does it bite?"

"Not . . . exactly."

"That really wasn't the answer I was hoping for."

A corkscrew tongue unfolded from the squit's mouth and spun in a counterclockwise direction. It poked through the fabric of Lucas's frock and began to burrow. Lucas tensed as a tiny pinpoint of blood rose to the surface of his skin.

"Stay still," Kara said. She was afraid that if she tried to grab the squit, she might accidentally scare it into burrowing even faster, so she laid her index finger flat against Lucas's back. "Come here," she said, and the squit retracted its tongue and slipped onto her finger. She cupped her hands around the tiny creature, and its wings thrummed with obvious pleasure.

What does it mean, she thought, *that something so deadly regards me with such affection?*

"You're wrong," she told Lucas, her voice no more than a whisper. "I'm just like her."

Kara uncupped her hands and released the squit. It flew north.

THREE

The general store was packed with people. Kara held Taff's hand tightly as they maneuvered their way through the other shoppers. She knew that crowds made Taff nervous, though he refused to admit it.

"Maybe we should go home first and check with Father," he suggested. "He might need the money for something we don't know about."

"I'm sure it will be fine," Kara said. Her brother didn't know it, but she had been handling their dwindling finances for the past year. If she gave Father the gray, he would probably just lose it, though she didn't want to tell Taff that. Despite everything that had happened, Taff still looked up to their father, and Kara wanted to preserve that feeling for as long as she could.

Suddenly Taff dropped her hand and coughed deeply. A tall woman pondering a new bonnet spun around, shooting him a nasty look.

"Keep your foulness away from me," she said. The woman stormed off to the other side of the store, but not before Taff reached out and wiped a long strand of snot on the back of her dress.

"Taff," whispered Kara. "That was not kind."

"She wasn't kind to me."

"Two broken boards do not . . ."

". . . a ladder make. Yes, sister. I know."

Kara allowed herself a small smile. "Still," she said, "it is kind of fitting."

Taff returned her smile with his own. "How so?"

"She was rather . . . snotty."

Taff howled with laughter, causing the other shoppers to turn in their direction. Kara knew it was never a good thing to draw attention to themselves, but Taff's laughter was so bright and infectious that she didn't care.

But soon enough his laughter changed to coughing, and Kara could hear the wetness clearly now, creeping into his lungs. She would have to spend the money on medicine. Luckily she knew what they needed; it was a simple tonic that did not require a trip to Doctor Mather. They wouldn't be able to afford the entire bottle with just a gray, but Tanner Stormfield, the shopkeeper, would allow her to pay for a single dose and give it to Taff right in the store. They had done it before.

"No, Kara," Taff said as they approached the aisle that held bandages, corked bottles, and various ointments. "I'm *fine*."

"You're not, Taff. You know what'll happen—"

"I don't want to waste the seed!"

"Your health is hardly a waste."

"*Please,* Kara," he said. "Don't spend it on me."

She bent down next to him.

"Sometimes children are sick a lot when they're young, but then they grow out of it later. That's what's going to happen with you, Taff. Right now things are hard, but when you're older, you're going to grow big and tall. And when that happens, I know you're going to take care of us—both me and Father."

She ran a hand over his cheek.

"But until that day, I get to take care of you. And you have to listen. Okay?"

Taff gave one curt nod. He didn't like it, but he trusted his sister more than anyone else in the world.

"Do you really think I'm going to be tall?" he asked quietly.

"As a Fenroot tree. Strong, too."

Their conversation, as it often did, turned into a playful game.

"How strong?"

"You'll be able to toss entire bales of hay from here to the ocean. And knock down trees with your bare fist."

"Will I be able to juggle cows?"

"Of course. But you won't. Because that would be mean."

Taff giggled. He asked if he could meet her outside; the other kids swore there was a tree nearby with Sordyr's face imprinted in its bark, and Taff wanted to see for himself. Kara had heard the same silly rumor when she was in the Younger School, but there was no reason to ruin his fun. She said she would meet him in a few minutes.

Kara found what she was looking for beneath a box of taffy intended to soothe stomach pains. The medicine looked like it had been sitting on the shelf a long time. She didn't think that would diminish its effectiveness, but she intended to ask the shopkeeper first.

When Kara turned around, Grace was standing right behind her. She was smiling.

Never a good sign.

"Good afternoon, Kara," Grace said, her voice sweetness itself. "So nice to see you."

There was no doubt that Grace was the most beautiful girl in the village. It was, however, an odd sort of beauty. Her eyes, the sharp blue of a freshly mined jewel, were emphasized by long, silky white hair gathered together in a pink ribbon. By all rights, Grace should have been forced to hide such unnatural hair beneath a hat or bonnet; physical anomalies of any sort—from cleft lips to the smallest birthmarks—were often viewed as a sign that a child had been "touched by magic" and should be watched carefully. This did not seem to apply to Grace. She wore her hair proudly, tying it neatly with a different-colored ribbon each day, and the villagers were moved by her "courage."

In their eyes she could do no wrong.

Grace stood in the looming shadow of her constant companion, a giant of a boy named Simon Loder, his mouth hanging open in a permanent expression of bewilderment. At only sixteen Simon should have been tilling a field—with his size he could have done the work of three men. He might have even had his own farm one day; Simon came from good stock and had been, by all reports, an energetic and even intelligent little boy.

All that ended when Simon was eight, on the night he entered the Thickety.

No one had dared search for him, not even his own parents. The boy was given up for lost, taken by Sordyr. In a way, they were right. The child who returned two days later, stumbling into the village with blood-soaked clothes, was a different boy altogether, his mind broken beyond repair. Simon now spoke rarely, and when he did it was only to Grace.

Kara felt bad for him, but he scared her too, the way his eyes shadowed Grace at all times. Others spoke of Grace's charity, how she walked the Path by befriending such an unfortunate soul. But Kara knew it wasn't kindness. Simon was a tool at Grace's constant disposal, as dangerous as an ax—and for her, far easier to wield.

"You weren't in school," Kara said, keeping her voice as dispassionate as possible. She did not feel like playing any of Grace's games today.

Grace leaned on her cane, carved from an ash tree felled by lightning. "My leg pained me this morning. I was unable to get out of bed."

"I am sorry to hear that," Kara said. "It must be a difficult thing."

"Yes, Kara. It is. You cannot imagine the pain."

Although Grace remained smiling, her eyes burned with blue fire.

No one had ever seen Grace's left leg; the women of De'Noran never wore skirts above the ankles, and Grace did not swim. But rumor had it that it was a gnarled, withered thing.

Grace blamed Kara for that.

"Did I miss anything in class?" she asked.

"No," Kara said.

"When I am fen'de, my first order of business will be to send Master Blackwood to the Clearers. He tires me."

Kara nodded politely and took a step toward the counter. "Good health, then."

Simon blocked Kara's path.

"Let me guess," Grace said, eyeing the medicine in Kara's hand. "The whelp is sick again." As she spoke she straightened the bottles on the shelf until they were lined up in a perfect row. "When I'm in charge, things are going to be different. Whelps like him will just get their necks broken. It's better that way. Even with those useless Clearers working nonstop, the Thickety still advances a little bit each year, and our part of the island gets that much smaller. We don't have space to waste on the sickly."

As always, Grace's cruel words were disguised by the tone and cadence of general conversation. The smile never left her face. To anyone else in the store, she might have been any young girl sharing idle gossip with a friend.

Kara met her eyes. "Don't talk about my brother like that."

The words came out louder than Kara had intended. Tanner Stormfield peeked out from behind the front counter.

Grace put a small hand on Kara's shoulder, as though comforting her.

"The truth hurts, Kara. You should know that better than anyone." She paused. "This bottle costs a yellow, at least. How did a poor farm girl like you come across such an amount?"

"I'm not buying the *bottle*, Grace."

Grace sighed dramatically. "You weren't planning on stealing—"

"Of course not! Mrs. Stormfield will give Taff a spoonful for a gray. I'll figure out the next dose tomorrow."

"You have a gray? Excellent news. Give it to me."

"What?"

Grace sighed, as though she were explaining something

to a small child. "The trade ship returned last week. They brought a new type of candy from the World. I want one, I've left my purse at home, and as I said—my leg pains me today. Hence: I need your gray."

"Right, Grace. And of course you'll pay me back."

"No. I won't." She held out one hand, close to her body so it couldn't be seen by anyone else. "The seed, please."

"Why would I do that?"

"Because in the end you're going to give it to me anyway. I'm simply trying to save you some embarrassment. By the Clen, Kara—it's like you can't tell who your friends really are."

Grace continued to hold out her hand. Waiting.

Kara could feel the anger spreading through her body like wildfire. It was always this way with Grace. To everyone else she was all smiles and sugar, the gift of the village. No one knew her dark heart except Kara.

Usually she could ignore Grace. But the small injustices

of the day, each building on the other, had pushed Kara too far.

She slapped Grace's hand away.

Kara immediately knew she had made a mistake, but by then it was too late. Grace was already pinwheeling backward, trying to find purchase on the shelf behind her but only succeeding in knocking a jar of preserves to the floor. Glass shattered everywhere as Grace's crippled leg suddenly gave out. She crumpled at Kara's feet.

Her sobs of pain were quite convincing.

"I barely touched her," Kara said quietly.

It didn't matter. No one was listening.

With one fluid motion, Simon lifted Grace to her feet; despite his size, he was as quick as a cat. Within moments concerned bystanders surrounded Grace, asking if she wanted her father. Grace waved their concern away with a resolute expression, which implied that the pain was actually excruciating, but she was far too unselfish to bother them about it.

After it was ascertained that Grace had not been hurt, the group turned its attention to Kara.

"Heathen," said Bethany James, an old crone with a crescent-shaped scar on her chin. "Hasn't this poor girl suffered enough?"

"She was the one who—"

"Don't listen to her lies," said Wilhelm Eliot. He was a bearded man no taller than Kara. "Her mother was the same way, quick with her tongue. And we all know how *that* turned out." Wilhelm examined Kara, stepping so close she could smell the fried onions on his breath. "Looks just like her. Maybe a night in the Well will teach her a lesson, before it's too late. I'll get a graycloak so we can register an official complaint."

Before Wilhelm could reach the entrance of the store, however, Grace shouted, "Wait! It wasn't Kara fault. She didn't push me very hard. I just . . . it's hard for me to keep my balance . . . because . . . because . . ."

Tears welled up in Grace's eyes.

Mrs. James wrapped an arm around her shoulders. "You are too good, sweetie. Trying to defend this one despite what she's done to you. Timoth Clen himself would have difficulty being so forgiving."

Tanner cut in, all business. "What exactly were you two arguing about?"

Grace looked down at her shoes. Demure and innocent.

"You, then," Tanner told Kara.

Kara shrugged. It was useless to say anything. They wouldn't believe her anyway.

Tanner crossed her arms, which were as strong and capable as any man's. "Girls," she said, "this is my shop, and I'll know what happened here."

Grace mumbled something, too softly to be heard.

"What was that?" asked Tanner.

Grace spoke again, louder this time.

"She took my gray."

Kara was aghast. Not by what Grace had said—but

that she hadn't seen it coming.

"I did not!" she exclaimed.

Even to Kara's ears, the words sounded desperate and false.

"Quiet, you!" Wilhelm snapped at Kara. He picked Grace's cane off the floor and handed it back, patting her hand gently. "Tell us what happened."

Grace took a deep breath, as though the experience had been so trying that it was still painful to describe.

"I came here for some ointment for my leg. I saw Kara, so I came over, thinking we could talk about school. I couldn't go today, on account of my infirmity, and I didn't want to fall behind in my studies. I thought maybe Kara could tell me what I missed. But all she kept doing was asking me if I had any money. I guess there's a new candy, and she really wanted to try—"

"Sweetrock," said Tanner.

"Yes, that's it. The problem was, she didn't have any money. I offered to buy her a piece, of course. I hoped this might convince her to help me with my schoolwork, because I get worried when I miss my lessons. But the minute I took out a seed, Kara grabbed it out of my hand, and I fell. It wasn't really that Kara pushed me. I mean, if she did, it was just an accident. She would never do anything like that on purpose. Kara is a really good person, once you get to know her."

"That gray is mine," said Kara. "I did some work this morning at the Lamb farm. You can ask them if you don't believe me."

She may as well have been talking to the wind.

"We should call one of the graycloaks," said Wilhelm.

"Yes," agreed Tanner. "Thievery cannot go unpunished."

"An hour or two in the Well, wouldn't you say?"

"At least."

"Oh, please don't!" Grace exclaimed, grasping Tanner's hands. "I know Kara was only joking around. She has a strange sense of humor, and it might seem unspeakably cruel to some, playing a trick on me the way she did—but at least it makes me feel like one of the able-bodied. I know she meant to give it back. Right, Kara? Weren't you going to give it back?"

Everyone turned to Kara, waiting for her response.

She thought about proclaiming her innocence once again, but there seemed little point to it. Grace would simply smile or fret or cry, and any excuse Kara made would shatter into pieces.

"I was going to give it back," she said, her voice a lifeless monotone. "It was just a bad joke."

Grace brightened instantly. She looked at Kara with what could only be called pride, as though Kara were a dog that had just done an excellent trick.

Tanner slipped behind the front counter and retrieved a mop. "I won't stand for this childishness in my store, girls. Someone needs to clean up this mess, too."

Grace nodded, as though that was the most reasonable thing in the world. "Kara, it's a bit hard for me to bend down, but if you hand me the mop, I can——"

"Nonsense!" Mrs. James exclaimed, extending a bony finger in Kara's direction. "It's the witch's daughter who caused the whole fuss in the first place. She's the one who should be punished."

"Too true!" Wilhelm exclaimed, nodding so ferociously that Kara thought his teeth might pop out of his mouth. He placed a hand on the small of Grace's back. "You aren't picking up a thing, sweetie. Come on, let's walk you back home."

Tanner nudged the handle of the mop into Kara's hand. "Aren't you forgetting something?" she asked.

"That's right!" Mrs. James said, and Kara remembered—with shocking clarity—the way the old woman's face had wavered in the torchlight the night of her mother's execution. "You soft in the head, girl?"

"The gray," said Tanner.

Kara, her movements sluggish, dug the money from the folds of her school dress. She considered it one last moment—*Just a useless seed, can't even grow anything*—before dropping it into Grace's outstretched hand.

"I just want you to know," Grace said, her tiny fingers closing around the prize, "that I forgive you."

She placed a small, dry kiss on Kara's cheek. Her lips were cold.

FOUR

The Westfall land had once been a verdant paradise of apple trees, cornfields, and green, flowing pasture. Although she often tried to re-create the farm in her mind, Kara was left with only fragments. Her father: tawny and brown, working in the fields, pausing to give her a wave or rolling a pumpkin up the giant hill that bordered their farmhouse. Mother guiding Kara's tiny hands as she planted seeds. The earthy smell of Mother, as though she had grown from the soil itself.

It seemed such a long time ago.

Walking across their land now, Kara reminded herself to be grateful for even these flashes of happier days; Taff had nothing at all. He knew only the withered trees that fell over in the slightest windstorm, the brown stalks that bore sharp pebbles of corn. Since their mother's death, their land had become a haunted, barren place. The villagers said it was cursed, of course, but Kara knew that wasn't the case. Any farm would fail without field hands to tend to it and an owner who spent more afternoons sleeping than working.

"We went to the Pool of Recognition today," Taff said.

Kara tried to mask her surprise. *Is he that old already?* she thought.

"Did you see Timoth Clen's image in the water?" she asked.

Taff threw up his hands. "There wasn't nothing there! It's not even fancy or anything. It's just a puddle!"

"What did your teacher tell you afterward?"

"She said to go home and think about what you've

seen. Except I don't know how I'm supposed to do that when I didn't see anything!"

Kara smiled, remembering how confused she had been at his age, the feeling of crashing disappointment at seeing her own face in the water and not the Clen's. It wasn't until years later that Kara realized the point of the lesson. If they shunned magic and lived by the rules set forth in the Path, then they would be like Timoth Clen himself. He could provide the path for them to follow, but he couldn't appear in the water to guide them, nor would he listen to their prayers like one of the false gods in the World.

That would be magic.

Kara longed to guide Taff to this conclusion, but this was something her brother would have to figure out on his own.

"Annabeth swears she saw him in the water, holding his hammer and scythe."

"That's a lie," Kara said, "and she better hope the

graycloaks don't hear her. Timoth Clen died over a thousand years ago." It had been a dark time, the world overrun by all manner of witches and foul creatures. Timoth Clen had saved them all, leading the Gray Army across the land until every last witch had been killed. After his death at the hands of the Great Betrayer, the Clen's chronicles and teachings had been recorded in the Path. From this the Fold had been born, and for centuries they had dutifully watched for magic's return, even when the rest of the World had moved on and forgotten.

"I'm hungry," Taff said.

"Is there anything in particular you'd like for dinner?"

This got a slight smile.

"A giant slab of roast beef with mashed potatoes, if you will. With gravy. Followed by a slice of coo-berry pie."

"Would you like some hot chocolate with that as well?"

Taff nodded. "With lots and lots of whipped cream."

"That sounds splendid!" Kara said. "I'll start dinner right away. Only . . . we did have beef just the other day, but I served it to a traveling prince. And since he was a prince . . . of course I had to serve it with gravy."

"That makes sense," said Taff.

"And I just baked a coo-berry pie, but it was stolen from the windowsill, I think by a gang of fairies. You know how they can be. And the hot chocolate . . ."

"You fed it to that passing dragon," Taff said. "The one with the broken wing."

Kara smacked her head, as though remembering.

"That's right. Poor thing. But I do have some good news. I have . . . potatoes!"

Taff gasped with mock excitement. "Wow!"

"How about I'll boil them in water, and we'll eat that for dinner?"

"That sounds great, Kara. Much better than that first stupid dinner."

Kara usually loved playing these story games with Taff. It was like a secret language they shared with Mother, who had told Kara many forbidden stories about trolls and wereskins, foul kings and fair queens. Today, however, joking about dinner only made her sad. If Jacob Lamb had paid Kara what he'd promised, they could have afforded a special dinner like the one Taff imagined.

"The back gate's not closing right again," Taff said. "I'm going to see if I can fix it."

Kara had no doubt that he would; Taff had a special knack for such projects, and at seven was already handier than Father had ever been. She watched Taff run across the cracked, useless soil that used to be a wheat field, the bottoms of his shoes slapping against the dirt, and made a mental note to mend the soles again tonight.

Her eyes drifted past the far border of their dying land to the Thickety.

It was no more than an hour's walk, with trees that made the tallest spruces and sycamores of De'Noran look like children's toys in comparison. The stories about this forbidden place were many and varied. *Ancient trees scratch their names on you while you sleep. Almost-humans sprout from*

the earth. *Steaming rivers boil the very goodness from your soul.* Kara didn't believe *all* the stories, but she was certain that Sordyr, the ruler of the Thickety, was no tall tale.

Oh yes, Mother had told her. *The Forest Demon is as real as you or I, though he cannot cross the borders of his kingdom, thank goodness. But be wary nonetheless. Never journey past the Fringe, for though the Thickety is closed to most, I fear he may make a special exception for you.*

Suddenly a gust of wind caught the branches of the trees, black leaves shuddering madly like the rush of a waterfall and something else, some other sound she was sure she recognized. . . .

"No," Kara said, stepping back. "No. It was just the wind."

She walked faster, trying not to think about it. Surely it must have been her imagination.

For just a moment, she'd thought the trees had whispered her name.

Kara found Father sitting on the front porch. He was hunched over, writing in his notebook again.

The previous night their front door had been smeared with a mixture of dung and what smelled like sheep's blood, a new touch. Kara hadn't had time to clean it that morning, and her father had allowed it to bake in the sun all day long. She wasn't surprised. Before Kara's mother had died, Father would have not only cleaned the door but found those responsible for the vandalism and beat them soundly. Now she wondered if he even noticed. She sat next to him on the swing. Her parents had spent many long evenings here, holding hands, talking quietly, while Kara was supposed to be asleep but instead lay close to the window, drinking in their secret giggles.

"Greetings, Father," Kara said.

He continued to write. Kara felt no curiosity, no desire to look down at the page. She knew what it said.

Her father's blond hair hung in tangled curls over his

forehead and ears. His beard was uneven on one side, as though he had started to shave one morning and then given up. Streaks of gray shot through it like weeds.

He stank.

Kara remembered him as he was: handsome and strong, balancing her on his shoulders as they walked through De'Noran. The other villagers smiling in their direction, waving.

Before. All before.

She slipped a hand into his own, trying not to notice the dirt crusted beneath his fingernails. Smears of slick, reddish manure from their doorknob.

"Did your day treat you well?" she asked.

He turned his head in her direction. His eyes were barely open, as though he had just woken up.

"Kara," he said. "When did you get home?"

"Just now."

"How was school?"

"Fine. Everything is fine."

"That's good."

He turned back to his view of their land. Kara knew, from experience, that she could sit here for an hour and he might not speak another word. On some days that was enough, just being near him. But dinner wouldn't cook itself, and she needed the answer to a question.

"How long have you been sitting here, Father?"

"What time is it now?"

"Almost dinnertime."

"Is it?" He gave a quiet chuckle. "Looks like the day slipped away from me, then. I sat down this morning for a spell and—"

"Did you pick the hushfruit?"

"The hushfruit?" Father shifted uncomfortably, crossing one leg over the other. Taff did the same thing, when Kara caught him up to some kind of shenanigans. "Hmm. The hushfruit. Let me think on that."

Before she left for school each morning, Kara looked her father in the eyes and gave him one specific task for that day. Refill the wood box. Milk the cows. Cut the hay.

Most times he was able to complete these chores, but lately he had been going through a bad phase. This had been the third morning in a row she had asked him to pick the hushfruit, without success. By tomorrow the fragile crop would spoil.

Kara would have to take care of it herself tonight. She was already so tired, she could close her eyes and fall asleep right now. The sheer thought of the extra chore exhausted her.

Father seemed to notice the disappointment on her face.

"Are you mad at me?" he asked.

She was. But yelling at her father would do no good. He would sob and beg her forgiveness, she would feel as though she had just whipped a small child, and they would start the process anew tomorrow. There was no point to it.

Instead she forced a smile as she rose from the bench. "No, not at all."

"I'll pick the hushfruit tomorrow. I promise. It's just, sometimes things escape me."

"There's no need, Father. You already did it."

"I did? Oh, that's good. That's very good indeed." He stretched his arms into the air. "No wonder I'm so tired."

Dinner was better than expected. Taff had found some wild herbs to flavor the potatoes, and Father had actually volunteered to help, kneading the dough and spooning the rounded scoops into a cast-iron pan. While the biscuits and potatoes cooked, Kara sent Taff to pick a few of the overripe hushfruits. These she diced and tossed with their last remaining spoonful of sugar and a dash of nutmeg. She folded the mixture into a pie dish lined with dough, creating a simple but serviceable cobbler.

By the time Kara served dinner, the mouthwatering

smells from the oven had already called Taff and Father to the table. Kara would never be Mother—who could take ordinary potatoes and turn them into a dish fit for a king—but she was a fair cook, and the food vanished quickly. She liked to think it was because her family enjoyed her cooking, but she knew the truth: They were starving.

For this reason Kara waited ten minutes before bringing out the cobbler, which she served piping hot so Taff and Father couldn't just gobble it down. She hoped that if she could make dinner last longer, their stomachs might be tricked into thinking they had eaten a more substantial meal.

Besides, Father was talkative tonight. Instead of just staring blankly at the table, he told them about the time that he had gotten the paddle for sneaking back into school during recess and putting rocks in the pockets of the schoolmaster's cloak. Kara and Taff had both heard the story before, but they smiled politely and laughed in all the right places. For a few minutes, they felt like a normal family.

Then Taff ruined it all.

"Someone was talking about Mother today," he said.

Father took a bite of his cobbler and chewed it thoughtfully. It was still far too hot to eat, but he didn't seem to notice.

"Is that so," he said.

"A boy in my class. Wilson Redding. His parents own the farm out past—"

"I know the Reddings," Father said. He placed his fork down and folded his hands together. "What did the boy say?"

"Wilson got in trouble. Actually he was already in trouble, and then he got in trouble again. He was clapping the erasers because he—"

Kara held up a hand. "Wait. He got in trouble for talking about Mother?"

"No," Taff said. "He got in trouble because he dared

James to eat a caterpillar. That was yesterday. I'm getting to the part about Mother, but I have to tell you this other stuff first."

Kara and Father waited for him to proceed.

"I forgot where I was," Taff said.

"Wilson was clapping erasers. . . ."

"Out the window. And Master Blackwood walked by, but instead of stopping, Wilson clapped the erasers harder than ever and got chalk dust all over Master Blackwood's robes. Wilson told Master Blackwood he just didn't see him, but I think he was lying."

"Why?" Father asked.

"Because he told me he lied. Which I thought was weird, because usually Wilson doesn't talk to me. But then Wilson asked me his question about Mother, and I understood."

Kara met her father's eyes and shook her head: *Nothing good can come of knowing.*

Father asked anyway: "What was the question?"

"Master Blackwood had also been the one who caught Wilson trying to make James eat the caterpillar. And now Master Blackwood was going to be giving Wilson the paddle, so he was pretty mad. So . . . he wanted to know if I was like Mother. If I could make something bad happen to Master Blackwood."

Kara was not surprised. Others had come to her with similar questions. Children—and adults—who tried to befriend her in secret because they were interested in Mother's supposed powers. A little *too* interested, in Kara's estimation.

"What did you tell him?" Father asked, his voice surprisingly calm.

"I told him that everyone knows that boys can't be witches, and I didn't know any spells or anything like that, and even if I could, I would never hurt anyone, not even Master Blackwood, who probably deserves it. But Wilson just got mad. He told me that my mother had no problem hurting people. That she had once made a little girl eat her own tongue because she had mispronounced her name. That she could break a man's bones by snapping her fingers."

Kara had heard these stories as well. These and more.

"Is it true?" Taff asked. "Could Mother really do all that?"

Father stared at a point just past Taff, his bearded face lax and expressionless.

"No," he said quietly. "And even if she could—she wouldn't."

Father scooped up a fresh spoonful of cobbler.

"This is delicious, Kara," he said. "It's nice that the three of us can—"

Taff slammed down his plate. Cobbler crumbs skipped across the table.

"Then what *could* she do?" he asked. "Everyone talks about her, but the stories are all different. Ryan says she could make your blood boil with a single word. Maggie says she could make the clouds swallow people whole."

"They don't know anything," Kara said. "They were just babies when she—"

"But they're telling me what their moms and dads said, and they knew our mother. But no one says the same thing. It's so confusing."

As often happened whenever Taff became excited, he began to cough. Kara offered him a cup of water, but Taff pushed it away. She settled with stroking his back, trying to calm him down.

"I don't believe them," he said, "any of them. I don't believe what they say about her."

"This was a long time ago, son. Just let it—"

"Everyone hates us, and it's not fair. They say she's a witch, but . . ."

"Taff."

". . . no one has ever actually *seen* anything."

"It doesn't matter!" Father exclaimed, slamming his fist on the table. And then, quietly: "The details might be different, but in the end it's all the same. Magic destroyed your mother. Plain and simple."

Taff opened his mouth as though to say something more but instead slumped into his seat. Kara ached for him. He wanted to love his mother so badly, but he had been told his entire life that she was a monster who didn't deserve his love. How different it would be if she were innocent. How easy to treasure what might have been.

Father rose from the table.

"I'm sorry," he said. "For everything."

He shuffled down the short hallway and closed the bedroom door softly behind him.

He's not even forty yet, Kara thought, *but he walks like an old man.*

Taff finally stopped coughing, though his face remained flushed. Kara slid Father's unfinished cobbler to him.

"Someone should eat this," she said. "It's getting cold."

While Taff cleaned the dishes, Kara attended to the mess outside. By the smell of it, the manure/blood mixture had been left to fester in someone's wheelbarrow for a few days before being packed into a pillowcase and slung against their front door. Kara went at it with a trowel, scraping away the bits that had already dried in place, and then got down on her knees and scrubbed the door with a rag until it was spotless. Finally she dumped bucket after bucket of sudsy water on what remained, liquefying the waste so it drained between the wooden boards of their front porch.

By the time Kara finished, the last vestiges of light had been squeezed from the sky. After washing up at the well, she went inside to check on Taff. He had already settled beneath the covers of his bed; a single candle burned by his bedside.

"Story?" he asked.

Kara sat on the edge of the bed. Without thinking, she raised a hand to his forehead, checking for a fever. *Only a little warm tonight.*

"Sorry," she said, shaking her head. It was already so

late, and the hushfruit wouldn't pick itself. "Tomorrow. I promise."

"You can tell me quick and skip the boring parts. I know what happens. I just like to hear the words."

"Tomorrow."

Taff smiled at her: warm and playful and just a little bit devious.

"You know you're going to say yes in the end," he said, "and you're already in a hurry. So why not just skip the you-saying-no part and get on with it."

The matter settled, Taff arranged his head comfortably on the pillow and waited for her to begin.

"Fine," Kara said, "but just this once." After a quick glance out the window—one could never be too cautious, not in De'Noran—Kara pulled out the book hidden beneath Taff's sleeping pad. It was small and oddly shaped, a conglomeration of discarded schoolbook pages that had been sewn together with black thread. Easing into bed, Kara wrapped her arm around her brother and turned to the first page.

"Long before remembrance there was a boy called Samuel. He and his sister liked to play with tadpoles and climb tall trees and dance to the music of the river, until one day Samuel was visited by a dread sickness and could play no longer."

The writing—ordinary and simple—was hers, but the drawings were Taff's, and they were extraordinary. Samuel and his unnamed sister, rendered in charcoal and chalk, seemed ready to step off the page and into their lives.

Kara lowered her voice to a whisper.

"Though she knew it was forbidden, Samuel's sister visited an old woman who lived on the edge of the forest. People called her Spider Lady and said she knew secret things." Before they had written the story down—when it was just something she told Taff at bedtime—Kara had actually used the word *magic*. But speaking the profane word out loud and committing it to the permanence of paper were two very different things, and in the end Kara couldn't bring herself to write the letters. The risk, if the book were ever found, was too great.

"Spider Lady told Samuel's sister that there was a beast called a Jabenhook that could lift the illness from her brother like an unwanted blanket, but in order to find the beast, she would have to journey into the forest and complete three tasks. . . ."

Kara read the pages quickly, skimming over the describing parts and allowing the pictures to do the work. Taff did not seem to mind. When she reached the final page, however, his eyes opened wide. It was his favorite part.

"The Jabenhook sat on Samuel's chest and wrapped its magnificent, speckled wings around him. There was a glow of light, as bright as a miniature sun, and then the creature set off into the air, a mass of squirming, worm-like shadows—plump with the spoils of disease—held fast between its golden talons. And from that day on,

Samuel was never sick again."

Taff, caught somewhere in that blurry realm between sleeping and waking, smiled gently. "The end," he said.

"The end."

His eyes opened just enough to meet hers. "Wouldn't it be wonderful? If something like that could really happen?"

"That sounds almost like a wish," Kara said. "And that, as you well know, is forbidden. Besides, there is no need for wishing if you follow the Path. All your needs will be met."

"You don't really believe that. Do you?"

She leaned over and kissed him on his forehead.

"Good night, brother," she said.

Kara slid the book into its hiding place, thinking once again that the story felt incomplete. What happened to the sister? She succeeded in her quest, but did she ever return from the forest? Did the siblings know happiness together? Taff had suggested that they add another leaf of parchment and give the characters a proper ending, but Kara refused: Although she wanted Samuel and her sister to be happy, she didn't want to lie about it. Happy endings, she had often suspected, could only be earned through some sort of sacrifice.

FIVE

The night was clear and cold, as it often was in the weeks leading up to the Shadow Festival. Kara drew her tattered black cloak around her and crossed what remained of the cornfield, her boots crunching against the untended soil. Walking through the abandoned field always made her sad. She remembered playing hide-and-find among its once-flourishing stalks with her neighbors from the adjoining farms, children who would now deny ever stepping foot on Westfall land.

It would be so much easier, Kara thought, *if I could bring myself to hate them.* The villagers had certainly given her enough reason, clouding Kara's days with disdain, despite the fact that she had never hurt anyone. But Kara had always been slow to anger, easy to forgive. She saw the way they treated one another: the smiles, the easy conversation. There was good there.

Besides, it was not difficult to understand their fear. Like them, Kara had been taught from birth that nothing was more obscene or inhuman than magic, and the idea that her mother had been a witch filled Kara with deep shame and revulsion (and occasionally, late at night, a thrill of excitement—which only increased her shame). Nothing could be more profane to the Children of the Fold than one of their own succumbing to the evils of witchcraft, and Kara, the mirror image of her mother, was little more than a walking reminder of what had happened.

But what, exactly, had *happened?*

If she knew, for certain, her mother's role in the deaths that night, Kara thought things might be better.

Even if the knowledge broke her heart, it would be easier than not knowing whether she should love her mother or hate her.

As though searching for the past, Kara raised her lantern high and stepped into the darkness of the orchard.

Three people had died that night; Kara knew this much at least. Her mother had been the third.

The first death was Abigail Smythe, Mother's childhood friend and a constant fixture at their farm. Kara remembered sitting on Aunt Abby's lap, tracing her freckles with one small finger while Abigail and her mother laughed over what Father, with a gentle shake of his head, called "some womanly foolishness." Constance Lamb would often be there as well, though she was Constance Bridges at that time, her face unscarred and smiling.

Kara didn't remember her mother having any other friends besides Aunt Abby and Aunt Constance, but they had seemed like enough. The three of them were inseparable. Kara couldn't count the number of times she fell asleep under the kitchen table, cradled against her mother's foot, the sounds of their pleasant, innocuous conversation more soothing than a lullaby.

Aunt Abby was married two days after Kara's fifth birthday. Her wedding was particularly festive; although the villagers had already begun to regard Mother with suspicion, Abby, with her smiles and freckles and pies, was beloved by all. The celebration ran long into the night. The next morning the entire community, as was their tradition, worked together to raise a new barn for the couple. Aunt Abby's body was found there two months later. She had been torn to shreds. Or her head had been replaced with that of a crow. Or maybe she had simply vanished, leaving nothing but her boots behind—there were a dozen different variations to the story. No one really knew for sure, except the fen'de and his graycloaks. And, of course, the person who had found the body.

Mother.

Aunt Abby's new husband was the second victim that night. His name was Peter, and although Kara hadn't known him well, he had once given her an apple and told her she had pretty hair. He had been found in the field just outside the barn, his body unharmed but his face frozen in a nightmarish scream.

Taff was not due for another six weeks, but the shock of finding her friends this way sent Mother into early labor. That was what Kara had always wanted to believe. Everyone else claimed it was the stress of using her dark magic to murder her best friend. In either case Kara's mother managed to make her way to Constance's farm before collapsing, and it was Constance herself who delivered Taff, only three pounds and no bigger than a loaf of bread.

Kara wondered if there had been time for Mother to hold her son before the graycloaks pounded on the door and dragged her into the night. It was something she had always wanted to ask Constance, along with where she had gotten her scars. From that night on, however, her mother's friend ignored Kara. She had asked Father what happened many times (though less often as the years passed), but he refused to talk about it. When Kara asked if Mother was really a witch, he simply nodded and spent the rest of the day writing in his notebook.

Only once, when he was deeply in his cups, had he given Kara anything resembling a clue. Stumbling into her room in the middle of the night, he said that Mother had never wanted to hurt anyone but "made a terrible, terrible mistake."

Kara had pretended to be asleep.

Kara picked up a gathering basket and flinched at the smell of rotten hushfruits. At some point Father had actually done some picking but abandoned the project midway. A soupy mess crawling with bugs was all that remained in the basket.

Turning her head away, Kara dumped it on the ground.

Although delicious, hushfruits were extremely fickle. There was only a small window of opportunity to pick the fruit when it ripened, after which it would shrivel and die on the branch. Luckily, it was easy to tell the proper time: The hushfruit's color changed from an unappetizing gray to vibrant purple, and the branches of the tree sagged as though begging to be picked.

Looking through the orchard, Kara saw tree after tree with branches so low the hushfruit grazed the ground.

It was going to be a long night.

She moved quickly. Some fruit was already too far gone and exploded in her hand the moment she touched it, dyeing her fingers a dark purple. Nonetheless, she managed to fill four baskets in two hours. By then, however, exhaustion had caught up to her, and Kara found her progress slowing considerably. There was no way she could pick it all, and her heart sickened at the amount of money they would lose. She cursed herself for trusting Father, who had promised to take care of this days ago. *I could wake him up right now. Taff too. Together we might have a chance.* But she knew that wouldn't work. Father would just feel guilty about not having done the work in the first place and would spend more time apologizing than actually working. Taff would be eager to help, but there was his health to consider. The temperature had plummeted in the past hour, and she couldn't make him come out into the cold like this.

No, the only solution was for her to work as quickly as she could. If Kara could gather another six baskets, that would be enough to fetch them a handful of yellows. She wasn't convinced it would see them through the winter, but it was a start. In the next hour, she was only able to gather half a basket, however, which she then knocked over with her numb hands, sending fruit rolling everywhere. Kara had to spend another half hour on her knees, looking for the scattered hushfruit with her lantern.

She actually felt relieved when she squeezed one too

hard, and it burst in her hand. At least its innards were warm.

I'll just rest, she thought, sitting at the base of a tree. *In a few minutes, I'll feel refreshed. Then I'll be able to work faster than ever.*

Kara closed her eyes. When she opened them again, she couldn't feel her feet, and a bird with an eye in its chest was perched on her knee. Kara's first instinct was to scream, but she felt so tired, so sluggish, that she was unable to open her mouth. She realized, somewhere in the back of her mind, that this was a very bad thing. That she really needed to get to her feet and move around.

Her body refused to listen.

She stared at the bird before her. Its feathers were a deep, rich blue that rippled like water in the moonlight. There was nothing but a bump where its head should be, with a small, dark hole that might have been a mouth. Its single eye was the dark green of murky swamp water.

As Kara watched, the eyeball rolled to the left, and a

second eye took its place, this one slate gray. No sooner had this new eyeball fixed itself in the bird's socket than it was replaced by a different eye, the same blue as the bird's feathers. If Kara had not seen it move into place, she doubted she would have known that the bird had an eye at all. This strange piece of camouflage quickly rolled to the side, replaced by an eyeball that glowed yellow and gave off a faint but welcome warmth.

At no point did the bird blink.

It's trying to get my attention, Kara thought. *It's trying to wake me up.*

The bird-thing's eye moved again, and a few eyeballs rolled by without stopping. Orange. Magenta. Albino white. Kara imagined the eyeballs lined up inside its body like marbles on the wooden track of a child's toy. There didn't seem to be enough room in its tiny body for all of them, but Kara supposed they weren't playing by the typical rules anymore.

Finally the bird settled on an eyeball that pulsed and

danced with the fiery red of an inferno. Kara's head burned just looking at it, but some of her exhaustion had drained away. As soon as Kara pressed her hands into the earth and began making the effort to stand, the bird flew to a nearby branch and watched her carefully.

"Thank you for waking me up," Kara said.

The bird hopped backward. Deeper into the orchard.

"Hey," Kara said. "Where are you going?"

The bird moved again. This time it took flight, not stopping until it reached the end of the row of trees, where it perched on a branch and faced Kara.

"You want me to follow you?" Kara asked.

The bird's eye changed color. A vibrant orange.

Yes.

Kara walked to the end of the row, her feet stinging as feeling returned to them. As soon as she reached the bird it took off down a different row of trees.

Found a branch. Faced Kara. Waited.

They did this several more times. They were nearing

the opposite end of the orchard, which also marked the northern border of her family's farm. Beyond that was only the . . .

Of course. Where else could such a strange creature have come from?

"No," Kara said. "I can't go there."

The bird's caw cut through the night, a strident burst of sound with no end in sight. Kara clamped her hands to her ears. Above her the fragile hushfruits suddenly burst, their purple innards raining to the ground.

"Stop it!" Kara screamed. "Please! I'll follow you!"

The bird stopped, changed eyes. Pink. Kara thought it was pleased with itself.

It flew out of the orchard and into the wind-torn night, Kara close behind.

Kara crossed the border of her family's land and stood before the Fringe, an expanse of wild growth that separated De'Noran from the Thickety.

Although it had been cut just this morning, fresh stalks and saplings already stood as high as Kara's knees. Mother had taught her about the different types of plants—so, unlike other villagers, Kara knew which could heal and which should be avoided. But the Fringe was always changing, and in the darkness it was difficult to differentiate between the red moss that could soothe sore throats and the moss that would make your fingernails fall off.

This is crazy, she thought. *Besides, if someone sees me, it will be the Well for sure. Maybe worse.* Yet Kara continued to follow the bird. Soon she reached a point farther than she had ever dared travel, even with Mother. Only Shadowcutters—those Clearers assigned to remove flora located within the shadows of the Thickety—were permitted to go so far. Kara's heart quickened as she slid past drooping, willowy stalks from which hung a dozen mustard-yellow spheres. She knew that each sphere would burst under the slightest pressure, producing nightmarish hallucinations.

Finally the weeds cleared. The Thickety stood before her, massive and ancient and foreboding, with leaves that remained black no matter what the season. The branches here were knitted into an impenetrable wall, save one spot: a small opening no higher than her knees. She noted, with a slightly sick feeling, that she would fit perfectly.

The bird waited patiently, its eye a glowing yellow. Showing her the way.

She thought about Simon Loder and his blank, haunted eyes. The Thickety had done that to him. He had experienced something so terrible that his mind had chosen to shut off completely rather than remember it. Who was to say the same thing wouldn't happen to her?

"I won't go in there," Kara said.

The bird cawed once, a gentle pleading.

Kara took a single step forward, and her mother's words returned to her through the mist of years: *Never journey past the Fringe, for though the Thickety is closed to most, I fear he may make a special exception for you.*

"No," Kara said, backing away. "Never."

The bird stomped its feet up and down.

"I should never have come this far." She was exhausted and light-headed and had nearly frozen to death. But now that she was thinking clearly, Kara understood that she needed to get as far from this place as possible.

The bird's eye swiveled: lavender. The precise hue of her favorite flower.

I'm sorry, it seemed to say.

Before Kara could swat it away—before she even knew what was happening—the bird swooped onto her neck. Kara heard a *snap* and watched the bird disappear into the Thickety, her necklace held fast in its talons.

"No!" Kara exclaimed, grasping the spot on her chest where the locket had rested for the last seven years.

It was all she had left of her mother.

And it had been stolen.

Without thinking, Kara crawled through the hole in the Thickety, determined to get it back again.

SIX

Kara found herself inching along a narrow, branch-lined tunnel. Her only source of light was the bird's yellow eye, hovering before her like a ghostly sun. The air was warmer here, and smelled of growth and flowers. She thought it might have been a very pleasant smell, had it not been so overpowering. Branches laced together into a tight, impenetrable net pressed down against her back, increasing in pressure as the tunnel became narrower and narrower. She reached up and could not even find an opening big enough for her hand.

At one point something with far too many legs skittered across the back of her hand and vanished through a seam in the branch net. Kara's shriek of surprise was answered by a thousand rustling sounds from the trees above. If the creatures of the Thickety had not known she was coming, they did now.

Suddenly the ground opened up, and there was only air beneath her hands. She tumbled free of the tunnel, down a short slope of dark, damp earth. On her back Kara clenched her hands together and breathed in the warm, humid air, unwilling—quite yet—to open her eyes.

"I'm inside the Thickety," she whispered, but saying the words out loud did not make them feel more real. She felt shame and excitement but above all fear, its shadowy wings spread wide enough to encompass all other feelings.

Kara opened her eyes.

It was dark. High above, a canopy of black leaves created a labyrinthine shield that blocked out the sky and any light whatsoever. On the branches below, however, clung gossamer threads of silver web that gave off a radiant glow like moonlight. These webs trailed off after a few hundred feet, and the remainder of the Thickety was cloaked in impenetrable darkness. Looking into it Kara felt dizzy, as though she were standing on the edge of a great precipice.

A stray strand of web dangled before her eyes, glowing softly. *Perhaps my people have been wrong all these years*, she thought, staring at its mesmerizing light. *Perhaps this is a place of wonder.*

Kara touched the thread. It immediately went dark.

This sudden darkness spread to the glowing web above, like a fire along a line of kerosene. Strand by strand the silver light extinguished itself.

But before Kara was plunged into complete darkness, something large and fast swung into action. She couldn't make out its exact features—it was just a blur of motion—but she did see a large number of legs and what appeared to be long, boneless arms. Spinning new thread between two impossibly fast hands, the creature repaired the web. It chattered at Kara angrily, berating her for ruining its work.

When the creature was finished, the web looked different than before, but it lit the area just as admirably. The webspinner gave Kara one final look of warning, then slipped between a small opening in the branches and disappeared into the darkness.

"Thank you," Kara said. Her voice sounded strange in this place, distant, as though she were shouting to herself across a stream.

Kara didn't know what to do next. She would leave the moment the bird returned her locket, but she didn't think that would happen until she . . . did what she was supposed to do. *Perhaps if I look around a bit, something will occur to me.* It wasn't as though she had to explore the whole Thickety, after all—just the area beneath the silver light. If she found nothing of interest, Kara would go straight home, locket or no locket. No matter what, she wouldn't go near the dark part of the forest. Even Kara's curiosity had limits.

Thus decided, Kara began her search. She had no idea what she was looking for, so she walked with great care, examining her surroundings closely. If there was something to be found, she prayed she would sense its importance.

She did.

Although it was the right size and shape, Kara did not think the shell belonged to a tortoise—at least not any sort of tortoise she had ever seen. For one thing, the shell was inscribed with burnt-orange spirals that seemed to impart some vague meaning. When Kara bent forward to examine the symbols more closely, however, a painful buzzing exploded in her head.

She quickly looked away. If the symbols did hide some secret meaning, it wasn't one she wanted to know.

When Kara turned back, the one-eyed bird was sitting on the shell, the necklace dangling from its talons.

She reached for it, but the bird hopped away.

"Give it back!" she exclaimed.

The bird regarded her, its eye a solemn but encouraging brown.

In time. This first.

Kara thought about making another attempt for the locket but knew it was pointless; the bird was far too fast. She knelt next to the shell, hesitant to pick it up. *There might be something dead under there. Or alive.* Kara dug her hand beneath its underside, trying not to imagine a pair of pincers groping for her fingers in the darkness. She lifted her hand, just hoping to get the shell a few inches off the ground, and jumped back in surprise when it flipped over completely. It was much lighter than it looked.

At the very least, Kara thought, *it will make a great sled for Taff this winter.*

The bird cawed, and the strident sound reverberated

into the darkness, emphasizing the unnatural silence of the forest.

"Yes?" Kara asked.

The bird, standing on the spot previously covered by the shell, marched in place. It rotated eyeballs until it reached a faded blue.

Help me.

"Help you do what?" Kara asked.

When the bird opened its eye again, the color was a purple so deep you could fall into it. *Pay close attention.*

The bird dragged its feet backward, with a slight hesitation each time. Drag . . . stop . . . drag . . . stop . . . drag . . . stop. It hopped over to the shell and perched on it, gazing at Kara expectantly.

"You want me to dig?"

The bird hopped up once.

Yes!

"That's what the shell is for, isn't it? For digging."

The bird hopped again.

"Is something important buried here? Is that why you wanted me to come with you?"

The bird's eye rotated for a long time. Finally it settled on dark gray, a stone wet with rain. For some reason Kara had trouble understanding the meaning of this one. It seemed a bit ambiguous, but as far as she could tell, it either meant "most important" or "not me."

Picking up the shell with two hands, she began to dig.

The black soil made no sense. Cupped in her hand, it felt much heavier than the earth from her farm, like a fistful of iron filings. Yet even after Kara filled the large shell with dirt, she could lift it with ease; if anything, a soil-packed shell was slightly lighter than an empty one. This was completely impossible, of course, but Kara was quickly learning not to question things in the Thickety.

She continued to dig.

Surprisingly soon she was standing waist-deep in a hole of her own creation. Kara tried to remember how long she had been digging. She could not.

And then, on her next scoop into the dirt, the shell made contact with something solid.

Immediately Kara knew this was the end of her search. It wasn't that she had a bolt of intuition. It was that the shell crumbled in her hands, spilling between her fingers as it disintegrated into black soil. Within moments there was no sign that her makeshift shovel had ever been there at all.

Kara plunged her hands into the dirt and unearthed a rectangular object wrapped in cheesecloth.

This belonged to my mother, she thought. *She wanted me to have it, which is why she hid it in the one place on the island it could never be found. Or . . . something wants me to think that.*

It was too dangerous. She should leave the object here and return home before someone saw her. That was the smart thing to do.

But what if it really was Mother's? This might be my only chance to learn the truth.

Before Kara could make her final decision, the bird

fluttered in front of her and dropped the locket. The ivy cascaded gracefully into Kara's palm.

"Thank you," she said, tying the locket around her neck. Its familiar weight made her feel whole again.

The bird's eye shifted to a sullen blue. It was a difficult shade to read, but Kara thought it might be some form of sympathy. No: not just sympathy.

Sorrow.

With a final caw, the creature disappeared into the darkness, leaving her alone.

That one means me no harm, Kara thought, *and would not guide me to something dangerous.* She began to unwind the cheesecloth. There was a second layer, made of different material, beneath the first. Kara thought it might be some sort of animal skin, though it was none that she recognized. She flipped the object over and saw that the skin had been sewn together with black thread, creating a sealed pouch.

Whatever was inside, Mother had taken great care to protect it.

Kara withdrew a small penknife from the folds of her cloak and cut carefully along the stitches. The thread had been pulled taut and snapped easily.

The skin slid to either side, revealing a black book.

It was bound in a strange material, cold and shiny and oddly moist when Kara touched it, though when she removed her hand, her fingertips weren't the slightest bit damp. Like the black soil, the book seemed to take exception to the natural laws of the world; though it was larger than the Path—a hefty tome, to say the least—it barely had any weight to it.

Vaguely she remembered seeing the book before. She had been four or five, her mother still alive.

In the barn . . . exploring . . . bored . . . a secret trapdoor . . . black book inside . . . Mother tearing it out of my hands . . .

Kara struggled to remember what happened next, but there was nothing more. She wasn't sure it mattered, though. The most important part of the memory had already been conveyed.

The book had belonged to her mother.

What if it's a witch's book? A grimoire? You need to bring it straight to the Elders.

But this voice of reason crumbled beneath the weight of Kara's curiosity. She started to open the book—*just one peek, just to see what's inside*—and that's when she realized she was no longer alone.

The figure of a man stood at the edge of the darkness. A pumpkin-orange, hooded cloak draped around his body and flowed through the trees like mist. He was far taller than a man should be, at least seven feet. Shadows obscured his face, and for this Kara was grateful. She knew that if she looked into his eyes, a part of her would be lost forever.

His hand reached out to her, clearly revealed in the glow of webs above them. Branches, shifting and curling like fingers, but branches nonetheless.

Kara felt her body go cold.

Sordyr.

A half-formed moan of terror slipped from her lips. Her breath came in short, needy gasps.

Run! she told herself. *Get away!*

But Kara could not move. Her feet felt encased in ten feet of dirt.

The Forest Demon regarded her from the darkness. His perusal made her feel weak and insignificant.

Kara found herself walking toward him.

What are you doing? she screamed. *Turn around!* But Kara's body had become a distant thing, too far away to hear her. Slowly but inextricably she made her way toward the cloaked figure.

With a single branched hand, Sordyr reached into his chest, pushing through the barklike skin. Kara heard digging sounds, and a moment later he produced a large, black seed, covered with dirt.

He held out the seed to her.

"Yours," he said.

Suddenly her mother's words floated down to her.

The Forest Demon will offer you a part of himself. You must refuse it, or you will become his forever.

Sordyr shook his branched hand impatiently.

Click, click, click.

Kara held the unearthed book before her like a shield. "This was my mother's," she said. Strength flowed through her. She thought of Taff, her father. If she allowed Sordyr to keep her here, she would never see them again.

Kara turned and ran.

Behind her Sordyr's branch hands clicked together, a strange and terrible language. The webspinner reappeared, using its segmented legs to string itself, upside down, along its glowing web. It was joined by another of its own kind. Then four. A dozen.

Sordyr's hands clicked together again. Louder this time. A command.

With shocking speed the creatures began to dismantle the web.

Kara ran as she had never run before, dodging the

suddenly appearing pockets of darkness. The black soil pulled at her feet like sand. Above her, webspinners chittered loudly as they worked. Strands of dead web floated to the earth, becoming tangled in her hair, her hands. Kara kept running. The opening was close, less than five hundred feet away, but there wasn't much time; the light had dimmed to a faint glow. If she didn't reach the opening before darkness overtook her, she would have no chance of finding it at—

A webspinner struck her shoulder. It was a glancing blow, but Kara was unprepared and lost her balance. She fell to one knee just in time to see a second webspinner leap in her direction. Kara swung the book. It connected with a satisfying *thunk* that sent the webspinner sprawling. She turned toward the tunnel in time to see a third webspinner, already airborne. Kara rolled out of its way. And ran. The Thickety was almost completely dark now, but Kara could still make out the entrance to the Fringe. Less than a hundred feet away, a welcoming sort of darkness.

Two webspinners landed on her back, but Kara ignored them, the frantic tugs on her hair, the wild chitterings in her ear.

The moment she slipped into the opening between the trees, the webspinners let go. She could hear their voices, soft and defeated, as they retreated. Their master would not be pleased.

Crouching, Kara took a few steps into the shelter of the tunnel. She could feel the branches just above her head, but they no longer made her feel trapped. They felt like armor. Safety.

Then Kara heard the voice behind her, as soft as a knife pulled from a sheath, as old as life itself.

"Kara," it whispered.

She felt warm breath on her ear. It expanded throughout the tunnel, filling it with the smell of autumn and fungus and dead things.

"Kara," Sordyr whispered again.

Branches clicked as he reached out to touch her.

Kara scrambled along the tunnel at a frantic, clawing pace. The scrapes and scratches along her knees and back meant nothing. The pain didn't matter. Nothing mattered except the small beacon of morning light in the distance.

She scampered into the fresh air of the outside world. The book in her hands felt substantial and real, and she hugged it to her chest as she navigated the Fringe. Only when she was a good distance away did Kara look back at the Thickety.

The opening between the trees had closed. Nothing pursued her.

But Kara could still feel his breath on her ear, hear his voice in her head.

Kara.

Her name. He had known her name.

Wondering if she would ever feel safe again, Kara opened the book.

Book Two
THE SHADOW FESTIVAL

*"A child who touches magic
is lost forever."*

—The Path
Leaf 928, Vein 116

SEVEN

Despite her exhaustion, Kara rose early the next morning so she could stop by the Lamb farm and check on her patient.

The wounds in Shadowdancer's hoof had not scabbed over yet, but they were well on their way. Kara flicked a few pieces of dried pus away with her penknife and ran a hand over the mare's foreleg.

No warmth. The infection was completely gone.

Kara smiled and stroked the horse's mane.

"You're getting better, girl," she whispered. "But try

to take it easy for another few days, just until your muscles get used to running again."

If Shadowdancer had been a different horse, Kara might have said the words with a singsong, soothing intonation; animals, particularly runners, loved the rhythm of it. But Shadowdancer would have found this babyish now that she was whole again, so Kara spoke to her directly, as she would a person. The proud horse demanded that sort of respect.

Leaving the stable, Kara almost walked into Constance Lamb.

"What are you doing here?" she demanded.

"I'm checking on Shadowdancer."

"No one asked you to do that."

"I know. I just wanted to make——"

"Where's that brother of yours?"

"He's sick," Kara said.

Taff had woken up with a fever and a small rash on his chest. She had begged Father to let her stay home from school and care for him, but he refused. Father might forget to pick the crops or bathe for a week, but he never ceased being a stickler when it came to attending school.

"He's sick a lot, that child," Constance said, and Kara was surprised to see a furrow of worry crease her brow. "What do you think—"

Suddenly the farm woman's eyes widened. She clasped her hands together and squeezed tightly.

"Where did you get that?" she asked.

Kara followed Constance's eyes to her mother's locket, hanging in the morning sun for the entire world to see. It had somehow slipped from its usual position beneath her school dress, though she didn't know how; Kara had threaded a lining inside the high collar of the dress to ensure the necklace stayed out of sight.

"I asked you a question," Constance repeated.

"I've always had it." Kara clasped the locket protectively. "Mother left it for me. Beneath my pillow, like she knew what was going to happen."

"Let me see it."

Before Kara could protest, Constance stepped forward and took the wooden locket in her hand, running her thumb over the simple shell embossed on its surface. Kara watched her carefully. If she tried to take the locket—or open it—Kara would slap her hand away and run off, no matter what the consequences.

I entered the Thickety to get this back, Kara thought. *No one will take it from me.*

Constance, however, seemed content to just hold it for a few seconds. When she looked up her eyes were moist.

She slipped the locket beneath Kara's shirt.

"There are grains of sand inside, from her home village. Before Helena was brought here."

Kara nodded.

"This was her most precious possession," Constance said, a new softness in her voice. "You'll want to keep it hidden, Kara. Close to your heart."

Without another word Constance Lamb made her way back to the farmhouse.

Kara continued to the schoolhouse alone, using a slightly circuitous path that avoided any view of the Thickety whatsoever. Since she had entered the forbidden forest, just looking at the trees filled her head with a low rumbling noise, like a river crashing between her ears. Kara had not had time to bind her hair properly, and it whipped wildly in the late-autumn wind, obscuring her view. She had heard that in the World girls could let their hair flow unrestrained, and although Kara admired the freedom this represented, she couldn't imagine how this would ever be practical on a windy day.

Her thoughts drifted to Constance Lamb, whose uncharacteristically kind reaction to Mother's locket confused her. Along with poor Aunt Abby, Constance had been her mother's closest friend but afterward had offered neither assistance nor compassion to the remaining

Westfalls. She had brought Taff into the world, of course, and Kara would be forever grateful for that. But the fact remained that until today she had shown Kara little more than cold indifference.

So why did Mother's locket bring her to tears?

Was Constance ashamed that she did not defend her best friend against the charges of witchcraft? Did she regret the way she had abandoned the Westfall family?

If so, it might finally be time for Kara to talk to her. More than anyone else, Constance would know what really happened that night.

This might be Kara's chance to finally learn the truth.

Resolute that she would speak to Constance as soon as possible, Kara returned her focus to getting to school on time—and was astonished to find herself sitting in the middle of a field, the black book open in her lap.

She had no recollection of coming here. Kara knew the place, of course—she had walked every inch of De'Noran, from Fringe to ocean. Father said a young couple used to live here when he was a boy, but they had abandoned the Fold and returned to the World. Their farmhouse had been left to rot in shame. Kara could see it from where she was sitting, a sagging skeleton overtaken by the elements. A short rope stubbornly clung to a tree branch where a swing used to hang, waiting in vain for its owners to return.

The farm—*the Thompson Farm*, Kara remembered—was not even on her way to school. In fact, it was in the opposite direction: north, toward the . . .

Thickety. I've been walking toward the Thickety.

With a cold shudder, Kara turned the book in her hands. She did not remember taking it out of her satchel (or putting the book *in* her satchel, for that matter). And yet here it was, open in her lap as though she had been reading for hours. Which was impossible, of course.

She felt watched.

Shooting to her feet, Kara turned to find Lucas

standing behind her. She felt her face turn red, as though she had been caught doing something wrong.

"What are you doing?" he asked.

"I'm just . . ." She searched for the right word. "Reading."

"That doesn't look like the Path," he said, eyeing the book with interest. "What is it? Did someone smuggle you a story from the World?"

Lucas stepped forward to peek at the pages, but Kara closed the book before he could see inside.

"It's nothing," she said.

Kara tucked the book into her satchel and hooked it shut.

When Lucas didn't respond, Kara knew she had hurt his feelings. They walked toward the schoolhouse in awkward silence, Kara wondering why she was being so secretive. There was no good reason *not* to show him the book. What harm could it do?

She was relieved when Lucas finally broke the silence.

"I found my family," he said.

Kara immediately felt guilty. No doubt he had been working himself up to share the news, and she had been too absorbed in her own troubles to notice.

"Are you sure?" she asked.

Lucas smiled.

"Yes," he said. "I think this time it's really them!"

Like all Clearers, Lucas had been born in the World. He had absolutely no memory of his birth parents: no vague recollection of a mother's warmth, no stirrings of familiarity upon hearing a certain lullaby. Most of his peers harbored little curiosity about their parents, choosing instead to curse them from afar—understandable, since they had sold them into a life of servitude. Lucas, however, remained obsessed with finding his blood relatives, certain that they had a good reason for abandoning him the way they did.

"They live in Dunn's Landing, right on the shore," he said. "They fish. The woman has brown eyes, just like mine. They have a little girl too, younger than Taff. I have a sister, Kara!"

She nodded, trying to keep her face as impassive as possible.

"They're far from rich now, but when they were first married, things were really bad. They didn't have enough money to feed their newborn son, so they . . . sold him to the Children of the Fold for two red seeds." Lucas looked away. "But they loved me, Kara. They didn't want to give me up. They were forced to in order to survive. That's different, isn't it?"

"Who told you this?" Kara asked.

"Hanson Blair. He's one of the oarsmen on the Ferry, and he's been asking around for me when they dock."

Kara knew Blair, a liar and a thief, and was sure that Lucas had paid well for this "information." Her friend was one of the most intelligent people she knew, but when it came to his family, he was blindingly optimistic.

"What are you thinking?" Lucas asked.

Kara hesitated. *Why do I have to be the one to crush him?*

He deserves a little happiness, even if it's a lie.

"That's wonderful news," Kara said. "You'll find them someday, when you visit the World. You'll be together again."

Lucas smiled, the big, relaxed grin that was both goofy and endearing.

"I have to go!" he said, and started on his way to the Clearer School. He took about fifteen steps and then called over one shoulder: "I'll return your book later!"

Kara was on him in ten steps. She grabbed his arm and spun him roughly around. There it was, in his hands. Open.

The black book. *Her* black book.

"Give it back!" she exclaimed.

Kara snatched it away, harder than she needed to. *When he put his hand on my arm, that's when he stole it. I should have known better than to trust him. To trust anyone.*

Lucas raised his hands into the air, the smile fading from his lips.

"Kara? I was just kidding around. I didn't meant to—"

"It's my book!" she exclaimed. "You have no right to touch it with your filthy Clearer hands. It's *mine*!"

Clutching the book to her chest, Kara set off toward school. Lucas remained at the top of the hill, dumbfounded. Finally he called after her: "Why are you so upset? It's nothing but blank pages!"

Kara kept walking.

EIGHT

Lucas is right. The book is useless.

Kara resisted an urge to toss it across her room. She could barely keep her eyes open, and yet here she was again, flipping through the pages in the middle of the night, searching for . . . she didn't even know what. A clue?

The pages remained as blank as ever.

When Kara had first opened her mother's book the night before, she had been thunderstruck by disappointment. She wasn't sure what she had expected to find, but anything would have been better than this: white page after white page after white page. She had risked her life by entering the Thickety . . . for nothing.

The worst part was that she had *believed*. Holding the book in her hands, Kara had felt the strange sensation of hope flood over her. *This is my mother's journal—it has to be!* Finally she was going to get the answers she longed for all these years.

She felt like such a fool.

Maybe there's some sort of trick to reading it, she thought, flipping through the pages. The book had been moved from its place beneath the floorboards of their barn— a perfectly adequate hiding spot—and hidden in the Thickety itself. Whatever secrets it held had to be amazingly important, otherwise Mother would have never taken such a huge risk.

More determined than ever, Kara tried everything she could think of to unlock the book's meaning. She examined the tome page by page, running a finger across every inch of white space, searching for some kind of telltale bump or groove. Each page was perfectly smooth. She knew that some of her classmates passed messages with what they called "vanishing ink," a simple mixture that remained invisible on the page but was easily revealed by the glow of candlelight. Kara tried it. Nothing. Since the blank pages invited her to write, Kara put quill to ink and wrote her name. Here, at least, the results were curious: The ink ran down the page like tears before dripping onto the floor.

The book was blank—and determined to stay that way.

Despite this, Kara could not get it out of her mind. Her thoughts had been wandering to the book all day, distracting her from Master Blackwood's lessons and making her forget her duties around the house. And now, despite her exhaustion, she remained awake, unable to stop flipping through the pages.

I need rest. A clear mind.

Sliding the book beneath her pallet, Kara blew out the bedside candle and forced herself to close her eyes. It was no use. Scattered thoughts about the book immediately bombarded her. *Perhaps pages once held writing but Thickety soil dissolved ink flesh from bones no Mother would know that so wouldn't hide it there could be something hidden inside cover cut it open whole book could be a hiding place . . .*

Kara flipped over on her side and tried to think of something else. Her thoughts wandered to Lucas. She couldn't believe how cruel she had been to him today. Lucas had done nothing wrong. He was just curious about the book.

I'll apologize tomorrow, she thought. *I'll let him look at the useless thing all he wants, and then I'll get rid of it forever.*

Feeling a little better, Kara closed her eyes. At some point in the night, her hand fell off the bed and slipped beneath the pallet, touching the book with a single finger.

Her dreams were dark.

After school the next day, Kara walked to the Fringe.

The infectious flora in this area had been carefully removed from the ground, but not all of it had been burned yet. As Kara walked between the towering piles of unearthed plants, she passed two Clearers using long pitchforks to poke at a mound of bulbous pods, draining any fluid at a distance before they risked transporting the weeds to the Burning Place. Both Clearers were large, bald men who wore heavy gloves and bandannas over their mouths and noses. They did their job without speaking. Kara, who did not have a bandanna, kept her mouth clamped shut. The air here was acrid enough to burn your tongue.

She continued toward the thick plumes of smoke that rose in the distance. Several Clearers were heading in that direction, pushing wheelbarrows overflowing with weeds. A stout woman nodded, and Kara returned the greeting with a small wave. She wasn't sure if she could call these people her friends, but they certainly afforded her more respect than anyone else on the island. In some ways, she was one of them. Her mother, being an orphan from a foreign land, had begun her life in De'Noran as a Clearer. She would have remained a Clearer had Father not insisted on her hand. As one of the most respected men in the village—some had even predicted he would be the next fen'de—his decision to marry so far below his class was openly questioned. But Father would have none of it. He loved her; it was as simple as that. Later most would claim he was bewitched. But Kara had witnessed her parents' love on a daily basis, and though she would agree that there was magic involved, it wasn't the kind they meant.

She was close to the Burning Place now, the greenish smoke hanging in the air like a pestilent fog. Kara tried not to gag on the smell, and though she kept her eyes slitted she would see the world with a greenish haze for hours afterward. Luckily she found Lucas before she had to get any closer. He was in his usual spot, shoveling up the less dangerous Fringe weeds with the rest of the younger Clearers.

"Kara?" he asked. "What are you doing here?"

Kara started to reply, but Lucas shook his head and handed her a bandanna. She covered her mouth.

"Can we talk?" she asked.

"Not now. There was a huge growth spurt last night— the usual weeds and some kind of yellowish plant we haven't seen before. Not deadly, but one touch is enough to make you really sick."

"I wanted to explain about yesterday."

Lucas ran the back of one gloved hand across his forehead, damp with perspiration. He nodded toward a short woman already heading in their direction, an exasperated look on her face.

"Can you come back in a few hours, after my duty ends? Framer's in charge today. You know how she is about breaks."

Kara shook her head. "Don't worry about that." She

opened her satchel, revealing the three pouches of ointment she had made that morning. Although it would not heal the more serious wounds, the medicine would soothe the everyday burns that came from working with the Fringe weeds. It was worth its weight in gold to any Clearer.

Lucas whistled beneath his bandanna.

"That'll buy me some time, for sure. But I still don't feel right leaving my friends to do all the work. Maybe I can just—"

"The book belonged to my mother."

Lucas put down his shovel.

"Come with me," he said.

He brought her to an empty section of the Fringe that had been completely cleared that morning. Already Kara could see weeds sprouting from the ground, however. Within a day or two, it would need to be cleared again.

"Can I see the book now?" Lucas asked, smiling with

mock caution. "Or are you going to yell at me again?"

"Sorry," Kara said, trying to return his smile but failing. Slowly she withdrew the book from her satchel but did not yet hand it to Lucas. It felt so *right* in her hands.

"Or I could just stare at it from here," Lucas said. He gazed at her strangely. "Kara?"

What are you doing? This is Lucas. You can trust him.

"Here," Kara said. She held the book forward, but she could not bring herself to put it in his hands. "Please take it."

He did. Kara resisted the urge to snatch it right back.

What's wrong with me?

"Don't tell anyone about this," she said.

"Why would I? It's just a blank book."

"People are sensitive when it comes to my mother. They might think it's a spellbook or something."

Kara saw Lucas tense.

"It's not," she said. "A spellbook."

"I know," he replied, too quickly. "If it was a spellbook,

there would be spells inside. Because that's what's in a spellbook. Which this is not."

Lucas flipped nervously through the pages. He did not blame witchcraft for every misfortune, as did many of the villagers, but you couldn't grow up in De'Noran without some fear of magic.

"I was thinking," Kara said, "that there might be some kind of hidden message inside. Maybe something my mother wanted me to know."

"Have you tried the trick with the lemon juice?"

"Yes."

"There's no writing. Anywhere."

"I know that."

"The paper feels like . . . paper."

"Wow," said Kara. "I feel like we're really sorting out this mystery now."

Without looking up Lucas playfully nudged her shoulder.

"*Good* paper," he added. "That might be important."

"Why?"

Lucas closed the book and ran his fingers over the binding.

"This leather is so weird," he said. "It feels wet. It should be wet."

"But it's not," Kara said.

"I don't like touching it," he said, handing the book back to her. Kara held it tight.

"I wonder what type of animal it comes from," he said. "Maybe we should ask the tanner."

"No!" Kara exclaimed. "No one else can know about this."

"But that part could be important. Depending on the animal, the book could be worth a lot."

"Why? It's just a book. It doesn't *do* anything."

"True—if you sold it in the general store, I doubt you'd get more than a couple of whites. But that's here in De'Noran. I have a friend who's apprenticed to a Trader. He makes the ferry run every month, across the water to the shore of the World." He shook his head in disgust. "They don't even get off the boat, you know—not allowed. How do you make that trip and not even get off the boat?"

"Lucas? Point."

"Some traders from the World meet them there, and my friend, he says those people have strange notions of what's valuable and what's not. They may have no interest in a perfectly good fishing rod, but show them a shiny rock they've never seen before and they get really excited. It's not so much what something does but how rare it is."

"That doesn't make any sense," said Kara.

"But maybe that was your mother's plan," Lucas said, thinking out loud. "Maybe she knew she might not . . . always be here and that things could get hard for you later on. Maybe she left the book for you to sell, so you'd have enough money to start a new life."

"You mean in the *World*? Don't be ridiculous!"

Lucas's gaze drifted toward the ocean. "Is it so strange," he asked, "to want to see it, at least?"

In school they had been taught that the World was a cesspool of greed and violence, populated by fools who chose to ignore the dangers of magic. These people had forgotten how the witches nearly destroyed everything almost two thousand years ago, how Timoth Clen saved them all. "The people of the World live only within their own years," Master Blackwood had told them. "They have never seen magic, and so many of them assume it doesn't exist." What they were good at, Kara learned, was war. Realm against realm, town against town, never ceasing. That's why Children were not allowed to leave the ship; strangers were killed instantly.

Stories of the World were enough to keep anyone from wanting to leave De'Noran.

Except Lucas.

"How can anything be worse than how we're treated here?" he asked, looking down at his green-tinged fingertips. "Both of us. Maybe your mother wanted you to leave."

"Maybe," Kara said. "But she didn't want me to sell this book. It can't be that simple."

"Why not?"

Because she buried it in the Thickety. Because it sends me strange dreams in which coiled snakes spring from my fingertips and fearsome beasts kneel before me.

The book was magic. She knew it. She just didn't know *how.*

Kara was trying to decide how much of this to tell Lucas when the trees of the Thickety parted and a creature of pure nightmare ran straight at them.

NINE

The gra'dak was short and squat but powerfully built. Its furless skin, the dark gray of overcooked fish, had flaked off in patches. Although the gra'dak's beady eyes were comically small, nature had more than compensated by giving it five mouths so different from one another that it seemed impossible they were part of the same creature. Chest mouth: the serrated teeth of darkwater fish; rear mouth: acidic tongue; forehead mouth: pincers. From within the gaping hole that passed for a normal mouth extended a pair of huge, boar-like tusks.

To Kara, however, the most disturbing mouth was also the least dangerous: a minuscule aperture concealed beneath the left forepaw that featured a full set of human teeth.

The gra'dak was still a good distance away, but Kara didn't need to see the telltale foaming of the mouths; only a sick animal would be confused enough to leave the Thickety. Though rare, this wasn't unheard of, which was why the Clearers always had their strongest fighters stand guard while they worked.

Unfortunately this wasn't a work area. Kara and Lucas were alone.

"Don't run," Lucas said, out of the corner of his mouth. He was trying to act confident, but she heard his voice tremble. "Their eyesight is bad. They react to motion."

Dust plumed into the air as the gra'dak came at a mad gallop.

"He's heading straight toward us."

"That's just a coincidence. He can't see that far."

The gra'dak squealed. Its mouths worked in unison, emitting a sound like a chorus of rabid boars.

"I really think it can see us," Kara said.

Lucas wrapped one arm around Kara, his grip firm. "I've dealt with these before. They're dangerous but stupid. We just need to move out of its path. Slowly."

Together they slid to the left. With the gra'dak bearing down on them, Kara found it difficult not to move quickly, but Lucas held her tight and determined their pace. By the time the creature passed where they had been standing, they were a good ten feet away.

"Okay," Lucas whispered. He was still nervous but pleased that his plan had worked. "Now we have to warn the others before—"

The gra'dak almost flipped over as it came to a sliding, violent stop and charged straight toward them. They turned to run, but there wasn't enough time. The creature plowed into Kara at terrible speed and knocked her off her feet. She felt the immense weight of it on her back and grimaced with the anticipation of pain, wondering which mouth would bite her first. Instead she heard five discordant howls of pain. She turned over. Lucas had succeeded in kicking the beast off of her, but the gra'dak had already regained its footing and Lucas wasn't sure what to do next. He searched for a weapon, but the field had been cleared of everything, even rocks. At the worst possible time, the Fringe was the least dangerous place on the island. The gra'dak swung its body in a powerful arc and knocked Lucas to the ground. Before Kara could even get to her feet, the monster had used its pincers to snip off two of Lucas's fingers, snapping both out of the air with its fish mouth and swallowing them whole. Lucas started to scream, but the gra'dak leaped onto his chest with surprising agility and suffocated the sound. The monster bent its head down, preparing to gorge itself.

Kara screamed.

She wasn't scared, not for herself. But the thought of this beast erasing her only friend from the world was unacceptable. The genesis of her scream was not fear. It was fury.

Stop this now!

The gra'dak froze in midthrust, its deadly incisors pressed against the flesh of Lucas's stomach. All it had to do was jerk its head forward, and it would be done. Lucas, his eyes wide with fear, stared up at the creature.

Without another sound the gra'dak stepped off Lucas and made its way back toward the Thickety. It did not turn around. By the time Kara had torn off the hem of her dress and wrapped it tightly around Lucas's bloody hand, the gra'dak was gone. Kara looked up just in time to see the trees closing together. In a few moments, it was as though the creature had never been there at all.

Kara assumed that she would somehow be blamed for the attack, but the Clearers were remarkably sympathetic. They praised her bravery and quick thinking, especially for binding Lucas's wounds with gemroots in order to stop the bleeding. She was hugged and patted and forced to drink two cups of their bitter tea. Kara, obviously still in a state of shock, did not even gag.

Lucas had fallen asleep as soon as they reached his house, leaving Kara alone with his "family," a motley crew of noisy Clearers as different from Kara as they were from one another. Light skin, dark skin, red hair, tawny hair, freckles, wide eyes, slanted eyes . . . the diversity in the room stunned her. In the village it was so easy to mistake one blond-haired farmer for another; only Kara, with her mother's foreign features, stood out. These Clearers, however, had been plucked from lands all over the World, and although they were not related by blood, they seemed to enjoy a bond and camaraderie most families would envy.

In time it began to get dark, and although Kara longed to check on Lucas, she knew she should start home. The women of the house assured her that he was going to be fine and encouraged Kara to visit again as soon as possible.

She gathered her things and set off, stopping three times on the journey home to make sure the black book was still in her satchel. It was.

Taff sat at the kitchen table, sketching the plans for some sort of invention. This one would be made, as far as Kara could tell, from chicken wire, a broken feed chute, and some sort of pulley system.

"What's that supposed to be?" Kara asked.

"A potato shooter."

Kara looked at the sketch closely.

"Why do you need a potato shooter?" she asked.

"To shoot potatoes."

Taff's laugh quickly turned into a cough. Kara reached out to touch his forehead, but he brushed her hand away.

"I'm fine," Taff said.

"Did you eat anything?"

He shook his head. "I was hungry before, but I can't find Father. He must be out in the fields somewhere. They got our barn instead of the door this time. I don't know what it is, but it smells *disgusting*, and not in a good way. Did Father clean it yet?"

"I'm sure he meant to," Kara said. *Except he's too busy feeling sorry for himself to actually do any work.* The thought came unbidden, and Kara scolded herself for such unkindness. *I really do need sleep.* The important thing was that their barn was clean again; before entering the house, she had scraped off the chunks, then used a brush and hot water to scrub away the smaller pieces.

Kara boiled some potatoes, then mashed them with salt, butter, and cinnamon. Using her fingertips, she molded the mixture into simple shapes—a star, a boat, a flower—and placed the plate in front of Taff.

"You need to eat," she said, kissing him on the forehead. It was clammy.

She found Father curled beneath the front porch like an animal seeking shade. At first she thought he had been drinking, but there was no alcohol on his breath. It had simply been one of his bad days. His clothes were torn and filthy, and his tangled beard was crusted with mud. Kara tugged on his arm gently, and Father looked up, recognition coming seconds later. Kara guided him to the bathroom. He sat on the floor and mumbled quietly as she filled the tub with water from the well outside, adding a kettleful of boiled water at the end to warm the lot. She closed the door behind her and was relieved to hear, in a few minutes' time, the sound of her father easing himself into the water.

She brought his clothes downstairs to soak but removed the notebook from his pants pocket first. The book fell to the floor and spread open on its thin spine, revealing the same two words scrawled across every inch of white space:

FORGIVE ME FORGIVE ME FORGIVE ME

After his bath Father stopped for a few moments in Taff's room. Kara heard their soft voices through her wall. She couldn't make out the specifics of their conversation, but at least he was talking. That was a good sign.

After telling Taff good night, Father walked the few steps to Kara's room. He paused outside her closed door before retiring to his own room. Kara wasn't surprised. Father was always hesitant to talk to her after one of his bad days. Tomorrow she could expect some unusual kindness as recompense, such as Father making breakfast or doing some of her usual chores. Kara looked forward to it.

But that was tomorrow. Tonight, there was still work to do.

She waited until she heard Father's thunderous snoring before withdrawing the grimoire from her satchel. As soon as she touched the cover a jolt shot from her fingers to her shoulder, as though her arm had been asleep and feeling was returning to it all at once.

The gra'dak had listened to me.

It sounded crazy, especially now that several hours had

passed since the incident, but Kara knew it was the truth. She had commanded a creature of the Thickety.

The book had to be responsible.

Placing it on her bed, Kara held the single candle on her bedside table as close to the cover as possible. As the flame danced and sputtered, dark figures seemed to move along the book's surface, shadows upon shadows. Kara opened the book. As always, it gave off the faint fragrance of gingerblossoms and melted candle wax.

The gra'dak waited on the first page.

Charcoal lines rendered the creature more vividly than any other drawing she had ever seen, as though the gra'dak itself had been pressed between the pages. Kara ran a fingertip along the page, feeling for the bump of a crushed skeleton, the pinch of pincers. There was nothing but flat lines.

Except, looking closer, Kara saw that they were not lines at all.

She balanced the grimoire against her headboard and

moved the candle so close that she was sure the paper would begin to blacken and shrivel. It did not. Instead the lines-that-were-not-lines grew darker, as though the illustration were rising to the surface, eager to be discovered. Kara was able to see the tiny, interconnected swirls and dots that composed the image of the gra'dak, the spaces between them so minute that they looked, upon first glance, like simple lines. She traced a finger along one of the strange symbols, and then another, starting at the thing's ratlike tail and then working her way along the body.

It was only when Kara reached the gra'dak's head that she realized she was mumbling something.

She clapped a hand to her mouth, momentarily forgetting that she was holding a candle, and then, without thinking, tossed it away as she felt a burst of unexpected heat sear her forehead. The candle rolled across the wooden floor. Kara sprang out of bed, intending to stomp out the flame before it could cause any damage, but the wick had already extinguished itself.

The room was plunged into darkness. Kara remained crouched on the floor, listening for the sounds of her brother or father waking from their sleep. Nothing. There was, however, another sound. Or rather, sounds. A piglike snorting coupled with high-pitched wheezing, the sounds simultaneous but emanating from the same source.

Kara crawled onto her bed and looked outside. Her bedroom window was only a few feet off the ground, but her view was unobstructed by bushes or trees, and she could see for a good distance. She saw nothing unusual.

And yet the noise continued.

Kara was considering unlatching the window and peeking her head out for a better look when the gra'dak leaped into view, balancing on the window ledge with its forepaws. It breathed out hot air and fogged the glass.

Kara fell backward in surprise. She hadn't seen the gra'dak, because it had been right below her window.

But how had it gotten there in the first place?

The gra'dak stood still. It pressed its paw against the glass, giving her a clear view of the human mouth.

"Hello," Kara said.

The gra'dak stared back at her with its absurdly small eyes. Up close Kara could see that they were a rather pleasant shade of green, like dew-grass. She hadn't noticed that earlier.

She pressed her hand against the glass. The gra'dak, shocked by this sudden movement, lost its purchase on the ledge and slipped out of sight. *It's scared of me,* Kara thought, assuming that it would now run away. But the gra'dak quickly regained its original position and began licking her hand through the window.

Kara knew animals. This wasn't a sign of affection. It was submission.

It sees me as its master. Because I called it here.

She knew what the symbols were now. They were words. And somehow Kara had known how to read them.

I just cast a spell.

This thought and its repercussions hit her like a physical force. The room started to spin. Kara clung to the window casing, refusing to let go, even when one of her nails split against the wood. She was terrified that she would be thrown off into the night, not stopping until she reached the Thickety.

I just cast a spell, she thought again. Her breathing came soft and fast.

The gra'dak stood patiently at the window, waiting for a new command.

"Go," she whispered. Kara merely mouthed the word, her throat too dry to make the sound, but it didn't matter. The gra'dak took off, streaking into the night, a writhing, breathing shadow.

Kara remained at the window and watched the animal until it was gone. The windowpane was cold beneath her fingertips. *Everyone was right*, she thought. *I'm a witch.* At least she knew now. She had been the bane of the village her entire life, the embodiment of fear and evil.

All their hatred had been warranted. There was darkness within her.

I'm a witch. Just like my mother.

Kara started to shiver. She pulled a blanket around herself, but this coldness was nestled deep in her heart and would not be subdued by lambskin or burning coal. This coldness was a part of her.

TEN

When Kara woke up the next morning, she knew what she had to do: Destroy the grimoire. She decided when and where she would set the fire, even how much wood she would need. But as Kara stepped out the front door she wondered if she was being hasty. This was, after all, the only connection she had to her mother. Perhaps the book held other secrets, other answers.

Kara found herself returning to the abandoned Thompson farm.

I am a Child of the Fold, and I do not want to use magic,

she thought, *but I might have to, in order to learn the truth. And the truth is a good, righteous thing! Wasn't it Timoth Clen himself who said, 'Truth is the flame that reveals all'? He would understand: I just need to cast a single spell so I know that what happened last night wasn't a figment of my imagination. After that I'll destroy the book.*

Kara sat in the weeds in front of the house and placed a small stone on the ground. *Moving an object without touching it. That sounds like something a witch should be able to do.* Kara stared at the stone. *Move*, she thought. When this didn't work, Kara took the grimoire out of her satchel and held it in her lap. She willed the stone to move once more. It didn't. Kara opened the grimoire to a blank page and placed her hand on it. Stared at the stone.

"Move!" she exclaimed.

Nothing.

Kara realized, with a sinking sensation, that she had no idea what to do.

She hadn't meant to control the gra'dak; it had simply

happened. Trying to cast a spell intentionally was completely different. She wondered if it was even possible.

It has to be. I just have to figure out what I did the first time.

A plump rat scampered across the roof of the farmhouse. It settled inside the rain gutter but peeked its head out, pink eyes intent with curiosity.

Kara held the stone in her hand and tried it that way. Nothing. *Perhaps it's too large.* She tried a smaller stone and then a smaller one than that, eventually working her way down to a pebble.

"Move!" she exclaimed. "Please?"

Kara thought the pebble trembled just the slightest bit. Then she realized that she was the one shaking—with frustration. This was ridiculous. What was the sense of having powers if she didn't know how to use them?

But you're not going to use them. You're going to destroy the book.

Of course she was. But when Kara set out to do something, whether it was chores around the house or copying passages on a slate, she expected to get it done. If she could control a beast from the Thickety, she should be able to move a stupid little rock. She had assumed this would be easy, and the fact that it seemed completely out of her control made Kara angry.

It struck her, then. The answer.

Anger.

When she had cast her first spell, she had been furious. Terrified and desperate too. The gra'dak was going to kill her friend, and she would have done anything to stop it. The magic of the spell had been generated through strong emotion.

That felt right to her. Emotion was the key.

Kara looked back at the pebble. She thought of all the people who had wronged her through the years. The fen'de. Grace. She remembered her mother, the future that should have been hers. All of this and more she focused into her next word.

"Move!" she exclaimed, throwing her arms into the air.

The pebble, unimpressed by this dramatic display, remained still.

"Ahhhhh!" Kara threw the pebble as hard as she could toward the abandoned farmhouse. It struck one of the remaining windows but, not being large enough to break the glass, bounced away with a pathetic little *plink*.

Still watching from above, the rat regarded Kara with what might have been amusement.

"Stop looking at me!" Kara screamed.

The rat froze as though caught in a beam of light. Slowly, like a marionette on a string, it spun on its hind legs until it was facing away from her.

It remained that way. Motionless.

"Hey!" Kara called out. She clapped her hands together. "Hey!"

The rat trembled slightly but remained in place.

It can't move, thought Kara. *Unless I let it.*

She flipped opened the grimoire. A perfect illustration of a rat had appeared on the second page, constructed from the words she would need to conjure it again. She compared the sketch in front of her to the rat on the roof. The details, surprisingly, were not exactly the same. In the illustration the rat was thinner, fiercer-looking. Nothing like the pathetic creature before her.

"The drawing isn't just this rat," Kara said. "It's any rat. All of them."

Kara wondered how long her little friend would stay on the roof. Would it be released the moment she left? Or, if she came back two weeks from now, would there be nothing left but a tiny pile of bones?

Why not try it?

Kara was tempted. It was only a rat, after all. Any farmer would kill it instantly. She would be doing the community a favor.

But then she thought of how the innocent creature must feel—like a prisoner in its own flesh—and suddenly felt ill that she would even consider enslaving it a moment longer.

"Go," she said. "I release you."

The rat scampered over the far side of the roof and was gone in seconds.

No matter what I did, I never would have been able to move the stone, Kara thought. *I can only control animals. That's my gift.*

Kara had never thought of witches as having specialties, but she supposed hers made sense. She had always had a way with any sort of animal, from horses and sheep to the smallest mouse. Truth be told, she felt a closer connection to them than to most of the people in her life.

She ran a hand over the illustration of the rat. It was slightly warm to the touch, as though the symbols had just been branded into the page. Kara felt a temptation to speak the words and let them course through her. If she wanted to, she could make dozens of rats rush to her feet. They would have no choice but to obey. How nice it would feel, after all these years, to finally be the one giving orders. To be in control.

Kara slammed the grimoire closed.

She needed no sermons or parables to know that forcing a living creature to do her will was wrong. She thrust the spellbook into her satchel with a solemn promise that she would never open it again. Her purpose today had been to learn what it could do. Now that she had, she could destroy the grimoire and be done with it forever.

She imprinted the next creature in the grimoire by accident. Kara had been sitting in class, thinking about the best place on the island to build a secret pyre for the book, when a fly landed on her desk. She swatted it away, but the persistent insect returned, its incessant buzzing disturbing Kara's thoughts. Before she could even think about what she was doing, the fly had suddenly paused in midair, hovering before her face.

Go away, she thought.

The fly darted out the window. She found the new addition to the spellbook after class. Having never seen a fly in such detail, Kara stared at it for some time, entranced. This made her curious about what other insects looked like up close. She skipped her chores and learned how to conjure a beetle and an earthworm. *Just to see the pictures*, she told herself. Then she began to wonder how the illustrations appeared. Did they simply rise up from the paper, all at once, or were they scrawled by an invisible hand one symbol at a time? Kara took to capturing animals with the grimoire open in front of her, hoping to see the new entry in the process of appearing. In this way she learned how to conjure a nightjay, a bloomjacket, a black beetle, and a ladyspider. Kara never did see a page in the process of being illustrated, but in time she forgot that had even been her intention and just continued to gather different species. Hummingbeetle, lilysnapper, batterkay. She spent one glorious day knee-deep in pond water. Trestlefish, snapping turtle, orangeray. Kara promised herself each and every day that she would destroy the grimoire, but somehow that never happened, and after two weeks she stopped promising. Controlling the animals would be wrong; she admitted that. But all she was doing was gathering them into a beautiful book. She was like a naturalist, except instead of using charcoal and paper she was using her gift.

By the end of the month, she had filled the first forty pages of the grimoire.

Spells, apparently, had weight, and the grimoire grew much heavier. Kara's shoulder ached from carrying it in her satchel, so she started to keep it hidden in its original spot beneath the floorboards of the barn. During class she stared into space and recalled the touch of each page, the music of the symbols. At night she slept with the book under her pillow. She listened carefully to the sounds of the sleeping house, eager to hear the telltale pitter-patter of a mouse, even the soft rustling of a bedbug. They were small—insignificant, even—but she would take them. Finding that she no longer needed as much sleep as she used to, Kara began to spend the nights with her face pressed up against the window, gasping with anticipation at the slightest movement in the dark. Perhaps it was a new creature, one she lacked.

This was how she came to hear the people outside.

There were four of them, dark shapes huddled together in the night. One shape loomed over the others, and Kara quickly identified this as Simon Loder. It was the first time she had ever seen the giant without Grace, though Kara had little doubt that the white-haired girl was behind his appearance here.

The group made its way toward the barn, laughing and hushing one another. A huge sack dangled from Simon's shoulder. Something black and viscous leaked from the bottom.

Kara knew why they were here.

The bedroom window creaked when Kara opened it, but she doubted anyone heard; it had been windy lately, and this night was no different. She slipped through the small opening and onto the ground below. Although Kara was wearing only a nightshirt, the frigid temperature didn't bother her.

Standing on tiptoe, Kara reached back inside her room and grabbed the grimoire.

She kept close to the shadows of the house and then dashed across the property until she could see the four boys gathered outside the barn. In addition to Simon, the group included Aaron Baker, Silas Goodson, and one of the Lambs' farmhands, a burly youth no older than fourteen. All of them paced with nervous energy except for Simon, who watched the proceedings with his usual blank-faced wonder. The three other boys were arguing among themselves about who would get to "do it" this time. Kara found their whisper-shouting so silly that she had to stifle a laugh. She couldn't believe that these children, none of them much older than herself, had been vandalizing her house all these months. Why had she ever been frightened of them?

Finally Silas—a weaselly, red-haired boy—snatched

the sack from Simon, who reacted with about as much emotion as a log.

"She told me I could do it this time," Silas said.

He must mean Grace, Kara thought. *Surprise, surprise.*

Silas opened the sack slightly, wincing at the smell. He raised it up, preparing to throw the contents at the barn door but first smiled back at his cohorts.

"This is going to be good," he said.

Kara sent the rats.

They came from nowhere, a writhing mass of fur and teeth that swarmed around Silas's feet. The sack fell from his hands, and Kara watched with no little satisfaction as the brackish contents intended to humiliate her family splattered across Silas's pants.

The farmhand—easily the smartest of the four—took off.

Silas slapped at himself and screamed—a high-pitched, surprisingly feminine shriek—as white blurs slipped up his pants. Aaron tried to help him, but the rats bridged the gap and covered his arms and chest. Simon, his face as impassive as ever, calmly plucked a rat off the ground and crushed it in one hand. Kara screamed as a sharp pain pierced her chest.

It hurts me when they die, she thought.

She looked up and saw all three boys looking in her direction.

"Witch," Aaron said. "Witch!"

Simon took a step forward, but Silas grabbed him by the collar, guiding him across the field. Kara allowed the rats to pursue them for a few minutes before releasing her hold.

The night was quiet once more.

Kara searched the ground until she found the rat Simon had killed. Cradling it gently in her arms, she returned to the house and buried the fallen soldier beneath her bedroom window. It seemed the least she could do.

ELEVEN

Sordyr chased the Leaf Girl through the village.

The people of De'Noran, lining either side of the dirt road, blocked any escape route. Many were eating popcorn or candy apples, and not even the smallest child was frightened. For one thing Sordyr hardly looked real; the farmer playing him was wearing a tattered orange cloak and a papier-mâché mask that kept slipping from his face. And although Tammy Little was an exceptionally adorable Leaf Girl, her mother had done a poor job attaching the leaves to her clothes. They had been falling off since the chase began, and a trail of them, like bread crumbs, led back to the starting point.

Despite all this, Kara still had to clasp her hands together to keep them from trembling. Images from the Thickety swarmed her mind. Sordyr's branched hand digging in his chest. The way he had whispered her name as though he had always known her.

Doing her best to shake free of such dark thoughts, she smiled up at Taff, who was perched on Father's shoulders. The Leaf Girl would be passing their way in a few minutes, and he wanted the best view possible. Someone began singing "Night's Long Journey" in anticipation, and the crowd joined in, filling the afternoon with music. The song had never been Kara's favorite, but she sang along anyway, clapping her hands during the chorus.

She realized, with a tremor of surprise, that she was having fun.

Usually Kara dreaded the Shadow Festival. For everyone else it was a ten-day respite from the strict rules of their religion, an invitation to relax and frolic. Yet for some reason this freedom encouraged the villagers to heap abuse on the Westfalls to an even greater degree than usual. By Last Night their property would be in shambles, a wasteland of moondrink jugs and rotting vegetables.

This year things were already different. No one had insulted them as they passed through the crowd. Kara had not been hit in the back by apple cores or had lemonade "accidentally" spilled on her dress. Not that the villagers were friendly, of course. They simply avoided looking in her family's direction. In fact, Father was able to maneuver Kara and Taff to a prime position closest to the road. The crowd seemed to part for them as they passed.

A pinch-faced woman met Kara's eyes. She whispered something to her husband, and the two ushered their family away.

Suddenly Kara knew what had changed.

Word had spread about the incident at the farmhouse. Before, she had been a harmless little girl who they could treat any way they wanted, but now . . . they were afraid of her.

Good.

The crowd cheered as the Leaf Girl passed their way. Taff watched her, entranced, and Kara couldn't help but smile. She reminded herself to start on his costume that night. She had promised to make him something special, and there was only a week left to Last Night. *Real scary*, he had told her, *not kid scary*. At his age the final night of the Shadow Festival *was* scary: the only time of the year when demons could cross the borders of the Thickety and enter De'Noran. As the years passed, however, most children came to realize that this was only a myth, a bit of fun the adults had at their children's expense. Although older children still wore the masks, they no longer believed they *had* to wear them in order to remain hidden among the unwelcome visitors. Mostly they were just interested in who was going to the festival with who, as boys and girls who attended the Shadow Festival together usually wed when they were eighteen, the Marrying Age.

"Taff seems to be having fun," Lucas said, joining them. The stumps of his fingers had healed nicely. Since he could no longer lift a shovel or a pitchfork with ease, his duty had been changed. He was now an Observer, charged with keeping track of how much the Fringe was growing each day. It was a job usually reserved for the infirm and elderly, and although Lucas's pride had taken a hit, the work was much safer.

"I never actually thanked you," Lucas said. "You saved my life."

"No, I didn't," Kara said. "I don't even know what happened. The beast just turned and ran back into the Thickety."

The crowd erupted in applause as the Forest Demon tried to snatch the Leaf Girl and she dove between his legs, barely escaping.

Lucas turned to face her.

"We both know that's not true."

Kara started to respond, then stopped herself. She wanted to tell him about the grimoire and the things she could do—but not here. There were too many ears.

And can you really trust him? Friend or not, will he really understand?

"So," Lucas said, "your brother said his costume is going to scare even me on Last Night. You must have something special in mind."

Kara smiled.

"I'll do my best," she said.

In addition to making a costume for Taff, she wondered if she ought to start on a dress for herself. *Something long and red, like Mother would have worn . . .*

Just in front of her, the farmer playing Sordyr grabbed the Leaf Girl, who screamed in surprisingly convincing horror as he wrapped his cloak around her. The two figures remained motionless for a moment.

Kara felt the warmth drain from her body.

"Kara?" Lucas asked. "Are you all right?"

She did not move. Even when the crowd burst into applause, and the farmer and Tammy Little had taken their bows, Kara remained frozen in place. She could imagine, all too clearly, what it would be like to be lost in that cloak forever—and it terrified her.

When they got home, the graycloaks were everywhere, combing their property as though searching for something. *The grimoire*, Kara thought, her eyes flashing to the barn. The doors had been propped open, and inside she could see several graycloaks stabbing the hay with their ball-staffs while others tore open sacks of seed. Kara tensed her body, preparing to make a desperate sprint for the book, but Taff, as though sensing her intentions, grabbed her hand. She took a deep breath and tried to calm herself. Even if she did reach the book, what was she going to do? It would take more than just rats to drive the graycloaks off, and someone was liable to get killed.

Maybe all of them. And what would be wrong with that?

Two graycloaks approached, long ball-staffs held diagonally across their bodies. One end of the staff was a wooden ball packed with iron filings. The other end was sharpened to a point. Different ends for different situations.

"Get inside," the older one said. He spoke directly to Father, though it was Kara he eyed warily. "He's waiting for you."

At the sound of those words, Kara's heart was seized in an icy grip, and she wondered if she should have made a run for it after all.

He sat at their table, drinking coffee. As always his eyes immediately found Kara's.

"Work hard, want nothing," he said.

"Stay vigilant," they replied in unison.

Fen'de Stone turned to face her father.

"How are you, William?" he asked. "Could I get you a cup of coffee? I brought my own beans. It seemed uncharitable, using yours, given these unfortunate circumstances." Fen'de Stone waved his hand, and a fifteen-year-old boy wearing a band of gray around his arm poured a cup of coffee from the percolator. His name was Marsten Cloud; Kara remembered him from school before the fen'de stole him for a life of religious devotion. These days the two were never apart.

Marsten handed the coffee to Father.

"Freshly made," the fen'de said. "Incidentally I couldn't help noticing that you were all out of your own beans, so I refilled your jar from my own personal stock."

"How kind of you," said Father.

"Don't worry about paying me back," said Fen'de Stone. "I wouldn't hear of it."

He clapped a hand on Father's shoulder as though they were great friends.

This was nothing new.

In the years following Mother's execution, Fen'de Stone had been unfailingly kind. Again and again he arrived at their time of greatest need: when there weren't seeds enough to buy a single meal or when Father couldn't work up the will to get out of bed. It seemed that Fen'de Stone was always watching them, waiting to knock on their door at the last moment and save their family from utter devastation.

He had murdered her mother. He had made her family the outcasts of De'Noran. Kara hated him with a passion so black, it frightened her sometimes. Yet all she could do, upon seeing him in the street, was curtsy and say thank you.

Kara was certain he took great pleasure from that.

"Fine coffee," Father said, taking a sip from his steaming cup.

The fen'de folded his hands behind his head and leaned back in his chair, highlighting an ample belly. Somehow, even during the bad seasons when crops provided little sustenance, the fen'de found a way to eat well.

"Drink up, old friend. Then we'll talk." He sighed. "It

seems we have a bit of a problem here."

They entered, then, as though on cue. Silas Goodson. Aaron Baker. Simon Loder.

Last into the room, her cane clicking against the stone floor, came Grace. Kara was surprised to see her but not nearly as surprised as Fen'de Stone.

"What are you doing here?" he asked.

"I thought this would be a good opportunity for me to observe how you handle such a delicate situation," Grace said. Her eyes never left the floor. "This way in years to come—"

"You are not needed."

"Maybe I can offer some insight into—"

"Go home, Grace. *Now.*"

Kara expected Grace to argue, but instead she simply nodded.

"Yes, Papa."

She kissed her father on the cheek and clicked her way through the silent kitchen, Simon at her heels. Marsten

Cloud held the door for them both, sneaking Grace a victorious smirk as she passed.

Fen'de Stone took a sip of coffee before returning to business. "There has been a formal complaint," he said. "These boys were attacked, while on your property, by a vicious throng of unusually inspired vermin. They also saw your daughter at the scene of the . . . incident. It's unfortunate, but given your family's history, I can do nothing else but suspect witchcraft."

This is it, Kara thought, her heart pounding in her chest. *They're going to bring me to the rocky field just like Mother and hang me from a tree.*

"That's a lie!" Taff exclaimed. "They're making up stories just to get Kara in trouble!"

"Taff," Kara said softly. "Please don't get involved."

Silas held forth his forearm, a grotesque patchwork of oozing scratches and bite marks. "Does this look like a lie, you little runt?"

"So you got bit by something? So what? My sister never

touched you." Taff turned to the fen'de. "They're liars! And you're a liar if you believe them!"

"Enough!" the fen'de exclaimed. The room came to a halt as he turned to Marsten Cloud. "Remove him," he said.

The fen'de's apprentice grabbed Taff by the elbow, none too gently. From the corner of her eye, Kara saw her father tense.

"It's just not fair," Taff mumbled as he was guided outside. "It's never fair. It's never—"

The door slammed shut. Kara was relieved to see him go. If something terrible was about to happen to her, she didn't want him there to see it.

Father was first to speak again. "You're saying these boys were on my land?"

"That's right!" Aaron exclaimed. "We were here!"

"Might I ask why?"

The boys refused to meet his eyes. And Kara's father, in a moment of rare lucidity, understood.

"Ahh," he said. "You're the ones who've been vandalizing my property."

"That don't matter," Aaron said. "We were just having a little fun. Not hurting anyone."

"Not like this witch here!" Silas added.

Father made a low grunt deep in his throat and took a step toward Silas. The boy seemed to shrivel beneath her father's rising anger.

"So let me get this straight," Father said, jabbing a finger into Silas's chest. "You throw dung and urine and Clen knows what else against my door, and then you have the nerve to come into my house and say you were attacked by some kind of, what? Monsters?"

"Rats!" Aaron said.

Father turned his wrath on Aaron, who instantly studied his toes.

"Really, um, big rats," Aaron added.

"Right," Father said. "Rats. It's a farm. We have rats in our barn. In the stable. Did it ever occur to you that there might be a simpler explanation? Any animal blood in that wonderful concoction you were going to throw against my door?" When neither boy answered, he continued, "The rats smelled it. That's why they attacked you."

"It wasn't just a few rats. There were lots of them."

"And we *saw* her there!" Silas exclaimed.

"I live here!" Kara snapped. "Did you ever think of that?" She turned to her father. "I heard noises outside and came out to investigate. They were being attacked by rats, all right. That part's true. But I had nothing to do with it."

"Why didn't you tell me?" Kara's father asked.

"I did," Kara said. "You must have forgotten."

He turned his face away, accepting her lie as truth, and Kara instantly hated herself for telling it.

No need to be ashamed. You did what was necessary to protect yourself.

Silas turned to Fen'de Stone. "She's a witch, just like her mother."

"She did something near the Fringe too," Aaron added. "I heard she made a Thickety monster attack this Clearer boy. . . ."

Fen'de Stone rose to his feet and gave each of the boys a long stare.

"We're done here. My men have combed this place from top to bottom. If there were any evidence of witchcraft, they would have reported it by now."

Silas and Aaron stared at the fen'de, openmouthed.

"So, that's it?" Silas asked.

"Yes," Fen'de Stone said. "That's it. For now." He turned to Kara. "It's too bad that my pet is no longer with us, Kara. The nightseeker. Do you remember?"

A doglike creature snorting her blood . . .

"I remember," she said.

"Such a creature would settle this argument quickly. But there was something about that particular nightseeker that I just didn't trust. I dined upon it immediately following your mother's execution." He patted his stomach.

"Not much meat, but oddly filling."

The men left.

Father stood there in silence and leaned his forehead against the door. As Kara watched, he seemed to shrink before her eyes, as though his former self was a costume he could wear for only a short time.

"Kara," he whispered. "Tell me it wasn't you."

She wanted to. She would tell him anything, as long as he would stay like this: strong, a whole man, her real father. But although Kara could hear the right words in her head, the lie refused to pass her lips. Finally her father shuffled off. He would not leave his room again that day, and she knew that when she saw him the next morning, his fingernails would be stained with ink.

After making sure that Taff was unharmed, Kara entered the barn. It looked like it had been at the epicenter of some great storm. At least a dozen sacks had been torn open and emptied; no matter where she stepped, seed and chicken feed cracked beneath her feet. Tools, yanked from their wooden pegs, lay strewn across the floor. Those with wooden shafts had been snapped in two.

Kara knew she should be angry, but right now there was only one thing on her mind: the grimoire. After glancing back at the house to make sure that Taff had not followed her, Kara closed the barn door. *It's safe. It has to be.* If a graycloak had found it, he would have immediately brought it to the attention of the fen'de. She just needed to see it, hold it in her hands (*use it*) before she could rest.

Kara pulled on the trapdoor. She had oiled the hinges herself, and it opened smoothly, without a sound.

The hiding space was empty.

Not quite understanding, Kara held the lantern closer. Perhaps her grimoire had moved just out of reach in order to hide from the graycloaks? Given the book's extraordinary powers, the ability to slide a few feet did not seem beyond the realm of reason.

After a few minutes of careful examination, however,

Kara had no doubt that the book was gone. In its place were five tiny dots, nestled in the soil as though trying to plant themselves there. Kara dug them out with one trembling hand and gazed at her find by the light of the lantern. One brown seed and four grays. The significance of the amount was not lost on her: the two brown seeds she had been owed for healing Shadowdancer, minus the gray Jacob had paid her. She shook her hand, and the seeds seemed to jump, eager to provide Constance Lamb's message:

I have your book.

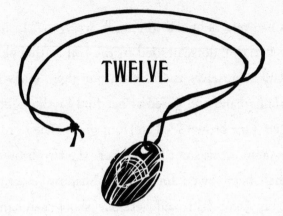

TWELVE

Kara wanted to confront Constance immediately, but this proved impossible; the woman, who had always seemed dispassionate toward her husband at best, suddenly clung to Jacob with the blind attachment of a newlywed. It was maddening—and more than a little confusing. If Constance had simply wanted to steal the grimoire for her own purposes, why had she left what amounted to a personal note informing Kara of her identity? And why tell Kara she had taken it but then make no effort to tell her *why*? All Kara needed was a few minutes alone with the farm woman, but even starting a conversation in Jacob's presence was out of the question. What would she say? *Pardon me, Mr. Lamb—I know you despise me because you think I'm a witch, but could I talk to your wife about my spellbook?*

Four days passed.

Without her grimoire it seemed like an eternity. Kara could barely sleep, and when she did she would wake up gasping for breath, as though she had been drowning in her dreams. One moment her body was cold to the touch, the next moment it burned with fever. She was constantly hungry, but the sight of food made her ill, and when she forced herself to eat, she spewed black vomit.

One day at their lunchtime meeting on the hill, Lucas told her she looked unwell and suggested she go home early. "Leave me alone!" Kara screamed, louder than she intended, and refused to open her eyes until she heard his footsteps fading in the distance. When she returned to the schoolhouse, everyone was giggling and chatting and building Straw Men for the festival. Kara stared at the ground and scratched at her forearms until they bled.

Why didn't they understand? Lucas, with his soft eyes; Taff, bringing tea to her room, trying to make it the way she did; her father, suddenly taking care of the farmwork in her stead. Kara didn't want their help. She didn't want to talk. She wanted her book back. She missed it, the power. She couldn't go back to being Kara Westfall. The others had been right to mock her. That girl was nothing.

It was only on the fifth morning that Kara felt slightly better. She still had a throbbing headache, but she thought she might be able to eat breakfast and keep it down this time. Taff knocked hesitantly at her door, and Kara gave him a big hug. He smiled and hugged her back, but she could tell from the way he scrunched up his face that she needed a bath. Kara laughed for the first time in close to a week.

After she had thoroughly scrubbed every inch of her body, she went outside to feel the sun on her shoulders. It wasn't quite warm enough to swim in the creek, but Kara thought she might at least dangle her feet in the water while Taff sat on his favorite rock and sketched a new design. Maybe Father could come too.

Excited by the prospect, Kara nearly passed Constance Lamb, sitting on their porch swing with hands folded primly in her lap.

"If you're finally done prettifying yourself," she said, "I thought it might be the appropriate time for us to have a little talk."

They did not speak again until they were deep in the orchard. The last of the hushfruits had fallen to the ground, leaving the air sickly sweet with the smell of rotten fruit.

"You stole my book," Kara said.

"Yes."

"Why?"

Constance sighed. "I overheard one of our farmhands

talking to my husband about some shenanigan him and his foolish friends were trying to pull over here, and how it went completely wrong. From the way he described it, I knew you must have the grimoire and that it was only a matter of time before the graycloaks found it. So I came to your farmhouse earlier in the day and took it before they could. Foolish girl—I didn't think you'd actually hide it in such an obvious spot."

"If you hadn't interfered, the graycloaks would have never found—"

"Wrong. They found the seeds I left and assumed it was just a hiding spot for a farmer's pathetic savings. You're not nearly as clever as you think you are. That might be something to reflect upon."

"Give me my book."

"A few questions first. Where did you find it?" Constance leaned against a tree and crossed her arms, waiting expectantly while Kara decided whether to tell her the truth.

If Kara admitted that she had entered the Thickety, Constance might report her to Fen'de Stone. But if Constance was her enemy, why hadn't she just told the fen'de about the spellbook in the first place? She could have handed it to him five days ago and been considered a great hero.

Kara took a deep breath. At some point she was going to have to trust somebody, and now seemed as good a time as ever. "I found it in the Thickety," she said.

Constance nodded. "Good. I wanted to make sure you were willing to tell me the truth."

"You knew?"

"Of course, Kara. I'm the one who buried it there."

Impossible, Kara thought. *This must be some sort of trick.* Constance Lamb was one of the most devout members of the Fold. She never missed Service, sewed the greatest number of words during Quilting, and read the Path to the elderly and infirm in her spare time. She had never been punished for any sort of infraction, even chastened for something minor. The thought of her daring to step foot in the Thickety . . . it just wasn't possible.

Unless . . .

"You're a witch!" Kara exclaimed.

Constance looked honestly shocked at the suggestion.

"Absolutely not! No—that grimoire is just another book to me. All I see are blank pages, as it appears to anyone without the talent." She looked straight at Kara, her eyes filled with sudden sympathy. "We're the lucky ones."

You might change your mind if you knew how good it felt, Kara thought, but then she remembered how she had suffered without the book and wondered if Constance might be right after all.

"Your mother was a wonderful woman, Kara. Don't let anyone tell you different. Oh, she had her faults, all right. She could be vain, as beautiful women are prone to be. And stubborn as a bull. Once that woman had it in her mind that she was right, there was no persuading her otherwise. But mostly she was kind and smart and funny.

And a good friend." Constance wiped her eyes.

I'm not the only one who misses her, thought Kara. She felt selfish that she had assumed otherwise, as though she were hoarding her mother's memory for herself.

"Why didn't you tell me this before?" Kara asked. "Why were you always so . . ."

"Cruel? Dismissive?" She sighed. "It's complicated. I can't look at you without remembering her. She was my best friend. It broke my heart when she died . . . and I was angry with her, besides."

"Angry that she died?"

"Partially. But mostly that she didn't listen to me."

Constance turned away from her.

"She showed me what the grimoire could do. Simple spells, so I wouldn't be frightened away. Turning a withered plant into a beautiful flower. Mending a wagon wheel. At first I was scared. This was against the natural way of things. This was witchcraft! There could be no greater sin! But everything that she did was so harmless—so helpful, even—that eventually it just became a part of our everyday routine." She shrugged. "I was the smart one. Abigail could bake. Helena could do magic."

"Aunt Abby knew?"

"Yes, Kara. She knew."

There was a sound from somewhere else in the orchard, the rustle of an animal passing their way. *If I had the grimoire, I could capture it.*

"So you knew my mother was a witch but didn't report her," Kara said.

"Yes."

"Then what happened?"

"Helena changed. It was small things at first. She started using her craft even when there was no reason for it. I came into the kitchen one day, and your mother stood at the counter, completely absorbed in making a pitcher of water pour itself into an empty glass. Without touching it, of course." Constance mimed the action with her hands. "And then the glass of water, back into the pitcher.

And then back again. Must have done it twenty times before she noticed me standing there. She just closed her grimoire and walked away. And that was the other thing. The grimoire. It used to be that she would leave it under the floorboards unless she needed it, but she took to carrying it with her everywhere. Even if she couldn't bring the whole book, she would tear off a scrap of paper and tuck it in her pocket. 'Just in case,' she said one time. I don't even know what she meant by that. Maybe she didn't either. Eventually she became paranoid that Abby or I were going to try to steal her precious book, so she stopped inviting us over. You were probably too young to remember, but—"

"No," Kara said. "I mean, I don't remember exactly what happened. Just that you and Aunt Abby were there every day, and then you suddenly stopped coming. But I don't remember Mother acting strange at all."

"Like I said, you were young. You might not have noticed."

Kara remained silent. After all these years of waiting, the last thing she wanted to do was interrupt.

"Helena became obsessed with that damned book. It was all she could think about. I knew—or thought I knew—that if we destroyed it, everything would go back to normal, so I slipped tighteye into Helena's tea. While she slept poor Abby took the book back to her house to burn it. I stayed behind. Just knelt by Helena's bedside and hoped that when my friend woke up, she would be my friend again. But the moment Helena opened her eyes, she clasped her hands around my neck and squeezed, and when I begged her to stop she just laughed—she *laughed*, Kara—and squeezed harder. Then she threw me across the room like I was an empty sack, face-first into a mirror." Constance ran a hand along her scars, each one a memory of that night. "When I looked up, there was blood in my eyes, but I could see your mother jerk her head into the air like a hound picking up a scent." Constance turned away and ran a slightly trembling hand along a gnarled branch.

"It was like the book had called out to her or something. Like it had screamed for help. I'm sure she didn't mean to hurt anyone, but . . . she killed them, Kara. Abby and her new husband. She killed them both."

Constance Lamb slumped to the ground, placed her face into her hands, and cried. When her shaking had subsided to a quiver, Kara asked her next question, the words barely louder than a whisper. It hardly seemed important anymore (*they were right Mother was* evil *they were all right*), but she still wanted to know how the story ended.

"If Mother had already killed two people, why didn't she fight back when the graycloaks came?"

"She had only one spell left. And all witches know never, under any circumstances, to use the final page in their grimoires. Helena feared the consequence of that far more than any heartless torture the fen'de might devise."

"Why?" Kara asked. "What happens?"

Constance propped her hands against her hips and looked at Kara in a way that made her feel five again.

"Did you really think all that power would come without a price?" she asked. "Haven't you ever wondered why the most infamous witches often vanished at the height of their powers? Minoth the Toothless? Mary Kettle? Elizabeth of the Soil? One day they're unleashing hellfire upon unsuspecting travelers or birthing a plague in the village well, and the next day . . ." Constance snapped her fingers. "Gone forever."

"Timoth Clen slayed them," Kara said. "Everyone knows that. It says so right in the Path."

Constance carefully scanned the farmland to make sure they were truly alone.

"In some cases, yes, I'm sure that's true," she said, her voice barely above a whisper. "But there's a lot more to it than that. I don't claim to know what dark entity gives the grimoire its powers. I'm not even sure your mother knew. But any witch who casts the Last Spell in a grimoire finalizes an eternal compact. From that point on, she belongs to it forever. And by forever, I do not mean until the day she dies. I mean *forever*."

Kara's stomach twisted into a cold knot. She had been certain that nothing could terrify her more than being alone with Sordyr in the tree tunnel, but now she wasn't so sure.

"How do you know all this?" Kara asked.

"Helena told me, a few days before she died. She was able to make her grimoire tell her things. Sometimes things that hadn't happened yet. It was one of her gifts."

"Well," Kara managed, trying to keep her voice steady, "those witches were clearly fools. Why cast the Last Spell at all?"

Constance fixed her with a knowing look. "I think you can work out the answer to that one on your own."

Because they couldn't stop themselves. Because their souls belonged to the grimoire.

"But what does it matter?" Constance stepped forward and studied Kara's eyes. "You're never using the grimoire again, so there's no risk. Correct?"

Kara nodded weakly. Apparently satisfied, the older woman continued, her voice hoarse and tired.

"After Helena was gone, I found the grimoire and tossed it in a fire, but the flames did nothing. I thought about giving it to Fen'de Stone, thinking he might know some kind of ritual to destroy it, but then I remembered the . . . relish . . . he took in your mother's death, and so I hid the book in the Thickety instead. When you passed the nightseeker's test—just like I prayed you would—I thought that would be the end of it. You weren't like her. But somehow you found the book anyway. It was the Forest Demon that led you to it, wasn't it?"

"No. He tried to stop me. I just barely escaped with my—"

Constance shook her head.

"You're wrong," she said. "If Sordyr truly wanted to stop you, you would not be standing here right now. He let you escape. Just like he let me bury the book in his forest. I don't know what he's planning, but clearly he wanted you to find the book and use it. You've been doing exactly what he wants, which should frighten you more than anything else." Constance took Kara by the shoulders. "Your mother spoke about him, Kara. He sent her nightmares as a kind of . . . she described it as a kind of present. To woo her, the way a young man might come to your door with a bouquet of wildflowers." The grip on Kara's shoulders tightened. "The only time I ever saw your mother frightened was when she spoke of Sordyr."

Kara got to her feet. She picked a hushfruit pit dangling low from a tree and rolled it between her hands.

"Why didn't Mother tell me all this herself?"

"Because you were just a little girl, Kara. And because she wanted to protect you. The greatest service you can do her memory is to destroy the grimoire and forget about it forever."

"I thought you said the grimoire couldn't be destroyed."

"Not by me—no. But since you are now its rightful master, I think you might be able to. That's just a guess though. I'll admit the rules of this craft confuse me."

"Why didn't you just tell me this in the first place, instead of stealing the book and waiting so long to explain?"

"How were the past few days, Kara? Pleasant?"

The pain, the weakness. There had been a reason.

"You wanted me to understand the power it had over me," Kara said, "so I would know what could happen if I continued to use it."

"Not *could* happen, Kara. *Will* happen. You'll end up just like her." She took Kara's hands in her own. "And neither one of us wants that. Not me. And certainly not your mother."

And suddenly Kara fell forward, and the woman who had steadfastly ignored her the last seven years of her life held her close and whispered soft words of comfort. Kara felt the tension drain from her body and realized how nice it was to stop thinking, just for a few moments, about whether things actually *would* be okay and just hold someone and believe.

"I miss her," Kara said. "I miss her so much."

"Me too," said Constance Lamb.

When Kara had finished brushing the tears from her eyes, Constance asked if she was strong enough to take the grimoire back and destroy it. Kara nodded. They walked to the place where Constance had hidden the book, a hollowed-out tree trunk just off the trail that led back to the village.

"You should burn it here," Constance said. "Just gather some firewood and get it done."

Kara could hear the doubt in her voice, the slight hesitation that meant *Let's do it before you change your mind. And let me be here, so I can make sure you go through with it.*

"I don't think it works that way," Kara said. "I think I need to be by myself. I think I need to want the book . . ." *Dead* was what she almost said, but that implied the book was alive—a possibility she was not yet ready to consider.

". . . gone," she said instead.

"Are you sure you'll be able to go through with this alone?"

Kara nodded. The grimoire was responsible for all the evil that had befallen her family. Destroying it would be easy.

"You have nothing to worry about," Kara said. "After what you've told me, I will never cast another spell."

It was only when she held the grimoire again that Kara realized she had lied.

THIRTEEN

She needed to cast a spell. Any spell. Anywhere. It had taken every ounce of self-control for Kara not to open the spellbook right in front of Constance and start conjuring creatures at random. Somehow she managed to nod and wave good-bye and not look as though she couldn't wait for this annoying woman to go away so she could *use her book*. But Kara knew it was important to remain calm. To look calm. If she didn't Constance might try to take the grimoire back, and then (*you would have to kill her*) Kara thought something bad might happen.

She ran into the copse of red willows that bordered the western edge of their land. Kara knew she should get farther from the main path that ran toward the village, but she couldn't wait a moment longer. She threw the book to the ground, and it opened to the last creature she had captured in its pages.

Fire ants.

Kara spoke the words that lined the small figure sketched into the book. Without looking up she turned to a new page. Burrclaws. She conjured them too. Instead of providing her body with an instant sense of relief, as Kara had anticipated, casting these spells barely diminished the pain. She needed more. Treeflies. Neirs. The words flew from Kara's lips until her tongue, unused to such foreign sibilance, became swollen and sore. Why wasn't it getting better? Wasn't she giving the book what it wanted? She cast more spells, not even cognizant of what she was summoning. It was so much easier this way, just to let it happen. Her hands trembled as she flipped through a series of inscribed pages, needing to conjure more, more, more . . .

The old pain faded. A new pain began.

Her right arm suddenly went numb as a flock of tiny neirs—their smiling faces belying a vicious nature—dug into a burrclaw and tore it to pieces. Meanwhile an army of fire ants overwhelmed a poor brightcay, slicing through its diaphanous wings before it could make its escape. Kara felt flames engulf her fingertips as the fire ants set to work.

"Enough!" Kara exclaimed.

The animals vanished. Some skittered away or flew off into the forest; some just blinked into nothingness. Kara collapsed to the ground, too spent to care about the difference. She did not feel the pain anymore, the need. She did not feel anything.

Kara closed her eyes.

When she opened them again, the sun had moved halfway across the sky, and Grace was standing above her.

Kara got to her feet, quicker than she should have, and

the ground tilted upward to meet her hands. She tasted bile on the back of her tongue and was forced to remain still until the dizziness passed.

Grace gently rubbed her back.

"There, there," she said. "Are you ill? Would you like me to get your father? I'm sure he would be a great help. He's an expert at not being well, isn't he, Kara?"

Kara longed to reach back and slap Grace's hand away, but she wasn't confident in her ability to balance her weight with one hand. Besides, she could see Simon standing just behind his mistress like a deformed shadow. His face might have been blank and lifeless now, but that would change the moment she struck Grace.

"This is a strange place to take a nap," Grace said. "Unless, perhaps, you were waiting for the Dark Man? Or perhaps meeting your little Stench friend? When I am fen'de, such inappropriate relationships will not be tolerated."

Kara tried to reply, but her mouth was too dry to talk.

She was ravenous too, as though she hadn't eaten for days.

I used too much magic. More than my body could take.

"What do we have here?" Grace asked, noticing something on the ground.

The grimoire.

Kara hurled herself toward the book, but Simon got there first, pinching the grimoire between two fingers and holding it at arm's length like a poisonous snake.

Propping her cane beneath the crook of her arm, Grace held out her hands expectantly.

"Give it here," she said.

Simon shook his head.

Grace's mouth fell open. It was the first time Kara had ever seen her surprised.

"Give it to me!" she repeated. "Now!"

Kara's strength had begun to return to her, and though the world was still not completely stable, she managed to get to her feet.

"It's nothing," she said, the words barely making a dent

in the silence. "Just a blank journal."

Grace ignored her. Using her cane she took a step in Simon's direction. Simon stayed in place but turned away from her. As Grace came closer he clenched his eyes shut and brought the grimoire to his chest and whimpered softly, as if its proximity caused him great pain.

"Simon," Grace said. Her voice was soft, hypnotic. "Simon, Simon." She ran a hand along his arm, and the giant shivered at her touch. "Be a good boy and let me have what I want. You want to make me happy, don't you?"

The giant nodded and looked up.

"Then give it to me. It's just a book."

The giant shook his head.

"Simon," Grace said. Her voice remained gentle, but the cracks in her patience were beginning to show. "You don't want to be punished, do you? You don't want me to leave you alone again. In the dark, where he can find you."

The giant's whimpering grew louder, but Kara noticed his hold on the book begin to slip a bit.

"Be a good boy, Simon. That's right. Be my Simon."

After she had taken the book from his arms, Grace spun one finger in the air. Simon nodded and turned away from her. He closed his eyes just before a whistle of air cut through the forest and Grace's cane snapped against his back.

"Never refuse me again!" Grace screamed. The ribbon in her hair—fuchsia today—unraveled and fell to the ground. She struck Simon twice more. "Never."

Grace's rage evaporated as quickly as it had come. She smiled at Kara and shrugged, as if asking *What can you do?* Then she opened the book. Kara waited for the look of disappointment when Grace saw the blank pages and realized that all this trouble had been for nothing.

Instead Grace's eyes shot open. Her entire body began to tremble.

"Goodness," she said.

Grace had turned to a random page near the middle of the grimoire, farther in the book than Kara had reached.

With the gentlest of touches, she used a single fingertip to trace the peaks and valleys of an unseen image.

"What is it showing you?" Kara asked.

When Grace looked up, her perfect face glistened with sweat and revelation.

"Everything."

Grace bowed her head forward until her nose almost touched the open book. From deep within her throat emanated a strange pattern of moans and grunts. Kara wondered if she sounded the same way when she cast a spell, like a conduit for something dark and far more powerful. The thought disturbed her.

"Grace," she said with a measured tone, "you need to stop. You don't know what you're—"

It started to snow.

There was no preamble. One minute it was an unassuming autumn day, and then the world was obscured by whiteness. Leaves rustled as animals rushed madly through the trees, their body clocks driven mad by this inexplicable change in seasons.

"Yes," Grace said under her breath. She tilted her head skyward, allowing the unusually frigid flakes to settle on her face, her forehead, her tongue. Snow vanished into her hair, precisely the same shade of white.

"So this is what it's like," Grace said. "Magic." Her voice dropped to a conspiratorial whisper, as though she and Kara were just two girls trading secrets. "I've always wondered. They don't tell you, in the stories, how *good* it feels. Not that I'm a witch like you, of course. I follow the Path and will certainly seek penance afterward." She turned to the next page. "But first: just one more . . ."

Kara snatched the grimoire from her hands and ran toward the village. She expected Simon to give chase, but the giant let her pass. "Bring it back!" Grace screamed after her. "Bring back my book! Bring it back now!" Kara continued to run, chest pounding, branches cracking beneath her feet. She was almost home before she noticed that it had stopped snowing.

FOURTEEN

The Fenroot tree at the village's center was the reason the last remaining Children had chosen to pilgrimage to De'Noran, despite the dangers of the Thickety. Fenroots had grown increasingly rare throughout the centuries, and you could not have a community that properly honored Timoth Clen without one. The villagers gathered around it now, waiting patiently on the smooth stones that encircled the tree. They were grouped by profession: Elders and their families sat in the first row, followed by the shopkeepers and farmers, and finally the fishermen and traders. Clearers sat in the last row, with a sizable gap between their people and the rest of the congregation so "noses could breathe."

The graycloaks were the only ones who did not sit. They roamed among the stones, staffs held at the ready, wooden balls up. Anyone who dared fall asleep during the sermon would be in for a rude awakening.

But even the graycloaks stopped moving when Kara entered the circle.

Over the years she had grown used to the murmurs of disapproval generated by her arrival at their weekly Service. This was hardly a pleasant way to be greeted, but the reaction was usually halfhearted at best, just another errand to be done: sweep your barn, till your field, shame the Witch Girl. Today was different. Kara watched, from the corner of her eye, as a father hugged his children close and an old crone spit in the aisle.

They had seen the snow, and they thought she was responsible.

"What's going on?" Father whispered.

Kara shrugged and led them to three stones in the farmers' section. Once they settled into their seats, conversations returned to the usual topics of crops, weather, and trivial gossip. Father turned to the Widow Miller and asked her how preparations for the Shadow Festival were going. There was nothing particularly exciting about their conversation, but it made Kara smile anyway; perhaps her father was finally getting better.

Taff twisted on the stone next to hers. "I don't see why we have to go to Service," he said. "There's only three nights left of Shadow Festival. We're supposed to be having fun."

"Don't worry. I hear Fen'de Stone's sermon is going to be even longer than usual today! Won't that be exciting?"

"I could be building something right now. Or climbing. Or washing my socks. Or anything that isn't this."

"Be good."

Kara eyed the graycloaks closely. *Are they going to arrest me on suspicion of witchcraft? How strange it will be if I get blamed for the one spell I did not cast.* Some kind of argument erupted between an old Clearer, his face cracked and wizened from years of service, and the blacksmith's apprentice, a haughty lad who was fond of causing trouble. The graycloaks did not bother to hear both sides. They simply dragged the Clearer away as the apprentice chortled with his friends.

No, Kara thought. *Nothing has changed. They may take me soon, but it will not be today.*

She could see Grace sitting in the first row, her pure white hair arranged in two fancy braids bound by a black ribbon. *Her magic is more powerful than mine,* Kara thought. *And the spell simply appeared for her. She didn't have to work for it at all.* The page Grace had used was ruined now, to Kara's eyes nothing but a shimmering black surface that rippled at her touch. *There's a spell here,* the book seemed to say, *but you're not worthy enough to see it.*

It was her mother's grimoire, but it liked Grace better.

"I think I have a fever," Taff said.

"Nice try. But we're not leaving."

Nevertheless, Kara placed the back of her hand to his forehead and was surprised to find that it was warm. She looked at her brother more carefully and noticed the ruddy cheeks and dried snot.

"See?" Taff said.

Kara nodded, feeling guilty. It was the first time Taff had ever brought an illness to her attention without her noticing first.

"I'm sorry," she said. "I haven't been paying much attention to you lately, have I?"

Taff shrugged.

She wrapped her arm around him and squeezed. "How about this? After Service we'll put your costume together. Just me and you."

"That sounds great," he said, even more crestfallen than before.

"But?"

"But you promised we'd make my costume yesterday. And the day before that."

Kara stared at him blankly.

"Do you even remember?"

She didn't. But she believed him.

Kara's apology was cut short as the fen'de, wearing the crimson robes of Service Day, took his position upon the Speaking Stone.

"Work hard, want nothing," he said.

"Stay vigilant," the congregation replied in unison.

After a sleepless night worrying about what might happen, Kara found it difficult to stay awake during the sermon. The fen'de could often be an excellent speaker—even Kara had to give him that—but he was just going by rote today, repeating homilies and stories they had all heard before. "When our people first came to this island, escaping the blind ignorance of a World that had forgotten all we had done for them . . ." Kara watched Grace closely. She expected her to still be angry that Kara had the grimoire, but instead her lips curled into a smile. Without turning in Kara's direction, she gave her a small, dismissive wave.

Why is she so happy?

". . . and on that glorious day Timoth Clen will return to us and cleanse the World of magic once more, and the Children of the Fold will be rewarded for never doubting the righteousness of the Path . . ."

The morning dragged on. Taff shifted in his seat, releasing an occasional sigh of boredom. Even Father looked ready to doze off. It was only hours later, when Service was finally drawing to a close, that the sermon took an interesting turn.

"Today is a special day," Fen'de Stone said. "A day of celebration." Men and women straightened in their seats as the customary zeal returned to their beloved leader's voice. "With the Shadow Festival drawing to a close, and spirits so high, I thought now might be the perfect time to make my announcement." He sighed theatrically. "I am nearing the twilight of my years and cannot be your leader forever." The crowd murmured its objections, but Fen'de Stone waved them away. "Don't worry, my Children. My time is still a long way off. I simply mean that the moment has come to begin training a new leader."

Grace smoothed out her dress and ran a hand over her hair, making sure every strand was in place.

No, Kara thought, though really she had been expecting this day for some time. *Not now. Not so soon.*

"Please come forth," Fen'de Stone proclaimed, gesturing toward the first row.

Grace leaned forward, ready to rise, before realizing that her father was pointing to the seat next to hers. Marsten Cloud rose proudly to his feet. Brushing past Grace he made his way to stand by the fen'de's side. "I am honored by your decision," he said, his handsome face dour and serious. "I shall do my best to serve the Fold."

The congregation clapped politely. Marsten Cloud was an excellent choice, a paragon of the Clen's ideals. He would make a fine leader.

Only Kara thought to look in Grace's direction.

The pretty mask had slipped away, replaced by an expression of rage so pure, it twisted her features into something dark and feral. Although Grace had shown her nothing but unkindness, Kara felt a rush of sympathy for her. She knew what it was like to feel betrayed by your own father.

The crowd rose to its feet, still applauding, and Grace Stone—her smiling face pure and beatific once more—joined them, clapping louder than anyone. Her teeth were perfect white rows.

After Service ended, Kara watched Lucas make his way toward her, maneuvering against the tide of worshippers leaving the Circle. "Filthy Stench," one of them muttered in anger. If Lucas heard he gave no sign.

"Can we talk?" he asked her.

Kara would have liked nothing better. She hadn't

realized how much she missed him until he was standing before her. But at the edge of the crowd, she saw Constance Lamb look meaningfully in her direction before heading toward the outskirts of the village.

She wants me to follow her.

"I'm sorry," Kara said. "I have to go."

Before Lucas could respond, Kara turned and walked away. She needed to talk to Constance about the night her mother died. Kara had been too overcome with emotion to question what Constance had been saying at the time, but in retrospect she was certain that a good deal of lies had been mixed in with the truth.

"Where was my father?" Kara asked, after following Constance to a secluded area behind the tannery.

Constance's eyes flickered away for just a moment.

Kara continued, her voice louder than she intended. "He told Fen'de Stone that he had seen Mother murder those people! He turned against her—his own wife! And yet he was nowhere to be found in your story."

"He arrived after me, but he could see what had happened. Anyone could."

"That's not right. He swore he had actually witnessed the murders. Why would he lie about that? He loved her!"

"No one is denying that."

"And yet you want me to believe that he denounced his wife without seeing her do anything wrong? That doesn't make any sense!"

"It was a long time ago, and I may have gotten some of the details wrong. William arrived after me, but it was only to bring the graycloaks. He had actually been there much earlier, before—"

"And when, during all of this, did you deliver Taff?"

Constance's face froze. "Before your mother left for Abigail's. I told you that, I'm sure."

"Stop lying to me!"

Constance looked her over, a bit of the old coldness returning to her eyes. "That's right," she said. "You've become quite the expert on lying, haven't you? Tell me, did destroying the grimoire simply slip your mind?"

Kara pulled her satchel closer. Since what had happened with Grace, she had been carrying the book everywhere.

"How did you know?" she asked.

"You don't see it—maybe you *can't* see it—but with the grimoire your eyes are different. Distant, even when you're standing here. It was like that with her too. From here it gets worse. Fast."

"I'm *going* to destroy it."

"Of course."

"It's just, things have gotten complicated."

"You sound like her. Making excuses."

"Mother never made excuses for anything!"

"I wasn't talking about Helena, you foolish child!"

Constance bit her lower lip, but it was too late: The words had been released. In the distance Kara heard the sounds of laughter and conversation as the Service-morning crowd congregated in the village square. The smells of fried dough and roasted hazelnuts drifted in their direction.

"What does that mean?" Kara asked. "If you weren't talking about Mother, who were you talking about?"

Constance shook her head fiercely.

"What's done is done. Destroy the grimoire. That's the important thing."

"Right. Or else my friends and neighbors will stone me to death and burn my corpse. It's a shame, really. They've been patiently waiting my entire life. I'd hate to disappoint them."

Constance looked at her with what might have been pity. "These are not bad people, Kara. They may do bad things out of fear or foolishness, but most of them want to live simple lives with their families. They are no different from anyone else, even you."

"I find that hard to believe."

"I know," Constance said, "and I'm sorry for that." While walking away she added: "I'll give you until Last Night. If you do not end this, I'm going to Fen'de Stone myself. I hate to threaten you, but I couldn't live with myself if it happened again. I owe Helena that much at least."

Constance left without another word.

For a few hours, as she patched Taff's costume together from various odds and ends, Kara was able to push the grimoire from her mind. It helped that Father stayed in the room with them. Ever since their encounter with the fen'de, he had been acting a bit more like his old self. Yes, there were still the long silences and lapses of memory, but as Kara watched Taff and Father shooting marbles across the wooden floor, she couldn't help but smile. *He's getting better. In time he will tell me the truth of that night.* She would ask him when the moment was right, but not this afternoon. Kara did not want to do anything to disturb a scene so tranquil—so *normal*—that she could almost imagine Mother walking through the door.

She did not feel the pull of the grimoire until later that night, when she lay in bed listening to Taff's worrisome cough and wondering if leaving his window open a crack had been the right decision. The need to touch the book started in the pit of her stomach and spread to the tips of her toes. It wasn't as bad as before, not yet. But it was rising.

She thought of the three-leaved weed the Clearers called tagen. "It may not seem it," Lucas had told her, "but it's the most dangerous thing in the Fringe. Just a bit of it under your fingernails, and you won't be able to stop smiling for two days. You won't feel any pain either. But by then the tagen has started growing inside your body, and it creeps into your heart and makes you want more, and you will want it even after it begins squeezing you from the inside out and your teeth have rotted away and the skin has begun to melt from your bones. With your last, strangled breath, you'll beg for it."

Kara wondered how long it would be before she reached that point. To where she'd rather die than not use magic.

Maybe you're there already.

There came a steady tapping at her window.

Kara flipped over in bed. Grace was standing outside, fingertips splayed against the glass.

"Were you thinking about me, Kara?" she asked. "I was thinking about you. That's why I came."

She continued to gently tap the window with the pads of her fingers.

"Why don't you let me in, Kara?" she asked. Her eyes were silver lakes in the moonlight. "Do you have it there? Can I see it?"

"It's not here," Kara said.

"Yes, it is. I already checked the farmhouse. Your secret spot. Father mentioned it to me. He might not have known what it was for, but I did. So clever of you to move it before the graycloaks came. Your mother's treasure." Grace paused, considering. "Do you think that when she touched my mother's stomach and made me like this . . . that she also made me like you?"

Grace continued to tap against the glass. The rhythm

was completely out of sync to her words, as though her hand had a mind of its own.

"She would never have done that," Kara said. It was one of the many stories that had developed after her mother's death, when the villagers seemed intent on blaming all their misfortunes on the dead witch.

"Of course you would say that. But I know the truth."

"I'm sorry, Grace. The truth is, there was no magic involved. You were just born wrong. No wonder your father didn't pick you to take his place."

The tapping stopped.

"You're not a very nice girl, are you? Can I hold the book? Just for a moment."

"No."

"Has it ever occurred to you how alike we are? We're practically sisters, Kara."

"No."

"Who knows? Maybe we are sisters. I've seen the glow in my father's eyes whenever he talks about the beautiful

256

Helena Westfall. Father used to be quite dashing. Stranger things have happened."

"You need to leave."

The sound of Taff's coughing broke through the night.

"Oh dear. The whelp has a leak." She looked up at Kara, honestly curious. "Why haven't you fixed him yet? Just think it, and the book will take care of the rest. Do you not want to waste the page?" Noting Kara's downcast expression, Grace broke into a huge grin. "Wait! It's not that easy for you, is it? You have *limitations*." She clapped her hands together. "He told me I was more powerful than you!"

"Who did?"

"You know who. He sends me the most wonderful dreams. Can I have the book, please?"

Kara pressed a hand against the windowpane.

"Grace. You can't listen to Sordyr. He's evil."

"Yes. The book? Can I have it? You might not be powerful enough to fix your brother, but I am. Give me the book and I promise I'll do it."

"Don't go near Taff! Ever!"

Grace's eyes widened. She drummed her fingers against the window. Her left hand had begun to shake.

"You are being so unreasonable, Kara Westfall. I walked all this way. Can you imagine how hard that was for me? I don't even need to hold it. Just let me see it. That's all. Just hold it up against the window." Grace folded her arms around her stomach and in the process lost her grip on her cane. She slipped to the ground. "Please, Kara. It hurts. You of all people should understand. I *need* to see it. He won't let me sleep until I do."

A coil of guilt twisted in Kara's stomach. If she hadn't been so careless, Grace would never have seen the grimoire, would never have known such suffering. *No one deserves this*, Kara thought, *even her.*

She drew the grimoire from beneath her pillow and pressed it against the window.

"Here," she said. "And now that you've—"

Grace hurled herself against the glass like a rabid wolf, her mouth stretched in an inhuman snarl of rage. Using the palms of her hands, she slapped the window so hard that Kara was certain it would break.

"Mine! Mine! Mine!"

Kara dropped the book. It fell open on the bed, and the pages turned until settling upon a meticulously rendered illustration of a squit. It looked different from the one she had plucked off Lucas but no less deadly.

Here, the book seemed to say, *try this one.*

Kara did not remember speaking the words, but that didn't matter: The result was the same. The first squit landed on Grace's arm and touched its corkscrew tongue to her skin. Grace yanked it off quickly before it could start to burrow. The second squit got farther, managing to dig into the flesh below Grace's elbow before she could pinch it out with two fingers and squish it to pulp. Kara felt a tiny pain in her finger, nothing more than a momentary ache. *I'm getting used to death*, Kara thought, and then the squits were everywhere, blanketing the bedroom window until Grace vanished behind a swarm of shifting bodies. Kara ran her finger down the inside of the window and a dozen squits clamored for position, longing to be close to their queen.

The book is mine. No one is going to take it away.

Grace screamed—the sound desperate and pure and surprisingly childlike—and Kara gasped. The world jumped into clear focus again.

"No!" Kara exclaimed. She pounded on the glass. "Stop it! Get away!"

As one, the squits flew off into the night. Kara pressed her face to the glass and watched Grace limp away. She had abandoned her cane, and her useless leg dragged behind her. *She's alive,* Kara thought. *Thank the Clen.* Grace turned back, once, and there was just enough moonlight for Kara to make out the expression on her face. Not gratitude, as it should have been, but a promise of revenge. Kara laughed. *That's what you think, cripple. Just try it again. See*

what happens. She laughed some more, and while a part of her realized that the laugh sounded wrong somehow, the majority of her body—still warm and satisfied from spell casting—rejoiced at the feeling.

"I'm better than you," Kara said. The grimoire nestled into her hands, home at last. "I'm better than all of you!"

She thought about conjuring something else to chase Grace all the way home. Her hand stroked the book. It would feel so good. So right. She would even choose something slow—a magslov, perhaps—in order to give Grace a chance. She touched the book again; this time it moved against her fingertips. *We have such fun things to do, you and I. I am my mother's daughter, after all.* A part of Kara that had grown disturbingly small wondered why all the noise had not woken anyone else in the house, and that's when she heard it: The sound that had been camouflaged by pounding glass and wandering thoughts and the buzzing of the squits.

Taff's screams.

Kara dropped the grimoire and ran to his room. Father sat on his bed, holding Taff in his arms. There was blood everywhere.

"Towels!" he exclaimed. "We need towels!"

There were two wounds—one in the center of Taff's forearm and the other behind his neck. The latter was nothing more than a deep scratch, but the forearm wound was deep. When Kara pressed a towel against it, blood bubbled to the surface, along with the body of a drowned squit that had burrowed too far.

Father picked it up between two fingers and flicked it outside. He shut the window.

"This is my fault, Kara," he said. The desperation in his voice brought sudden tears to her eyes. "Everything that has befallen our family. I didn't stand by her like I should have, and now we're all being punished!"

No, Kara thought. *It's my fault for thinking I could control the grimoire.*

She cleaned and bound Taff's wounds and made him

a poultice for the pain. He grimaced but fought tears the best he could. Eventually Taff fell asleep, and she watched him, his slightly flickering eyelids, the gentle rise and fall of his chest. Her beautiful brother, who had never hurt anyone.

He could have died tonight. I did this to him. Me.

No. Not just her.

"Where are you going?" Father asked moments later, when Kara swept through the kitchen, satchel swinging from her shoulder. He was sitting at the table, halfway through a jug of moondrink. "Kara?" he asked.

But Kara didn't answer. She just grabbed a handful of matches and continued on her way.

By the time sunlight streaked the sky, Kara had built a nice stack of branches. She dropped the grimoire onto the pile. The book crashed through the makeshift firewood like an anvil and plummeted several inches into the earth.

Kara took out the first match.

She wondered what tricks were in store for her. Would the grimoire suddenly come to life, grow legs, and skitter across the field? Perhaps Sordyr would materialize before her eyes and tempt her with promises of power and happiness.

At the very least, there was no way the match would catch on the first try.

But it did.

Kara watched the flame dance, waiting for a supernatural breeze to extinguish it. The morning remained calm. Still expecting something to stop her, Kara cupped the tiny flame and touched it to the wood. The branches, though slightly damp, caught easily enough, spreading the flames gleefully through the pile. Heat snapped at Kara's skin, but she remained still and watched the flames engulf the cursed book, certain that it couldn't be this easy.

But there were no tricks. The book did not rise up into the sky. It did not possess her mind and force her to reach into the flames to save it. A black dragon did not swoop from the sky and snatch the grimoire away.

It simply didn't burn.

When the fire worked itself out, Kara retrieved the book, dusted off the ashes, and returned it to her satchel. It wasn't even warm.

FIFTEEN

The skies opened up at dawn, and the rain continued throughout the morning. Angry darts of water pummeled the scarecrows that lined the village square and sent vendors hawking candy sticks and painted marbles running for cover. Within hours the outdoor area reserved for dancing had been reduced to a worthless quagmire. Optimistically wearing their costumes, anxious children pressed faces to windows and prayed for the rain to stop. The older girls gathered together and combed one another's hair with funereal anticipation, wondering if they would be able to wear their dresses at all.

The final day of the Shadow Festival was a disaster.

Even morning Service had to be held inside the school-house, and though it was the most important sermon of the year, the fen'de's words of wisdom were swallowed up by the incessant cascade of raindrops. But as the sermon came to a close the rain suddenly stopped. Fen'de Stone, who never wasted such an opportunity, said it was as though "Timoth Clen himself had reached out his battle-worn hands and squeezed those offending clouds shut."

By late afternoon, sunlight reigned supreme, and though there was hardly enough time for the mud to dry before the festivities began that evening, the residents of De'Noran were in high spirits. Villagers and Clearers worked side by side to make minor repairs and lay down plywood in the dancing area. The girls, laughing giddily, slipped into their dresses—the feel of them so different from the stiff, starched clothes they wore every other day of the year—while younger children spilled out into the streets, eager to see their friends' costumes. By the time the sun fell over the horizon, straining for a final look, the somber village of De'Noran had been invaded by foreign forces: ghosts and goblins, chatter-walks and woldy-beats, music and laughter.

Only two figures seemed out of place, hesitantly standing on the fringe of the merriment. Taff's black frock was long enough to conceal his shoes, but a simple metal wire sewn into the hem kept him from tripping and gave him the appearance of floating along the ground. His mask was a monstrous assemblage of tree branches, acorns, random bits of fabric, the bottom half of a broken spoon, cord, and shiny buttons. Peering out from two tiny eye-holes, Taff saw the mouths of the other children drop in awe. He smiled and squeezed Kara's hand.

She smiled back.

Unlike the other young ladies, her dress was black and plain. She wore her long hair straight. The only notable thing about Kara's attire was her locket, which hung outside her dress for all to see.

A group of Clearer children crossed their path, the sounds of their youthful laughter drowning out the distant fiddles. Lucas glanced in Kara's direction, and she raised her hand in a slight wave. *I haven't spoken to him since the start of Shadow Festival*, Kara thought, but before she could say a word, Lucas's friend pulled him along. Last Night came but once a year, and there was no time to waste.

Kara and Taff joined the crowd of children going from house to house, filling their burlap sacks with candy apples and sticky figs and other treats. When no one was looking, Kara touched the object inside her satchel and made sure it was still there. The weight of it made her shoulder throb with pain, but that didn't matter. By the end of the night, she would return it to the Thickety and be free of it forever.

She found Father serving pumpkinade at the center of the game booths. Kara had volunteered his services, and though he had grumbled about it at the time, he certainly looked happy now. She watched from afar as he chatted with the children in line, acting frightened when he saw their costumes up close. She remembered how much her father had once loved this village.

It wasn't too late for him.

Kara approached the table, and the little ones scattered.

"At least I don't have to wait in line," she said.

Father handed Kara a cold glass of pumpkinade. When she'd woken that morning, she had found him sitting by Taff's bedside, changing his bandages while humming an old song. Instead of driving him deeper into madness as she expected, his son's need seemed to be pulling him back to the world of the living.

"Taff having fun?" he asked.

She motioned behind her. Taff was attempting to toss a

beanbag into a small, wooden barrel. Pretty Tammy, once again wearing her Leaf Girl costume, cheered him on.

"Taff is having the time of his life," she said.

"I see that."

Kara tried her drink. Usually pumpkinade was too sweet for her taste, but this was perfect. She took another sip. If she was going to ask him, it had to be now. This might be the last chance she ever had to discover the truth. All she had to do was say the words: *Why did you betray her?*

The problem, however, wasn't the question—it was the consequences. What if talking about the past broke him again? Or what if the truth was so terrible that Kara was better off not knowing at all? It was a lot to risk just to satisfy her curiosity.

"Something on your mind?" Father asked.

Kara took a sip of pumpkinade.

"Actually," she said, trying to sound as though she had just thought of the idea, "do you think you could do me a favor? Taff wants to do the rounds in the houses just out-side the village——"

"That boy's got one serious sweet tooth."

"He does. But afterward——" Kara paused, forcing her voice not to crack as she told the lie. "I wanted to try my hand at some of the festival games. The ones for the older children. And so I was wondering if maybe I could send Taff back here, and you could take him home. Do you think that would be okay?"

"Of course." He shrugged. "Actually, it looks like the kids are getting tired of pumpkinade. I could just call it a night and take him off your hands now. You shouldn't have to miss your fun."

"No! Don't worry. I want to . . . be with him for a little longer."

"That's fine." He placed a hand on her shoulder and looked into her eyes. "You sure there isn't anything else?"

Kara leaned over and kissed him on the cheek.

"Good-bye, Father," she said.

The crowd of children moved as one toward the farm-houses that dotted the periphery of the village. The ground was wet and slippery, but since everyone's boots were already caked in mud it didn't seem to matter. Although one could still make out the sounds of laughter and singing, these had grown more subdued and were intermingled with the occasional yawn. It was getting late, particularly for the younger ones.

There was no one home at the Wilcox place, but the owners had left behind a bucket of lemon drops wrapped in cinnamon leaves, Taff's favorite. Kara let him take two. They did not have as much luck at the next farm: dried cranberries and splintered wooden tops.

"Had enough?" Kara asked Taff.

"Just one more," he said.

Kara kissed him on top of the head.

"Just one more."

The Miller house was a healthy trek from the village,

nearly twice the distance as the last farm. Nevertheless not a single child turned back. Widow Miller spent all year preparing for this night, and her legendary treats were not to be missed. Although Kara was anxious to return the grimoire to the Thickety before it grew any later, she couldn't bear the thought of denying Taff such a joyous experience. This night would be forever ingrained upon his memory, and in case something went wrong, she wanted his final memories of her to be happy ones.

"Look here!" Taff exclaimed. He gestured toward a narrow opening between the stalks of corn that bordered Widow Miller's land. Kara raised her lantern and shed light across a path that branched out in three different directions.

"It's a maze," she said.

The other children whooped with joy and spilled into the cornfield, tired muscles and aching feet instantly forgotten. The majority took the rightmost path, which Kara found curious only because there seemed to be no specific reason to do so. Before Kara could object, Taff took her hand and pulled her along. They went left, then right, then left again. It was darker in the corn, and although Kara could still hear the giggles of the other children, they were already growing distant.

"I think we're going the wrong way," she said.

"Or maybe we're the only ones going the right way!"

Kara disagreed. Although she couldn't see the Miller farm over the tall stalks of corn, her sense of direction had always been excellent.

"The house is in the opposite direction," she said.

"That's a *good* sign," replied Taff. "Any corn maze worth its seed is going to send you the wrong way first in order to trick you. Widow Miller wouldn't just make a path that goes straight to her house. She's a lot cleverer than most grown-ups."

Kara wasn't convinced, but Taff seemed so excited that she decided to just trust him and see what happened. Hand in hand they passed beneath the towering stalks through a series of interchangeable twists and turns that led to the farthest edge of the cornfield. At this point the path doubled back in the direction of the farmhouse, gradually becoming so narrow that Kara had to turn her body to proceed. Corn silk tickled her bare neck as she passed.

They turned a corner and saw the scarecrows.

There were at least a dozen of them, twine-bound to tall wooden stakes driven deep into the ground. The closest one, hay-padded into the form of a woman, wore a gray burlap sack in place of a face. Moonlight glinted off polished button eyes.

"This is creepy," said Kara.

"This is *great!*" exclaimed Taff.

Kara heard voices in the distance. Through the stalks she was able to make out the soft glow of lanterns, floating through the night like will-o'-the-wisps.

"There's another group just behind us," said Kara. "Maybe we should wait."

"I want to be first!"

"It might be more fun if we all go at once."

Although Kara couldn't see Taff's expression beneath the mask, she was sure he was smiling.

"You scared?" he asked.

She was, a little bit. Kara had never been frightened by thunder or the dark, but there had always been something about scarecrows that unnerved her. They were already so close to human in form—how easy it would be for one to leap to life, wraps its arms around her, and drag her deeper into the corn. . . .

"Wait!" Taff exclaimed. "This is Yaguth, the hunter witch! Remember the story? She tried to conceal herself in a broom, and Timoth Clen cracked it over his knee."

Kara followed his stare to a small scarecrow with a broken shaft in its hands and fox fur draped around its shoulders.

"They're all witches," Taff said, and though his voice was still excited, Kara also heard the first stirrings of doubt. "Look at this one with the bag of black stones. That's Lana the Raiser. And this one over here!" He pointed to a scarecrow with a dirty rag where its eyes should be. "That's Sable the Blind."

Taff dashed farther down the row, calling out name after name, filling the night with the titles of bedside tales: Shadow Lass, Elizabeth of the Soil, the Calling Woman, and Esmeralda the Red (two incarnations: one young, one old). The path grew wider but not so wide that Kara could slip past the scarecrows without brushing against them. She looked up at the wrong time and found herself face-to-face with seashell eyes bound to a head of blackened straw.

"Mary Kettle," Taff said, kicking the small cauldron at the scarecrow's feet. "She was a nasty one. Could enchant any object and make it do her dark deeds. And then there's how she got her name—"

"Enough of that," Kara said, pushing him forward. But Taff twisted away from her hands, staring up at the last scarecrow with a puzzled expression.

"I don't know this one," he said.

It was taller than the others and wore a brocade dress dyed the deep red of blood oranges and embroidered with golden swirls. Straight, dark hair snipped from a horse's mane hung down the scarecrow's back.

Kara felt the grimoire grow warm in her satchel as anger swelled inside her. *That's Mother's dress! Somebody stole it from the trunk where we keep her old things.*

"Who is it supposed to be?" Taff asked.

Kara placed a hand on his shoulder. "It's just a scarecrow," she said. "Come on. We're almost there."

She took her brother by the hand and pulled him around the next corner, where they could see the lights of the farmhouse and smell cinnamon and buttered popcorn. No doubt there would be hot chocolate as well, and maybe coffee. The night had settled into a numb coldness, and Kara would welcome either.

Unfortunately the Widow Miller had one last trick up

her sleeve. The path branched into three directions, each blocked by a wooden gate. Taff swung the rightmost gate open, then bent down to examine the hinges before he closed it again.

"It only opens in this direction," he said, stepping back onto the main path. "The other gates are probably the same. Once they shut we can't go through them from the other side."

"And if we go through the wrong gate, we'll probably end up back at the beginning."

"Probably."

Kara sighed. She had always liked the Widow Miller, but right now she could have cheerfully strangled her. If they took the wrong path, they might be at this all night.

Taff took the lantern from Kara's hands and shone the light down each path, trying to see as far as possible. "The left and the right paths bend out of sight. But the path behind this middle gate seems to head straight toward the farmhouse."

"A bit obvious, don't you think?"

"So we should take one of the other two."

"But which one?"

Taff shrugged. "The left one. If we're wrong we'll try the right one next. We'll be able to get back here faster this time, since we know the way."

Taff swung the gate open, but he paused before stepping through it.

"Wait," he said. "You're right. The center path is obvious. But maybe that's the point."

"You mean it's so obvious that no one would pick it?"

"Exactly! Especially after everyone figures out the path to get here was in the opposite direction of the farmhouse. Then they would think Widow Miller would do the same thing here. Which is why she wouldn't."

"You're pretty smart," Kara said.

Taff, too excited to be modest, simply nodded. He passed through the center gate, holding it open for his sister. Before Kara could follow him, however, she glimpsed a flicker of motion behind the left gate. She moved the lantern just in time to catch a tall figure walking away from her, pumpkin-orange cloak dragging along the dirt as branched fingers trailed through stalks of corn.

Kara slammed the center gate shut.

"Go," she told Taff.

"What are you doing?" He pulled at the gate, which rattled angrily but remained locked from his side.

Kara needed to get Taff as far away from here as possible. She hoped that his current path would take him right to safety, but what if it didn't? What if this direction led to another, deeper part of the maze? What if it took him directly to Sordyr?

"Why aren't you coming?" Taff asked.

Kara thought fast. "What if you're wrong?"

"I'm not."

"But if you are, you can just come back. I'll let you through the gate and we can try a different path. This way we don't have to risk starting all over again."

Kara hated lying to her brother, but she had to admit that her plan was sound. Even Taff seemed impressed.

"But I really think this is the right path," he said.

"If so it's a very short walk to the house. An even faster run. If you're not back in a few minutes, I'll know it's the right direction and I'll follow you."

"I'll just come back and let you know."

"No!" Kara shouted, so loud that Taff jumped. "No. Once you're at the house, stay there. I'll be right behind you. Here." She slid the lantern through the bars of the gate. "Take this."

"It'll be dark without a lantern, Kara. How will you see?"

"I'll manage. I can hear the others behind me." She leaned in and whispered, "I'll send them through the left gate."

Taff giggled. "I'll be fast."

"Run!" Kara said. "Don't stop running until you reach the house!"

She waited until the sound of his footsteps faded into the night. Then she went through the left gate.

Sordyr stood at the end of the row—a dead end—his cloak draped around him. His face was hidden beneath the folds of his hood, but his body looked smaller, as though being away from the Thickety drained him somehow. Even his stick fingers seemed weak and brittle.

Kara resisted the urge to turn and run.

It's me he wants. As long as I'm here, Taff is safe.

Sordyr strode toward her. Fresh straw, placed after the storm, crunched beneath his feet. She could hear children's laughter and the faint strains of a fiddle, the music muffled by cornstalks but still audible.

"Why are you here?" she asked.

His orange cloak rustled as he came closer.

"*How* are you here? You shouldn't be able to leave the Thickety, even on Last Night."

The grimoire pleaded to be used (*Yes, he is powerful but not more powerful than us*), but Kara refused its call. *Only ill can come from using its power. I just need to give Taff time to reach safety.*

When Sordyr was about ten feet away, he came to a stop. Kara was struck by how awkward he looked, nothing like the omnipotent presence she had met in the Thickety.

He held out his branch fingers.

"Give it to me!" he said.

The voice was fake-deep and all too human. With clear eyes she considered the figure before her. The cloak had been recently dyed. The branch hands were just . . . branches.

"Listen to what I say, witch!" the not-Sordyr exclaimed, his voice quivering. "Give me what you have stolen!"

Kara pushed him to the ground.

"Who are you?" she screamed, clawing at the hood of the cloak.

"I am . . . the mighty . . ."

"Who are you?"

"It's Aaron! Aaron Baker!" The boy scrambled away from her and pulled the hood back, revealing shifty eyes and a familiar patch of sweaty hair. He held his hands over his face. "Don't turn me into a bug or nothing! Please! She said you'd stolen something of hers, but you would give it to me if I dressed up like . . . him, because of you being a witch and all. I thought she was just playing some kind of trick. You know, some Shadow Festival fun. I didn't mean no harm."

Kara didn't need to ask Aaron why he had agreed to play his part; like most boys he had a terrible crush on Grace and would do anything she asked. From Grace's perspective it must have seemed like the perfect plan: "Sordyr" would demand the grimoire, Kara—his dutiful servant—would obey, and Aaron would bring the book back like a dog returning a bone.

"Whatever it is," Aaron continued, "I guess you couldn't just give it to me, could you? She promised me a kiss if I returned with it."

"No."

"Fine." He crossed his arms. "She said you'd probably figure out I wasn't him anyway. She said that would be fine, as long as I led you away from your brother and bought her some time—"

Taff!

No longer caring about the trail, Kara plunged through the dead end of the path and into the crops themselves. Tightly planted stalks slapped her face as she ran. After a few minutes, she stumbled out of the corn and into lights and laughter, several yards to the right of the true exit.

"The Witch Girl cheated!" a small girl said, pointing an accusing finger.

The front yard of the farmhouse was packed with people. Most of the children had removed their costumes but still had enough energy left to bob for apples or play chase the leader. Parents drank hot ale from wooden cups and passed the time in idle conversation.

Kara searched frantically through the crowd.

"Taff!" she called. "Taff!"

No one offered to help. Most didn't even look up. Only Widow Miller, oiling the wheels of a long wagon that would provide a welcome ride home, acknowledged her presence.

"Lost your brother, have you?" She wiped her hands on a rag before tucking it into the back of her pants. The widow, a large woman with a tight, work-worn face, never wore dresses.

"Have you seen him?" Kara asked.

"I have," she said. "Not so long ago, right over there. He was all tuckered out from the maze so the fen'de's girl got him a glass of cider." She shook her head. "I really think I overdid it this year, but I just can't help myself. I'm as dutiful as the next woman, but sometimes people need a little *fun*."

"Where are they now?"

Widow Miller clapped a huge hand against Kara's

back. "No need to worry. Grace volunteered to take him home."

"Taff *left* with her?"

"That's right. Her and that simple boy. Simon."

This isn't right. Taff hates Grace almost as much as I do.

"You *saw* my brother leave with Grace Stone?"

Widow Miller hesitated. "I didn't actually *see* him leave, but Grace told me she was taking him home. She didn't want you to be worried none. You should be grateful, Kara. That girl's got a touch of the Clen to her."

Kara could see it unfolding in her mind: Simon dragging Taff away when no one was looking, giving Grace the opportunity to appear like her usual helpful self. *She never expected me to be tricked by Aaron's costume. He was just a distraction—and I fell for it.*

"There was one more thing," Widow Miller said. "Grace mentioned that you had something of hers. She didn't seem mad about it or anything, but she said she'd sure appreciate it if you got it back to her quick. Tonight, if possible." The widow crouched down next to a wagon wheel and removed her oily rag. "I told her I'd pass it along."

SIXTEEN

K ara sprinted along the main road, past large groups of exhausted children shedding their costumes like skin. She stopped only when she had reached the copse of red willow trees that lay just beyond the Westfall farm.

Grace had brought Taff there.

Kara's certainty of this came not from fresh footprints or wagon treads, but an understanding of her foe. This was where Grace had first held the grimoire, and the fen'de's daughter, who coveted order in all things, would want to end this where it had begun.

The problem, then, was not in finding her brother—but what to do once she did.

It could be so easy. Grace wanted the grimoire; Kara wanted to be rid of it. But then what? Grace would promise to let them go (no doubt with hands clasped together and an expression of angelic sincerity lighting her face), but those were just words. Once the grimoire was in Grace's possession, Kara and Taff would be at her mercy. By trading her magic, Kara was also relinquishing any ability to protect them.

If she can make it snow without even thinking about it, what will she be able to do once she learns how to control her magic?

Kara couldn't let that happen. Grace had been dangerous enough before this; if she were given the power to match her ambition, there was no telling what type of tragedy might befall the island. Only one thing was certain: Innocent people would suffer, and their blood would be on Kara's hands.

But if you had to, would you trade their lives for Taff's?

The answer came instantly.

In a heartbeat.

And yet . . . surely they didn't *all* deserve to be punished. What about Constance? Her father? Lucas? And then there was Taff himself. How would he react if he found out that his freedom had been purchased with the pain and suffering of others? He might never forgive her.

It doesn't matter what I do, Kara thought. She closed her eyes and bent her head forward, as though in prayer. *People are going to suffer.*

She stepped into the copse.

The trees were still. As Kara passed between them dark shapes seemed to swirl just out of sight, vanishing the moment she turned her head. "Taff!" she shouted. Her instincts told her to be quiet, but given the fact that she had no plan, what advantage could surprise offer? "Taff!" She ducked beneath drooping red leaves, panic growing. "Taff!" Not a sound in response. It was as though the willows themselves had been turned upside down until all life was shaken out.

Then Kara saw the light.

A lantern hung from a withered tree at the far edge of the woods. It held only enough oil to burn for a single hour, so Kara knew that someone—probably Simon— had been here recently.

They must have used a wagon to get here so quickly. Grace could not have walked this far.

Kara saw a second beacon several hundred yards in the distance. She hurried toward it, finding an identical lantern resting on the stones of an abandoned well. Taff's mask had been propped against it.

By the fifth lantern, Kara knew where she was being led. She stifled a sudden, unexpected giggle. *Of course.* Grace knew that Kara would come here, but that wasn't good enough. She had planned an even better location for their encounter. More dramatic.

The final lantern, entirely unnecessary, hung from a wooden peg just outside the front door. Kara took it.

Aunt Abby's house hadn't been lived in for many years, and Kara thought it might need some illumination.

The stale air stank of death.

Rat bones lay in scattered piles. More recently something larger had crawled beneath the floorboards and expired. The walls were spotted with thick, black mold.

Crossing swollen floorboards, Kara made her way deeper into the house. She was frightened, of course, but beneath that was a deep sadness. Aunt Abby, more than anyone in her life, had treated her like a *child*: squeezing her cheeks, making funny faces, sneaking her extra treats when Mother wasn't looking.

She'd be doing those things for Taff right now, if Mother hadn't killed her.

Kara turned a corner and entered the kitchen. Aunt Abby's new husband had built it just for her, a newlywed surprise. It was twice the size of most kitchens, with an elaborate island at its center to hold all of Abby's pots, pans, and mixing bowls. Now it was a darkened ruin. The island had cracked in two under the weight of a massive ceiling beam. Shards of pottery crunched beneath Kara's feet.

A giant stood in the corner.

Kara spoke softly. "Where's my brother?"

Simon did not respond.

"Taff!" Kara called. She took a step forward, intending to investigate the next room. Simon blocked her path.

"Let me pass," Kara said.

Slowly Simon shook his head. He gestured to the satchel with one massive hand. The fingernails had been chewed raw.

"You need to see it? Before she'll let me come?"

He nodded.

"Fine."

Kara yanked the grimoire from the satchel and shoved it in his face. Simon opened his mouth in a silent scream, then backpedaled so fast, he nearly fell.

The book terrifies him. Maybe he's not as simple as he seems.

She stepped around Simon into the meeting room. Like the rest of the house, it had fallen into disrepair, but at least the impressive table at its center—long enough to seat a dozen people—had escaped damage. Grace sat at its head, elbows resting on the table, head propped daintily on two folded hands. She had chosen a red ribbon for the occasion.

"This house soothes me," she said. "Maybe I'll move here. Afterward."

A perfectly spaced row of candles lined the table, infusing the room with a soft glow. The tabletop had been scrubbed and polished.

"Where's Taff?"

"Upstairs. I had to gag him. Sickly little pup won't stop yapping, once he gets going. Give me the book, and I'll set him free. I'll even leave the gag on so you can enjoy a quiet journey home."

"I need to see him."

"Why? Do as I ask, and I'll send him down."

"I'll give you the book as soon as I know Taff is safe."

Grace slammed her fist against the table, rattling the candlesticks. Simon moaned softly, hiding his face in his hands.

"I need it! Now!"

Although Kara did not feel calm at all, she took a deep breath and slid into a chair two seats down from Grace.

"Let's talk."

"I don't want to talk. I want the—"

"Grimoire. I understand. Of course I do. Have you really thought this through, though? Everyone already knows I'm a witch, and there's little I can do to control my darker impulses. But you're the fen'de's daughter. What would your father think?"

"Do not speak of my father!" Her tone was venomous, but Grace's lips trembled with hurt as she spoke; it was the most human Kara had ever seen her. "The rest of the village accepts me, but my *own father* looks at this hair, this twisted leg, and sees an abomination touched by magic. Once he learns of my power, he'll be thrilled to know he was right the entire time."

Grace rose to her feet, candlelight reflecting off her crystalline-blue eyes.

"I can't wait to show him what his little girl can do," she said.

"Grace . . ."

"I will have the grimoire. Now. Or I will tell Simon to go upstairs and crack your brother's neck. He'll do it too. He'll do anything I want him to. Tell me that you believe me."

"I believe you," Kara said.

She's lost. If there were any good in her whatsoever, it has been swallowed up by her need for the grimoire. I have no choice.

Kara slid the book across the table so it lay midway between them. Grace pounced on it like a wild beast on a carcass. Struck by a sudden, desperate idea, Kara tried to look as unconcerned as possible.

"It's useless anyway," she said, stifling a yawn.

"Don't be daft. I've used it. I've felt its power."

"Oh, it can do some good *tricks*, if that's all you want. It's great fun at the beginning." Kara shrugged. "It just gets boring after a while. The curse doesn't let you wield any *real* power."

Grace ignored her and opened the book. Her look of triumph, however, quickly shattered as she flipped through the pages that held Kara's spells. "Why are these all black?" she demanded, anger rising. "What did you do? These are useless! Useless!"

Then, midway through the book, Grace found a fresh page. Her breath quickened as she traced the words of a spell that remained invisible to Kara. "Yes! That's just what I need." She looked up, her confidence restored. "Now tell me about this curse, or I will *make* you tell me."

"We had an agreement. I've done my part, and now—"

Grace spoke a single word, and Kara's tongue swelled into a snakelike mass. Tiny tendrils branched off, squirming down her throat and into the oxygen-providing cavities of her nostrils. Kara fell to her knees, gagging for air that would not come.

Grace waved a hand. Kara's tongue returned to normal.

"The curse," Grace said. "Or next time I'll kill you."

Although her insides had turned to ice, Kara forced herself to laugh.

"That's the point, Grace. You can't. You can't kill anyone."

Grace stared at her quizzically.

"Explain."

"I want to see my brother first."

Kara hopped up on the meeting-room table and swung her legs casually, as though she had nothing to fear. She hoped that such insolence would help make her story more convincing. She also hoped that Grace did not notice her trembling hands.

"Fine," Grace said. And then, louder: "Simon! Bring the whelp!"

Floorboards creaked as the giant entered the room, Taff slung over his shoulder like a sack of grain. He laid the boy across the table. Outside of a few scratches and bruises, Taff appeared unharmed.

Kara ran to his side and removed the gag.

"Are you okay?" she asked.

Taff sneezed in response. By instinct Kara felt his forehead. The fever that burned within him was a raging, monstrous thing.

"What's going on?" he asked. His voice was hoarse. "Why did they—"

Taff flew through the air, smacking against the opposite wall with a sickening *thud*. He slumped to the ground, motionless.

"The curse," Grace said.

Kara charged her with a scream of rage, but Grace spoke a single syllable and Kara was propelled backward, the world spinning as her head collided with the stone floor. She struggled to rise but was held in place by invisible hands.

Leaning carefully on her cane, Grace stroked a wisp of hair out of Kara's eyes.

"It's sad, really. We could have done great things together."

From the corner of her eye, Kara saw the grimoire sitting on the table.

"I know what you're thinking. You can't move, Kara. Besides, if you try anything, I'll make the book create the most horrible spell I can think of. And then I'll cast it on your brother."

Grace flipped to a new page of the grimoire. Looked down. Smiled.

"Speak," she said.

Suddenly Kara could move again. She talked quickly, trying not to think about how hard Taff had crashed into the wall. "My mother told me about the book when I was a little girl. She was the one who trained me." *Why hasn't he made a sound? Even a moan of pain . . .*

Grace scoffed. "She didn't do a very good job. I'm already a better witch than you'll ever be."

"That's what you don't get," Kara said. "I can do all the spells you do. I just choose not to, because I might accidentally kill someone."

"That's ridiculous."

"Remember that night outside my window? Letting my creatures kill you would have been easy. They wanted to—I could feel it. I had to exert all my power just to keep you alive."

"Maybe the book wouldn't let you kill me," she said. "Maybe it wants a real master."

"But what about everyone else in this town—did the book want them to live too? If I had the ability to take my revenge, don't you think I would have done it long before now? If I could use the book the way I wanted to, we wouldn't even be having a conversation right now! The moment you stole my brother, I would have *ended you.*"

This gave Grace pause. The cold logic of Kara's story made sense.

"Tell me more," she said.

Kara continued. "There's nothing more to tell. The grimoire gives you all the power in the world, but you can't use it to kill another person. If you do, you'll never be able to cast a spell again. It's nothing but a colossal tease."

Grace slumped into her chair, shaking her head. "No. That doesn't make any sense at all. Why give someone all this power if she can't use it?"

It took Kara a moment before she realized that Grace was waiting for an answer. She thought frantically. With each passing second, Grace looked more suspicious.

"Mother died before she could tell me," Kara said, but the lie sounded forced and weak.

Grace pulled the grimoire toward her. "Are you trying to trick me?"

"Just tell her, Kara," Taff said, rising to his feet.

Both girls stared at the seven-year-old in surprise.

"The Path is wrong," he said. "Not all witches are bad. A good witch cast a spell on the book so that it couldn't be used for evil."

Grace turned to Kara. "Is this true? Why didn't you tell me?"

Taff continued. "She was afraid if you knew it was another spell, you might try to break it. She knows how smart you are. She doesn't care about the others—neither of us do—but we want to be safe."

Grace nodded slowly, satisfied by the explanation. Kara resisted the urge to plant kisses all over her brilliant brother's face and took him by the hand, guiding him toward the door.

"We're going now," she said. Hopefully her story would keep Grace from doing any major harm, at least until she thought of a better plan. "Be careful. Even if you just hurt someone—it can cost you your powers for a few days. . . ."

"Stop," Grace said.

They were so close. Kara thought about running, but Simon's massive frame blocked the entire doorway.

"Perhaps your story is true," she said, "but if so, that just makes you more dangerous to me. You're the only ones who know my secret. If you tell someone, how will I defend myself?" She clicked her cane against the stone. "It's strange. I was going to let you live. I really do like you, Kara. The boy, not so much."

She turned to Simon, and her voice cracked only the tiniest bit when she spoke. "Start with him and make it quick. No need to be cruel about it."

Without a moment's hesitation, Simon curled his arm around Taff's neck and squeezed. The boy's feet dangled off the floor.

"No!" Kara screamed. She dug her fingers beneath Simon's arm and attempted to pull her brother free. "You don't have to do this! You don't have to listen to her!"

But then Kara looked into Simon's eyes and understood the essential falsehood of her words: He *did*, in fact, have to do this. There was no joy in the act, but there was also no doubt that he would see this through to the end. His blank stare was workmanlike, like a farmer slaughtering a hog. Kara tore bloody trails across the giant's arm, but his grip remained strong. It was only when she changed tactics and sent a well-placed kick to his manhood that Simon relinquished his hold. Taff fell to the floor, gasping for breath. Kara managed to get one hand around his shoulders before Simon regained his composure and pushed her away. It wasn't a hard shove, by Simon's standards, but it was enough to send Kara sprawling across the room. Her head connected with the meeting-room table. The right side of her face went instantly and completely numb, as though she had fallen asleep in the snow.

"Silly girl," Grace said. "There are other ways to kill people than magic. Didn't Mother teach you *that*?"

Kara rose to her knees, swallowing the sudden nausea burning her throat. The room teetered before her. She picked up a chair and raised it high in the air, struggling for a moment beneath its weight. Grace clapped her hands softly. "Go ahead," she said. "Throw it. Maybe you'll even give Simon a scratch."

Except Kara didn't throw it at Simon. She threw it at Grace.

It wasn't a perfect hit; even on her best day, Kara had neither the strength nor skill for that. But luck, at least for this one moment, was with her, and twenty pounds of finely crafted De'Norian wood skidded across the floor and clipped Grace's left leg. With no ability to balance herself, Grace fell to the ground headfirst, white hair spilling over her features like an angel's shroud.

The grimoire crashed open-faced to the floor.

Kara wasted no time. As Simon let loose a wail of almost bestial fury and Grace raised her head, the leaking gash in her chin marring those perfect features, Kara stumbled to the book and fell before its leaves. Grace said something that might have been *nonono*, and then Kara placed her hand upon the grimoire. The black page before her shifted, and her old spell appeared.

And then she was lost in the book, allowing it to have her fully and completely (*Why did I ever resist this?*), but still she could hear them. Simon's footsteps approaching like thunderclaps. Grace's nails scratching against the stone as she struggled to her feet.

No time to think. No time to ponder right or wrong.

She read the words.

They waited. Frozen. Listening intently for what this new spell might bring.

Seconds passed. A minute.

Nothing but silence.

"It's my book!" Grace finally spat out, her voice triumphant. "Mine! It doesn't work for you anymore! You've failed, Witch Girl! You've—"

Grace had just enough time to realize she was wrong, and then the swarm swallowed her whole.

The girl's pain was pleasure. Kara absorbed each tortuous gyration and flailing limb with ardent eyes, unwilling to miss a single moment. Grace had been transformed into a swirling mass of carapaces and mandibles; not even a single strand of her white hair could be seen. There were only Kara's creatures—her beautiful, loyal creatures—cloaking the girl until Kara gave them her final command. Then, and only then, would they take her life.

A merciless smile shifted Kara's features into strange new positions.

Something else was making a sound. Kara didn't know where it was coming from—she refused to shift her eyes from the show—but it was loud and annoying and made Grace's screams difficult to appreciate. Then Kara remembered. The giant. It was hard to tell, but she thought he might be sobbing.

Pathetic.

Kara stifled a laugh as the fool tried to rescue his mistress from the swarm. He was bitten several times for his troubles, and his hands began to swell even beyond their usual gargantuan size. She considered sending more reinforcements into the fray—the grimoire, nestled in her lap, craved attention—but it seemed unfair. These little ones had traveled so far, and they deserved their prize.

"Kara," said a voice, small and tremulous, "stop it. No matter what she did, this isn't right. This isn't *you*."

Kara swatted at the voice but ended up with a handful of soft hair instead. Hair that felt familiar, somehow.

Part of the swarm broke free, squeezing through a tiny gap in the roof and escaping into the night.

"Taff?" Kara asked.

The boy put his arms around her and nestled against her neck. Kara could still smell lemon drops on his breath. "Make them go away," he said. There was a new hitch in his breathing. Kara made a mental note to apply a mint poultice to his chest before he went to sleep that night, and another section of the swarm, larger than the first, fluttered reluctantly into the sky.

"I want to go home," Taff said.

Kara nodded. Home. Her own bed. Father. She rose, intending to release the remainder of the swarm and set Grace free, when Simon Loder grabbed Taff's head and slammed it against the floor. Taff lay instantly still— more still than any living human should be—and though Kara did not scream, a small murmur of surprise escaped her lips. Simon bent down next to Taff and took his head between his hands, positioning his body for a final, neck-crunching twist.

Kara killed him.

It was surprisingly simple. Kara willed her children to remove this life from the world, and they complied, lifting the giant off his feet with ease and pressing him against the ceiling as they emptied their stingers. Those with only one sting to give pattered to the floor like black rain, a sacrifice for their queen. Simon followed with far less elegance, his face already ballooning beyond recognition as the poison completed its work. He gasped once for breath, but his windpipe had already closed and all that came out was a defeated hiss.

No one would need to close his eyes. They had already swollen shut.

A solitary soldier landed gently on Kara's hand, as though awaiting further orders. It was only then that she recognized the insect: a haverfly. During summer they glowed briefly with a pretty bluish hue. Taff and Kara had spent many nights running along the stream, collecting them in glass jars. She had thought them harmless.

But anything can kill, can't it, Kara?

"Go," she told the haverfly. It lingered briefly on the end of her fingertip and then set off. The rest of its brethren followed.

Kara could hear footsteps in the distance, voices, but that didn't matter now. Taff wasn't moving. A pool of dark blood stained the floor beneath his head.

"Taff?" Kara whispered.

She held one trembling hand over his mouth, searching for a breath.

"Get her!" Grace screamed. *"She killed Simon! Witch! Witch!"*

Multiple hands shoved Kara to the ground, and she found herself looking up into the faces of half a dozen graycloaks. "Wait!" she screamed. "My brother is hurt. You have to help—" Before she could finish, something cold and foul-smelling was shoved into her mouth, suffocating further protestations. Kara had just enough time to see Grace's smile of triumph as she hid the grimoire beneath her cloak. Then someone pulled a sack over Kara's head and she saw no more.

BOOK THREE

THE LAST SPELL

*"There is no such thing
as a good witch."*

—The Path
Final Leaf

SEVENTEEN

The Well was her world. Her world was the Well.

The darkness was complete and unforgiving, a lack of light so all-consuming that Kara seemed to float in it. She saw things anyway. A crowd of people stretched across a field, hatred in their eyes. Grace tapping at her window. Taff's body, cold and motionless.

And Simon, always Simon. Bloody and ravaged. Eyes open, accusing her.

After Kara's throat became too hoarse to scream any more, she grew to accept the darkness. This was the way it was going to be. She was a witch. A murderer. Evil. She deserved to be punished. Perhaps she was going to be imprisoned down here forever. How long had it been already? Kara didn't know. It might have been days. It didn't matter. She didn't feel hunger. She didn't feel anything, not even the icy chill of water that rose to her chest. The walls of the well held her fast, like a vertical coffin.

She started to hear voices, not always in a language she understood. A whisper, tickling her earlobe. The steady cadence of her name, pitter-pattering into the dank water like rainfall.

There came a time when she realized she wasn't alone.

A soft blue light hovered just above her, close enough to touch. Holding a hand over her eyes, Kara was able to make out the bird that had led her into the Thickety. It was perched on a narrow stone ledge, the blue light emanating from its single eye.

"Are you real?" Kara asked.

The bird's eye swiveled, and the light changed to orange.

Yes.

"You can't be," Kara said. "The Well is covered at the top. How did you get inside?"

The light switched to a questioning mauve, blinking on and off in the darkness: *How do you think?*

"Magic," Kara said, and the light changed to orange again.

Yes.

"Can you get me out of here?" Kara asked.

The light turned red.

No.

"Can you at least *help* me escape?"

The light remained red.

"Then why are you here?" Kara asked, her voice hoarse and unrecognizable.

The bird's eye turned to a sullen blue that Kara recognized from their time in the Thickety. She had thought it meant sorrow, but now, as its depths and shades of meaning cut through the darkness, she realized that wasn't quite right.

"You feel guilty," Kara said.

The eye quickly returned to orange.

"Because you're the one who led me to the grimoire," Kara said.

Orange still.

"Well, what do you want? Do you want me to tell you it's okay? Fine. I don't blame you. You weren't the one who made me kill Simon. I'm just evil, like everyone says I am. Just like my mother."

The light turned red, deeper and more insistent than before.

No!

Its eye swiveled fast, eager to make its point, settling on a warm pink that instantly filled Kara with a sense of calm.

"Mother," she said.

A flash of orange and then the bird showed her a color she had never seen before. Somewhere between black and green but neither of them, the color of pestilence and extinction and nightmares better left forgotten, a color that had been exiled from the world long ago.

It was the color of evil.

The bird's eye flashed from pink to red to this color, and then again. Again.

Mother. No. Evil. Mother. No. Evil.

"But she was," Kara said. "She killed her best friend and her husband. She maimed Constance."

Red.

No.

And then the red light wasn't a light at all but a glowing orb projecting a series of images across the interior of the Well.

Images of the past.

It took Kara a few moments to recognize the place before her as the Smythe house. Not the ruin Grace had led her to on Last Night, but freshly painted and filled with promise. Kara was seeing it from above, as though sitting in the branches of a nearby tree, and she realized that she must be seeing the bird's memories.

Someone was sobbing.

Kara turned and saw Aunt Abby projected on the wall behind her, kneeling in the grass beside a dead man with a horrific expression marring his once-handsome face.

"What have you done?" a woman asked, out of breath from a frantic sprint across the field. Her stomach was swollen with child. "Where's Constance?"

"Mother," Kara said.

Kara reached out to touch her face, a faded memory suddenly bright and vivid with life, but felt only the cold stone of the Well.

Abby rose to her feet. Tears flooded her eyes but did not conceal the madness whirling within them.

She clasped the grimoire protectively to her chest.

"They tried to take it," she said. "They said it was controlling me. I didn't mean to hurt him. I didn't mean to hurt Constance either. She's inside. Alive. But her face.

Her face . . . I just wanted to get it back, I didn't mean . . .
I couldn't let them have it. I love him. Do you think he'll
still love me when he comes back?"

"It's over, Abby."

"It's not my fault."

Mother nodded patiently. She took a casual step in
Abby's direction. "You're right. I should have never taught
you such dangerous things. The fault is mine." Mother
held out her hands. "Give it to me."

Abby backed away like a wounded animal.

"No," she said, flipping open the grimoire. "I can fix
this."

Excitement pulsed in Abby's eyes as she riffled through
the spells, stopping only when she reached the last page.
She smiled with childish glee.

"It's here, Helena!" she exclaimed. "The words to
bring him back!"

Mother shook her head vehemently. "It's the Last
Spell," she said. "You know what will happen."

"Not to me. I won't let it."

Kara's mother took three quick steps and placed her hands on Abby's shoulders. The younger woman flinched but did not pull away.

"Look at me," said Mother.

It was a sharp, teacherly tone, and Abby responded. Without breaking eye contact, Mother spoke. "That day in the farmhouse, what was the very first thing I taught you?"

Abby spoke by rote, as though she had been asked to repeat the words a thousand times: "Do not, under any circumstances, complete a grimoire. The final page must remain unused."

"The most important advice a witch will ever hear. Heed it now."

"It doesn't matter if I die."

"You'll wish you had."

"He said he still loved me, even after he learned what I was. I just want to make things right."

Mother ran a hand along Abby's blond curls. "I know you do. But there are some things that not even magic can fix, my friend."

With great care Mother began to tease the grimoire from Abby's fingers, but just as the book was about to change owners, Abby snatched it back.

"Those rules might be true for you, but not me! Anything I want, *my* grimoire provides. I'm more powerful than you!"

"That's what it wants you to think. Nothing is more tempting than power. The book knows that!"

"You're jealous. You want to take it from me. Like him."

"Enough! Don't be a fool, Abigail! You can't cast the Last Spell!"

"Watch me."

Of its own accord, the grimoire flipped to the final page. Abby began to read. Mother rushed to stop her, but Abby mumbled a few words and rose high into the air. Once safely out of reach, she continued casting her spell, the words a blur of enigmatic syllables, her voice only vaguely her own.

The body of Peter Smythe spasmed slightly.

"Stop!" Mother screamed. But how could she be heard? Abby's voice was a tornado, a hurricane, a deafening roar. The windows of the Smythe house shattered outward, and a great crack zippered its way across the roof. Peter's fingers began to twitch in an unnatural, jerky rhythm.

Then the bird's eye flashed, and the images around Kara began to change. "Not yet!" she exclaimed. Though she saw nothing but chaotic colors swirling across the walls, she could still hear Aunt Abby's screams: *What is this? I command you to release. . . . I command . . . Helena! Help me! Heeelllp!"*

Kara had never heard such terror in her life.

And then the image of a bedroom, seen from the branches just outside an open window, stretched across the walls of the Well. The mattress had been thrown to the floor; on it rested Kara's mother, motionless and unblinking, her face drained of color. An overturned tureen dripped water onto a pile of torn and bloody sheets.

Somewhere a baby was crying.

That's Taff! Mother just gave birth!

Angry voices exploded from another part of the house.

"Fen'de Stone said no one can—"

"Let me through! Now!"

There were brief scuffling sounds, and then Father opened the door. He held a small bundle cradled in his arms.

"Please," Mother said, and Father carefully handed her the sleeping child. She nestled the small form against her chest and squeezed his tiny hand. "They never even gave me a chance to hold him. My little Taff."

"Taff?"

"It has a special meaning in the tongue of my people. Perhaps he'll learn it one day." She clutched Father's arm.

"Constance carried me here and delivered the baby all on her own. She saved our son's life! Make sure she knows how grateful I am. And that I'm so sorry I couldn't heal her face."

"You can tell her yourself."

"I couldn't save Abby. She was too far gone. How could I have let this happen? And don't say it wasn't my fault, Will. I was the one who wanted to share my craft."

"Once I speak to Fen'de Stone and explain what happened, he'll—"

Mother looked away from the baby. Her eyes were cold.

"You'll do nothing of the sort."

"Why not? These people trust me. They'll listen to what I have to say."

"Good. Then they'll be sure to believe you when you denounce me as a witch."

"What?"

"Tell them that you never loved me. That you were

only under my spell."

"Never!"

"Tell them that I'm guilty of all these crimes tonight— and more!"

"They'll kill you!"

"They will kill me regardless of what you say. If you defend me, you will only incriminate yourself. Who will raise this little one, then? And what about Kara? What kind of life will she know without a father to watch over her?"

"I won't betray you."

"You betray me if you do not do as I ask!" Helena drew him down and tenderly kissed his lips. "Please, William. You need to do this."

"You are my world, Helena."

"And you mine."

She stared into his eyes, and Kara saw something pass between them, something that had been grown and nurtured by laughter and tears and hands held by firelight—and all the other moments of a life shared together.

Father looked away first.

"You must hide the truth from them," Mother said. "Especially from Kara. Speak only ill of me when I am gone. Make her believe I was every bit the monster people whispered about. This way, when she begins to use her powers, she'll do so with respect for the dangers." Mother turned her head, unwilling to share her tears. "It would be best if her greatest fear in life was becoming like me. Here." Mother slipped something small into Father's pocket. "You'll know when it's time."

From the other side of the house came shouts and the sound of approaching footsteps. Father stepped toward the door, ready to prop it shut, but Mother shook her head. "Come, my love," she said, patting the mattress. "Sit by my side and look at this beautiful child we made. Is this not the most extraordinary magic of all?"

The bird's eye flickered out, and the walls grew dark.

"More!" Kara exclaimed. "Show me more!"

But there was nothing. No sign of the bird at all.

Suddenly sunlight tunneled cruelly into her sensitive eyes as the cover of the Well slid open.

A rope dangled before her.

Everyone was wrong, Kara thought as she looped it beneath her arms. *Mother didn't hurt anyone. She sacrificed herself to protect her children.*

Kara touched the locket around her neck and smiled.

"Mother was good," she said.

The rope grew taut, and Kara Westfall rose toward the beckoning day.

The graycloaks brought her to a small stable. One of the stalls had been prepared just for her, its walls reinforced and raised to the ceiling. They left her a simple brown frock and a bucket of hot water and departed. Kara heard the sound of chains being fastened on the other side of the door.

She washed herself and dressed quickly, then slept for almost two days.

When Kara awoke it was early morning. Faint beams of sunlight whispered through small holes in the stable wall. Past a narrow, barred opening in the door, she could see a small table and a chair. Fen'de Stone sat there trimming his fingernails with a penknife. Twin lenses encased in a thin metal frame dangled from the edge of his nose. Kara had heard talk of this kind of World magic, portable mirrors called "spectacles" that improved one's eyesight instead of casting a reflection.

Behind Fen'de Stone stood two graycloaks.

"My brother," Kara said. Her voice was a dry rasp. "Does he live?"

The fen'de nodded toward one of the guards, who produced a metal cup from beneath the folds of his cloak and filled it with water from his canteen. He passed the cup through the bars to Kara. She longed to throw it in his face, but her thirst was greater than her pride; she swallowed the water in three gulps. It was rusty and warm and the best thing she had ever tasted.

"My brother," she repeated.

"He lives," replied the fen'de. "But he's in a bad way, that poor child. Head swollen, the fever with him always. Doctor Mather, dedicated soul, has been at him with his leeches every day, but Taff's condition only grows worse. It's a baffling situation."

Kara felt her lower lip start to tremble and bit it viciously, nearly drawing blood. *I will not cry in front of this man. Ever.*

"It is such a relief to have you here, Kara," Fen'de Stone said. "To know that you're just like your mother. All these years, I *knew* that nightseeker was wrong. And I was right. I . . . was . . . right!" The fen'de leaned back, and his seat groaned beneath the weight. "Excuse the excessive pride, but I can't help feeling a trifle satisfied with myself right now."

"I'm very happy for you."

"Did you bewitch that useless beast so it couldn't identify you? And the death of Bailey Riddle—was that your doing? I suspected witchcraft, but—"

"I had nothing to do with it. I was only a child."

"You're still a child, Kara. And yet the things you can do! What you did to Simon Loder—it's quite a story my daughter tells."

"I'm sure it is."

Fen'de Stone paused and studied her for a moment, his expression perplexed. *He expected the Well to break me. He expected a docile girl begging for forgiveness.*

She was glad to disappoint him.

"Kara Westfall," he finally said. His voice was now measured and formal. "You have been accused of the most serious violation of the Clen's teachings: witchcraft. In addition, an eyewitness of the highest moral caliber has seen you use these dark powers to take the life of another. How do you plead?"

Kara was tempted to concede. All she had to do was say "guilty" and her fate would be sealed. No more anger. No more pain.

But what would become of Taff? He would die without her help.

"I do not know any witchcraft," Kara said. "I am a Child of the Fold. I walk in the footsteps of the Clen."

Kara stared proudly through the bars of the door, daring the fen'de to claim otherwise.

He removed his spectacles and rubbed his eyes.

"You're not going to make this difficult, are you?"

"You asked a question. I answered it. Who's being difficult?"

Fen'de Stone snapped his fingers, and one of the graycloaks handed him an ancient-looking red tome. The fen'de spread it across the table.

"This is my greatest treasure," he said. "A book older than even the Path. It was written by Abel Sanderson, one of Timoth Clen's greatest lieutenants. A man renowned for his bravery on the battlefield but also for a . . . shall we say, *talent* to convince witches to tell the truth. This is a guidebook of sorts. It's all in here, every technique. The Twisting Stick. The Melting Blade. The Screaming Collar. Which shall we start with, Kara? Do you have a preference?" He closed the book. "Or perhaps I'll just flip it open and choose at random."

Kara looked deep into his eyes and knew that he was not bluffing. She glanced through the bars and gasped at the illustration before her. If there had been any food in her stomach, she might have been ill on the spot.

"What do you want to know?" Kara asked.

Smiling, Fen'de Stone closed the tome and pulled out a smaller book. He removed a quill and black inkpot, brushed a hand across a new page.

"I have to document everything," he said. "So those fools in the World believe me. They didn't about your mother, you know. Said I was making it up to try to make my little *cult* seem *relevant* again." He straightened his spectacles. "Tell me what happened at the old Smythe farm. In your own words."

"Simon Loder was going to kill Taff. I stopped him."

"You murdered him."

Kara knew her actions were justified, but the words stung nonetheless.

"I was defending my brother."

"Why would Simon wish your brother harm? Simon's just an idiot. He can't even think."

"He doesn't have to. Grace does it for him."

Fen'de Stone picked up the red tome again and idly flipped through the pages.

"Do not speak ill of my daughter, witch," he said.

"Did she tell you her version of what happened?" Kara asked.

"You mean the truth? Yes. Grace told me everything. Every dark deed. Every unspeakable act. She's had nothing but nightmares since—"

Kara burst into laughter.

Fen'de Stone's eyes blazed. "Since you refuse to share the events of that night," he said, leaning forward, "allow me to do it for you. You trapped them in the old Smythe house. It was Simon you were after. The Forest Demon—your Lord and master—ordered you to kill him. Simon is the only one who ever returned from the Thickety, and Sordyr wanted to make sure he didn't share any of its secrets. Grace tried to reason with you, to convince you to rejoin the Path, but it was useless. You used your black magic to murder Simon. You nearly killed your own brother. If my men hadn't arrived in time, you would have taken Grace from me too."

"What a thrilling story! Perhaps Grace should leave the Fold and become a talespinner."

Fen'de Stone rose from his chair. "My daughter would never lie to me, witch. So just answer this one question, and I promise I will end your misery at the crack of dawn."

"You've already decided I'm guilty. What else could you possibly want to know?"

"Where's the grimoire?"

Kara was unable to hide her astonishment.

"That's right. I know about the source of your power," the fen'de said. "I didn't when your mother sat in your position, and I'm embarrassed by my ignorance now. Not even Timoth Clen himself knew that secret. But I've spent many years studying your kind, and you'll find I've grown quite knowledgeable." Fen'de Stone smiled, revealing an uneven row of yellowed teeth. "I understand why you'd want to hide the truth. Somehow it makes it all seem less impressive. It's not you who wields the power. It's the book."

"So where is it?"

Why don't you ask your daughter? She's a witch too.

She longed to say the words; to a man of such extreme faith, they would be just as deadly as a sword blow. But then Kara remembered the trade Grace had offered her: *You might not be powerful enough to fix your brother, but I am. Give me the book, and I promise I'll do it.*

"Your answer?" Fen'de Stone asked.

If Taff was badly wounded, Grace might be the only

one who could save him. For that reason she couldn't tell Fen'de Stone the truth about his daughter. He probably wouldn't believe her, but what if he did? His graycloaks would capture Grace and maybe figure out a way to destroy the grimoire. If that happened, no one would be able to save Taff. Of course Kara had no idea how she was going to escape her cell (let alone convince Grace to heal her brother), but even a small chance to save Taff was better than none at all.

"Answer!" Fen'de Stone exclaimed. A branchlike vein throbbed along his temple. Though still a child in years, Kara had lived hard enough to recognize madness when she saw it.

The fen'de waited a few more moments for Kara to reply. When she did not, he opened the red tome at random.

"Oh, yes," he said, gazing at the page before him. "I believe we'll start right here."

EIGHTEEN

Kara spent the next day alone in her cell. A graycloak came to bring her porridge and a moldy loaf of bread in the morning and returned for her chamber pot just before dusk. Other than that she saw no one.

For the first few hours of the day, Kara held her fingers beneath the single beam of sunlight that filtered through a crack in the ceiling. She turned and twisted her hand, watching the light play off her skin. If she focused hard enough, she could remove her mind from the lingering pain.

Instead she watched the sunlight dance and worried about Taff.

He must live.

The thought made no logical sense—why should Taff be exempt from death?—but she clung to it anyway. To think otherwise was the end of all.

He must live.

Eventually Kara realized that her legs were sore from sitting so long in the same position, so she got to her feet and did her best to clean the stall. She brushed the hay into the corner, making a serviceable sleep mat, and cleared away the mud and dried horse manure. Kara supposed that the animal odor might have bothered some people, but she found it comforting. She wondered how Shadowdancer was doing. She imagined riding him through the grassy pastures west of the village, but the thought only made her sad. There was no use dreaming of impossible things.

By lunchtime—though of course there would be no

lunchtime, not for her—Kara began pacing the floor from one end to the other. Six strides back, four across. Six, four. Six, four. She was used to a constant stream of work, of never having a free moment. It would have never occurred to her that waiting for one's death could be so *boring*.

That night her efforts at sleep were interrupted, time and time again, by the dead, accusing eyes of Simon Loder.

Cold water slapped her awake. A young graycloak stood before her brandishing an empty bucket and a smirk.

"Rise and shine, witch," he said.

He dragged her out of the stable by her hair. The sun had not yet risen, and Kara's teeth chattered uncontrollably as the morning chill bit through her soaking clothes. Four more graycloaks waited outside. One of them held a long coiled rope, which he used to bind Kara's hands together. He shoved her into an open wagon, and they started toward the village, Kara remembering a similar trip she had taken years earlier.

At least they didn't put a sack over my head this time.

When they reached the barren field where her mother had been killed, the large crowd gasped in horror. And why not? Kara was everything a witch should be: bloodied and filthy, her clothes torn and her face streaked with mud. Two graycloaks yanked Kara to her feet and dragged her forward. Tiny details suddenly seemed important. The way her toes scraped against the cold earth. The crowd parting in perfect unison as she passed. The wide, horrified eyes of the children.

The fen'de waited for her on a newly built scaffold, and the graycloaks tossed Kara to his feet. Behind him stood Grace, wearing the traditional brown robes of a fen'de apprentice (with a brown hair ribbon to match).

"What happened to Apprentice Cloud?" Kara asked.

"Don't speak that fine boy's name," Grace said. "There was a horrible accident, and I have agreed to honor his memory by serving in his stead."

Her voice was clear and pure, providing no hint that she had been the one behind Marsten Cloud's "accident." Kara, however, noted the way her fingers trembled slightly, longing for the touch of something they couldn't have. Being without the grimoire, even for a few minutes, tortured her.

She's losing control. Marsten Cloud won't be the last to die.

Fen'de Stone stepped forward. He wore his traditional Service Day robe, as clean as the day it was sewn. Kara resisted the urge to soil it with her muddy handprints.

"Kara Westfall!" he exclaimed. "You have been accused of breaking the most sanctified rule of the Fold by engaging in magic."

At the word *magic*, the crowd erupted, raucous exclamations blending together into one unified stream of violent intent.

SAVEUSBURNTHEDEMONWITCHJUSTLIKEITSMOTHER

The fen'de held his hand high in the air until the noise ceased.

"The evidence weighs heavily against you, Kara

Westfall. Very heavily indeed. However, we of the Fold are a merciful people, and we will give you a chance to confess your crimes." He knelt down and placed a hand on her head, and the crowd gasped—only a man as holy as their fen'de would dare touch such a wicked creature. "Admit that you have lost your path. Tell us how you forsook Timoth Clen and all his teachings and embraced those of darkness instead."

"Tell us!" the crowd intoned.

"Tell us how your mother, wicked woman, taught you her dark arts and corrupted your soul."

"Tell us!"

"Tell us how you took the life of Simon Loder, that poor, innocent boy."

"Tell us!"

"Tell us everything, Kara Westfall, and your death will be far quicker than you deserve. You will be washed in flames! The Clen's will be done, in death you will be pure again!"

At this Kara expected the crowd to erupt once more, but instead it grew eerily quiet. It took Kara a few moments to realize that they were waiting for her to respond.

Muscles groaning in complaint, Kara managed to get to her feet. She turned and faced the villagers sitting before her. Baker Corbett. Rancher Goodwin and her twins. Elder Carlye. She had known these people her entire life and recognized none of them.

Kara stood tall. She took a deep breath and spoke.

"I am innocent, like my mother before me!"

Her words were drowned out by an angry wave of voices. Only the Clearers, standing behind the back row of the congregation, remained silent. There was violence in the air, and although they might not have been its intended target, a lifetime of servitude had taught them how easily that could change.

Kara looked for Lucas but did not see him.

Once again Fen'de Stone raised a single hand. The crowd fell silent.

"The witch professes her innocence," he said. "But have no fear, Children. Your fen'de knows how to find the truth in all things."

The rest of the afternoon was a blur. They pinned her to the ground and laid a long wooden board over her body. One by one each member of the community placed an object on the board—stones and bricks and rusty tools—creating a crushing weight that pressed her deeper and deeper into the mud. Near the end a freckle-nosed toddler, overwhelmed by this fun game, jumped on the board himself. The crowd roared with laughter.

Periodically Fen'de Stone would wipe away the mud from Kara's lips and whisper the same question: *Where is the grimoire?*

Kara never said a word.

Her mind stepped away from the pain and attempted to formulate a plan. She needed to escape. She needed the grimoire. She needed Grace to heal Taff. Each need was more impossible than the last. Even when they dumped her back in her cell, her muscles limp and tender and screaming for sleep, Kara remained awake until it was nearly morning. Thinking. At one point she heard some sort of commotion outside: graycloaks barking orders, movement through the nearby trees. She thought about going to the window to have a look, but the idea of standing seemed as physically insurmountable to her as knocking down the stable walls with the push of a pinkie.

The plan finally came to her in that foggy land just before dreaming. Perhaps it was her idea alone. Or perhaps it wasn't. Perhaps it drifted through the barred window of the stable on a whisper of autumn mornings and rotting leaves. Even later it was impossible to know for sure.

"I hid the grimoire in the Thickety," she said.

Fen'de Stone placed his quill on the desk. He took a sip of tea.

"You're lying."

"No."

"Don't try to trick me. The grimoire is the source of your power. You would never hide it so far away."

"I would if I knew I was going to be captured."

"No. You would use it to defend yourself."

Kara sighed as though the fen'de's ignorance tested her patience.

"I was drained from dealing with Simon Loder. Witches can't just cast as many spells as they'd like. We get tired. Surely you knew that?"

Fen'de Stone's lips tightened. "Of course." He raised a pudgy finger. "But you had no time to bring it all the way to the Thickety."

"I didn't *bring* it. I *sent* it. With magic?" Kara sighed again. "Are you sure you've studied witches?"

Fen'de Stone got to his feet and paced back and forth. It was the first time Kara had ever seen him so uncertain. She considered this a good sign.

"I still don't believe you. And if you think I lack further ways to make you speak the truth, you are very, very wrong."

"You have the truth. It's only your fear that convinces you otherwise."

"I'm not afraid!"

"That's exactly the reason I sent my grimoire to the Thickety. What place on this island could be safer?"

Fen'de Stone paused, considering the soundness of her logic. After a few moments, he took his seat and clasped his hands together.

"Where?" he asked.

Kara shook her head. "That's not how it works."

"Yes. It is. Tell me where you've hidden it, and once I have the grimoire, I'll make sure you die the next morning. It'll be mostly painless—you have my word."

Kara casually moved to the rear of the stable so her back faced Fen'de Stone. She knew that this next lie would be the hardest to deliver convincingly, and if the fen'de caught a glimpse of falsehood on her face the whole desperate scheme would fall apart.

"It's not that I don't want to tell you. I *can't* tell you. I won't know exactly where the grimoire is until we're close. Only then will I be able to sense it."

Kara turned and was relieved to see Fen'de Stone nodding, as though that made sense.

"It doesn't matter," he said. "We cannot enter the Thickety. To do so is death."

"You fear Sordyr?"

"I fear nothing, witch. But the laws are clear. No one can enter that cursed place. And yet . . ."

Fen'de Stone stroked his considerable chin. Kara remained silent, knowing that he would either convince himself or not; there was nothing further she could do.

"I'm certain an exception could be made for such a holy task. After all, the Fold was created with the single purpose of *ending* magic, and even if no one in the World believes anymore, we know the truth! If we were

to locate this grimoire, and prove that magic still exists, it could usher in a new time for our people, a return to their former glory. Kings would enlist our services. Converts would rush to join us. Our days of cowering on this island would finally come to an end!"

Beads of sweat ran down Fen'de Stone's face. His eyes protruded from their sockets.

"Perhaps this is the great task that will finally prompt the Clen's return to his Children. And it shall be recorded that I was the one responsible."

Suddenly Fen'de Stone pounded his fist against her cell door, rattling the chains. His graycloaks exchanged a look of concern.

"If this is a trick, witch, I'll see to it that your loved ones are slaughtered for all to see."

Though her heart was racing, Kara managed to keep her face impassive. "Don't you remember? My mother is dead. I tried to kill my own brother. My father hates me. Who are these loved ones you speak of? I am all alone."

The fen'de nodded.

"For now," he said.

Two hours later a burly graycloak tossed Lucas into the cell with her.

"If the grimoire isn't where you say it is," Fen'de Stone said, "I'll slit this Stench's throat myself."

"No!" Kara shouted. "He has nothing to do with this!"

But Fen'de Stone was already walking away. "Sleep while you can," he said. "We leave at sunrise."

NINETEEN

A blackish welt darkened Lucas's left cheekbone. Blood seeped through his torn trousers. Despite all this, he was smiling.

"It's good to see you," he said.

Kara knelt by his side. Tearing a piece from the bottom of her frock, she rubbed the grime and dried blood from Lucas's face.

"This is all my fault," she said.

"You can think that. But I choose to blame the people who locked me in here."

"He must have known we were friends, that I would do what he wants if he promised not to hurt you. Only I can't do what he wants, because it's impossible, and now—"

"It's not like that."

"Was it terrible? How badly did they hurt you?"

"If you just let me—"

Without realizing it Kara had begun to scrub the bottom of his chin very hard. Lucas grabbed her hand and held it.

"First of all, that hurts. A lot."

"Sorry."

"Second—they didn't find me, Kara. I found them. Last night I was creeping through the woods that run out back, trying to get closer to the stable. They caught me."

Kara nodded, remembering. "I heard them chasing you! But why would you do that? You must have known that they would punish you."

She saw—to her surprise—that Lucas's cheeks had

grown pink. Kara couldn't remember ever seeing him blush before.

"I was trying to rescue you," he said.

Kara's first reaction was anger. She opened her mouth, intending to tell Lucas that she certainly didn't *need* to be rescued. That he had ruined her one and only plan, because now all she could think about was how to keep him out of harm's way. That he was a complete moron if he thought her life was valuable enough to be worth saving.

She meant to say all these things—she meant to *scream* them—but all that came out was a soft, hesitant "Oh."

For a few moments, there was silence. Lucas absentmindedly rubbed the place where his two fingers used to be.

"Not that I don't appreciate the effort," Kara said, "because I do—I really, truly do. But what were you *thinking*?"

"You're welcome."

"You're just one person. A boy. Did you really expect to sneak past an entire army of graycloaks?"

"Not the entire army. Just the ones guarding your cell."

"You've ruined everything!" Kara exclaimed. "We're going to the Thickety tomorrow to get the grimoire, because I told him the grimoire is there, but I lied, because I thought once I got out of here I would at least have a chance to escape, and when he finds out he's going to kill you, and it'll be my fault. That's if Sordyr doesn't get us first, of course. And Taff is so sick, and if something happens to me——"

"Kara!"

His voice was surprisingly sharp in the darkness.

"Do you remember Tanith? The old Burner who lives in the house next to mine? Too many years close to the flames, mutters about dry waterfalls and words made of minced sky?"

"Yes . . ."

"You're making her sound downright lucid right now."

"You're not funny," Kara said, but she couldn't help smiling anyway. "It's just—everything has spiraled out of control. I don't even know where to begin."

Lucas slid his hand into hers.

"I'm no talespinner, but I've found that the beginning is usually an excellent place. Take your time. We have all night."

She told him everything.

The one-eyed bird. Her trip into the Thickety. Finding the grimoire. Her first spell. The dark temptation of the book. Grace's power. Taff's kidnapping. Simon's death. Her vision in the Well.

Lucas remained silent, offering neither judgment nor sympathy. Just listening.

By the time she'd finished, dawn was less than an hour away. Though Kara hadn't slept, she felt more refreshed than she had in weeks. She was reminded of something

Mother had once told her, when Kara—plagued by guilt—had confessed to some meaningless fib: *Now you understand, child. Secrets and lies can weigh more than boulders.*

Lucas got to his feet and stretched in the dark. He looked out the tiny window.

"Do you think anyone can use this grimoire? Or just . . ."

"Witches?"

". . . people with the right sort of talent?"

"Constance said she couldn't use it. My guess is that Mother originally planned to teach both of them, but only Abby had the ability."

"Let me see if I understand this correctly. You see a blank page until you conjure a creature, and afterward its image appears in the book. But Grace . . ."

". . . opens the book, and whatever she wants appears."

"But what does that mean? How are you two different?"

"She's more powerful. All I can do is conjure animals. Grace can do anything she wants."

Lucas shook his head.

"I'm not so sure about that. Remember, it's the grimoire that decides what Grace can and cannot do. Your ability might have limitations, but it's still *your* ability. Even without a spellbook, you've always had a way with animals that bordered on enchantment. The grimoire just helped you focus your talent, take it one step further. With Grace, it's too easy. I get the sense that the grimoire is using her, not the other way around."

Kara had never thought of it like that. "It's giving her exactly what she needs so she'll keep using it, because once she casts the Last Spell, it'll have her forever, just like Aunt Abby." She shuddered, remembering the terror in Abby's voice. "What do you think happened to her? Is she still . . . alive?"

"I don't know," Lucas said. "Just make sure you never find out."

"You don't need to worry about that. I'm through with magic. Everything we've learned, all the Path's teachings—they're totally correct. Magic is evil."

"Really? After listening to your story, I'm not so sure."

"All of this happened because of magic!"

"No. All of this happened because Grace Stone—who, as you might have noticed, was not a very nice person to begin with—liked the feeling of power that magic gave her and became obsessed with getting more. You need to stop blaming yourself. As far as I can tell, your use of magic includes saving my life and Taff's."

"You're wrong. I've done bad things."

"Who hasn't?"

"I'm a witch, just like they say I am!"

"Sure. But that doesn't make you *bad*."

"I killed a man!"

"And if you had done nothing? Then Taff's death would have been your responsibility. You did what needed to be done, even though you didn't want to. That's not evil. That's courage."

Kara wrapped her arms around her legs.

"Then why don't I feel brave?"

"Because you're too busy feeling guilty. If this is going to work, you need to accept the fact that being a witch is part of who you are. Because, if everything goes well, you're going to have to use magic again."

"I don't know if I can."

"You will. When the time is right, I know you will. We just have to figure out a way to escape from the graycloaks . . ."

". . . sneak back into the village, past hundreds of people who will be hunting me down, and convince my greatest enemy to heal my brother."

"When you put it like that, my plan to rescue you doesn't sound half as crazy."

Kara rose and stood next to him.

"There's one thing I didn't tell you," she said. "I saw Sordyr."

Lucas didn't say a word, but Kara saw his grip tighten around the bars of the window.

"What was it like?"

"I'm not sure. It's like trying to describe a dream after you've woken. I only remember the way I felt in his presence. Cold. Lost."

"The Thickety is hundreds of miles deep. We'll make our escape as quickly as possible. Chances are, we won't come anywhere near him."

Lucas was trying to sound brave, but Kara could hear the fear in his voice.

"I want to believe that. But he spoke to me. He knows my name."

"You think he wants to hurt you?"

And finally Kara spoke her greatest secret, the thought—too horrible to say out loud—that had been circling through her head since the night she'd stepped into the Thickety.

"I don't think he wants to hurt me at all," she said. "I think he wants to keep me."

Lucas's eyes widened. He turned back to the window.

It was still dark, but a soft nimbus of purple light had appeared on the horizon. "We should stop talking," he said, "and save our energy. The only thing we can do now is wait for them to come."

TWENTY

They never came.

The sun rose and bathed the stall in light and warmth, but it remained quiet outside. No sounds of guards changing duty. No horse clops in the distance.

No one brought them breakfast.

"Fen'de Stone must have gotten distracted by something important," Lucas said. "We should try to get some sleep while we can."

Kara nodded, but she had trouble believing that Fen'de Stone had simply found something more important to do. *You didn't hear him. He aims to find the grimoire and restore the honor of his people. Nothing could be more important than that.*

Despite her swirling thoughts, Kara managed to fall asleep. When she awoke again, it was early evening and Lucas was standing by the window.

"Still quiet," he said.

It remained that way the entire night.

The next morning they combed the stall for possible weaknesses. At first they had no luck, but then Lucas saw a hoof file that had slipped between the cracks of the floorboards.

"I might be able to use that to pick the lock," he said. "If I knew how to pick a lock."

"Maybe we could use it to pry under the nails," Kara suggested. "Pull a piece of the wall away. Sort of dig our way out."

They tried everything to get the file: stomping on the floorboards, using their fingernails to dig beneath the wood, tying strands of hay together to lasso it up. Nothing worked.

Three days passed. The hunger was bad but nothing compared to the thirst. To conserve what little moisture remained in their cracked lips, they began to use hand signals. Mostly, though, they just lay on the floor and waited for something to happen.

"Why doesn't anyone come?" Lucas whispered when it had grown dark.

"He's trying to make us weak," Kara said. "This way he knows we'll do what he wants us to do."

"What if he changed his mind?"

"No. He wants the grimoire too much."

"He could have found it on his own. Caught Grace with it."

Kara shivered. She had not considered that possibility. "You're right," she said. "If he has what he wants, he might just leave us here to die. That's something he would do."

Lucas laid his hand on her arm.

"Forget what I said. You were right. He's just doing

this to make us weak. We can't let him win."

"Can we talk about something else?" Kara asked. "Just pretend things are normal for a little while?"

"Sure," Lucas said. The stable grew silent as Kara tried to think of something to say—something *normal*. . . .

Lucas spoke first.

"Hanson Blair lied. He has no idea where my family is. I caught him laughing at me with a group of his friends. I feel like such a fool."

"You're not a fool, Lucas. You just wanted to believe. There's nothing wrong with that."

An uncustomary desperation crept into his voice. "And now I'm never going to know who they are. I'll never be able to ask them why they left me here."

Kara longed to comfort him, but his wounds cut deeper than words could mend. Instead she put an arm around his shoulders.

"Well, I'm glad they did," Kara said. "You're my best friend."

In the darkness she saw Lucas smile. "You're glad my

parents left me to a life of servitude working in a field of deadly plants? Some friend."

Kara pinched his arm.

"We're going to get out of here," she said. "Watch. We're due a little luck."

She was awoken by the jingle of keys.

Through sleep-hazed eyes she saw a large figure, his face concealed beneath the folds of a hooded cloak, struggling to open the lock to their cell. The man's hands shook badly.

"Lucas," Kara said. "Lucas! Get up!"

Lucas mumbled something incoherent and turned over.

The man dropped a large ring of iron keys. Bent down to pick them up. Fumbled with the lock some more.

Kara shoved Lucas. Hard.

"What?" he asked. He was still groggy, but his eyes were open.

Kara pointed at the figure just as the door swung open. The man stepped inside and removed his hood.

It was Fen'de Stone.

Although he did not appear to be wounded, there was blood everywhere. His face. His clothes.

His eyes found Kara.

"You," he said.

The fen'de withdrew a long dagger from a sheath inside his cloak. The jeweled weapon seemed more ornamental than functional, though judging from its gore-encrusted blade, it could still serve its natural purpose.

Lucas stepped in front of Kara.

"Fen'de Stone?" he asked.

If the man heard Lucas, he made no indication. He continued to approach Kara, step by lumbering step, his mad eyes never leaving hers.

"You," he repeated. "You."

When he was only a few feet away, Kara felt Lucas tense, ready to pounce. But there was no need. The fen'de collapsed to his knees and laid his dagger at Kara's feet.

"You need to save us," he said, the words nearly incomprehensible through his blubbering tears. "I tried, but I can't do it. I'm not strong enough. You need to make her stop hurting my people!"

"Who?" Lucas asked.

Fen'de Stone looked at Kara with pleading eyes, and for a moment she almost pitied him.

"My daughter," he said.

Kara would never take freedom for granted again. She luxuriated in the warmth of the sun, the playful caress of the morning breeze. After the initial flush of pleasure, however, she realized that it was all wrong. The air should have been fragrant with the whistlebuds and landrils that bloomed this time of year, but instead it was as stale as a tomb. Eerie silence, bereft of the usual buzzing and fluttering, accentuated every footstep they made.

She felt like a stranger in someone else's dream.

"It started four days ago," Fen'de Stone said, moving with surprising speed along the crooked path. "Little things at first. Milk spoiling for no reason. Plants sprouting out of the ground, roots up. The Elders were convinced it was your evil presence leaking into our community. They promised that everything would go back to normal once you were executed."

Fen'de Stone stopped so suddenly that Kara nearly ran into him. He regarded her with bloodshot, bulging eyes.

"They wanted to kill you right away. It was me who saved you. I told them that they were wrong. I protected you, Kara! Remember that. Remember that I'm your friend."

He stood close, waiting for her to respond, his body rank with dirt and sweat.

You hurt me. You killed my mother and made me watch.

"I'll remember everything," Kara said quietly.

With a short grunt of satisfaction, Fen'de Stone spun on one heel and continued walking, his pace even more frantic than before. Kara assumed that they were headed toward the village, but although it would have been shorter to cut through the wooded area to their left, Fen'de Stone refused to leave the main path.

"It was the cattle that changed everything. Rancher Samuelson called on me—pulled me out of bed in the middle of the night. I'm embarrassed to say I didn't believe him at first. Thought maybe he had been tipping the moondrink again, as he was wont to do in his younger years. But he's been a good member of the Fold, so I donned my cloak and followed him out just the same. I noticed that Grace's room was empty as I left, but I didn't think much of it at the time. That girl always had some odd ways about her, and sometimes she just went walking. I punished her as a righteous father should, but it never did any good."

He's speaking about her in the past tense, Kara thought, *as though she were never his daughter at all.*

"What happened?" Kara asked.

The fen'de scratched a dried spot of blood on his scalp.

"Samuelson's property, as you know, borders the Clearer land on one side. That's nothing he's happy about, but his family was one of the last to settle here, and someone has to live close to those . . ." The fen'de hesitated, his eyes shifting in Lucas's direction. ". . . people. But Samuelson can be a stubborn sort, and he got it in his mind that if he built a stone wall along the northern edge of his ranch, he might keep away any unwanted guests. It's ridiculous, really—the wall is barely taller than I am. Any Stench with a mind for trouble could just—"

"The cattle," Lucas said.

"Dead, or well along the way. I am a great lover of animals—as our blessed Timoth Clen was before me—and this was the most horrible thing I've ever seen. Flanks torn apart, legs shattered. My soul twisted in sorrow for those pitiable creatures. I helped Samuelson put them out of their misery afterward."

"Something attacked them?" Lucas asked. He inadvertently touched his ruined hand. "Maybe something from the Thickety?"

"No. There were no bite marks. No unusual paw prints. As far as we could tell, the entire herd of cattle just kept battering the wall, over and over again, until they killed themselves."

"It was Grace," Kara said. "Isn't that right?"

The pained expression on Fen'de Stone's face was answer enough.

Kara pictured Grace standing on a hill overlooking the cattle, watching them graze peacefully for a time before opening the grimoire. And then, after she spoke the words, a sly smile lifting her lips as the first cow charged the wall.

Did she hesitate? For even a moment?

"But why?" asked Lucas.

"She was testing her powers," Kara said. "Just like I did at the beginning." She didn't like admitting this connection between them, but it deserved to be spoken. "Grace killed all those poor creatures just to see if she could."

They journeyed in silence for a long time after that.

Although Kara still had questions, the burst of energy that came with escaping the stable had faded, and exhaustion and thirst now made it difficult to concentrate on anything beyond simple movement. Glancing over at Lucas, she could see the same struggle in his eyes.

By midafternoon the ground had grown hazy, and her legs threatened to buckle beneath her.

"We need water," she finally said. "And food."

Fen'de Stone nodded. "Almost there."

A simple campsite waited around the next bend: one bedroll, a ring of stones where a fire had once burned, and, most importantly, two glorious water skins. Lucas snatched up the first one and handed it to Kara. She raised it to her cracked lips and drank deeply, limiting herself to three swallows. Vomiting would be very self-defeating.

Fen'de Stone produced a stick of dried beef from beneath the bedroll. He was about to slice off a considerable portion for himself when Lucas yanked it out of his hands.

"Give that back, boy!" the fen'de exclaimed.

Lucas ignored him completely and sliced the meat in two, giving the larger portion to Kara. It was fresh and moist, and although Kara couldn't help but wonder if it came from Samuelson's cows, she was too hungry to care.

After she had taken a few bites and another swallow of water, Kara turned to face Fen'de Stone.

"The cows were just the beginning, weren't they?"

Fen'de Stone kicked at the dirt. "Are you going to make me tell it all, witch?"

"Yes. If you want my help, I need to know everything."

"None of this is my fault!"

Kara broke off a piece of meat and handed it to the fen'de. "Just tell me what happened."

The fen'de nibbled the meat absentmindedly as he spoke but never swallowed a piece. "I haven't been a perfect father. I've often looked upon my daughter with shame. How could anyone blame me? I am the leader of the Fold, chosen to spread the Clen's message! And yet one look at Grace and all my Children see is her ruined body."

"You're wrong," Kara said. "They loved Grace. All of them."

"No! They snicker about how she's been touched by pagan magic. I know they do! They laugh at me, *and it's all your mother's doing!*" The fen'de leaped to his feet, eyes flaming with hatred, but his anger flared out as quickly as it had begun. He continued his story. "When I got back to the house after my visit to the Samuelson place, she was waiting for me. She opened that damned book of hers and patched the hole in our ceiling with a single word and then showed me my dead wife in a cupful of tea. 'Isn't magic wonderful?' she asked. 'I can bring Mama back to us for good, if you'd like me to.' When I shrieked at her to stop, she grew hurt and angry. She said that there were such good sheep on this island, but they were wasting their time on a . . ." He paused here, as though unwilling to say the words out loud. ". . . dead god. She said the real world mocked the Fold, a bunch of loons living—by choice—on a cursed island. 'Poor Father,' she said. 'I am going to give you all a gift: A god worthy of such noble devotion.'"

Fen'de Stone turned to Lucas, his voice suddenly calm and conversational. "Did you know that her hair didn't turn white until she was two years old? The mangled leg was there from the start—her mother screamed when she saw it, the last sound she ever made—but Grace's hair . . . it was extraordinary. Golden yellow, like saffron. Like she was touched by the sun."

They ate the rest of their meal in silence.

It was early evening when they found the graycloaks.

They waited over the next rise, as still as statues, ballstaffs held across their bodies. Six of them in total. Their heads were bowed down, concealing their faces beneath the shadows of their hoods.

"Maybe they can help us," Kara said. She started

forward, but Fen'de Stone snatched her arm.

"Those men belong to Grace now," he said.

Kara lay flat against the ground. The three of them were concealed by a tangle of overgrown weeds and several medium-size boulders. To the east Kara heard ocean waves crashing against the shore. The salty air teased freedom.

"They haven't seen us yet," Lucas whispered. "We can circle around. We won't reach the house till tomorrow, but—"

"That's too long," said Kara. "Taff needs me."

"Taff needs you *alive*."

"This is the only way," said Fen'de Stone. "The other path takes you too close to the village."

Kara replied with what she hoped was more confidence than she felt. "Fine. Then I'll face Grace now."

"You're not ready."

"I'll never be ready. Now is as good a time as any."

"No. You're exhausted and starving. You need to rest.

Strategize. You're only going to get one shot to save my village."

"I don't care about them. I only care about my brother!"

"Just a thought," whispered Lucas, "but maybe you two should lower your voices. . . ."

"Your duty is to De'Noran."

"Duty?" she asked. "Why should I help any of you? I've spent my entire life being tormented and humiliated, and I haven't deserved any of it!"

"Kara," Lucas said. He placed a hand on the back of her neck, but she shook it away. These were things that needed to be said.

"Did anyone try to help me after my mother was killed? Did anybody have a word of kindness to say? No. But now things are different, because now you *need* me. Even if I could save this place, give me one good reason why I should!"

Fen'de Stone's red-rimmed eyes gazed back at her with shocking desperation. *He loves them*, she thought, and the sudden realization that a man who could torture and murder was also capable of love shifted something in her irrevocably. The old man wiped a trail of snot from beneath his nose. "If there is any good in that heathen heart of yours, hear this: You are the only one who can help them. If you do not, they will die. Now get ready to run."

With more quickness than he had shown in two decades, Fen'de Stone leaped to his feet. The graycloaks, as one, turned in his direction.

"Men!" Fen'de Stone shouted. Kara kept her head pressed against the earth but heard his footsteps as he made his way down the hill. "Timoth Clen requires your skills one final time! To me, to me!"

Kara heard a whisper of grass as the graycloaks glided closer. "What's he doing?" she asked.

Lucas held a finger to his lips.

"You are lost, my friends," Fen'de Stone said. "But I am here to guide you back into the light. Take my hand.

Join me. Let us fight this demon together."

Kara lifted her head just enough to see over the weeds. There hadn't been nearly enough time for the graycloaks to walk so far up the hill, and yet there they were, surrounding the fen'de in an eerily perfect circle.

"We have to go," Lucas said.

Kara shook her head.

"We can't just leave him here——" she started, but then a flash of motion caught her eye as Fen'de Stone was struck across the knee with the ball end of a staff. A whistling noise filled the air, like steam from a kettle. Kara suspected it might have been laughter.

From his knees Fen'de Stone extended his hand out to his attacker. "Come back, my friend." For just a moment his eyes met Kara's, and while she might have expected to see terror there, all she saw was joy. "Come back to the Fold. Do not listen to her lies! Have faith! Timoth Clen will return to us. He will never allow such evil to continue!"

As one the graycloaks raised their ball-staffs high into the air. Their cloaks dipped far enough for Kara to see that they were not holding the staffs at all; rather, the wood had become an extension of their left arms, a weapon of flesh and bone.

Fen'de Stone bowed his head.

"Work hard, want nothing," he whispered.

"Don't look," said Lucas.

He pulled Kara to her feet, and the two of them ran away as fast as they could, trying not to think about the sounds behind them.

TWENTY-ONE

The Lamb house had been well fortified. Wooden planks, nailed together in tight rows, blocked the windows. A tower of seed sacks leaned against the side door. Stones and broken glass speckled the front yard.

All was silent.

"Are you sure this is a good idea?" Lucas asked.

Kara advanced slowly, careful to avoid the debris in her bare feet. "Fen'de Stone said my family was here."

"Maybe at some point. It sure looks empty now."

"I have to see for myself."

They climbed the porch steps. Kara remembered her last visit to the house. It had been an unusually cold day, and Mrs. Lamb had given Taff a pair of mittens.

Hardly a season ago. It seemed like a lifetime.

"Hello!" Lucas shouted. He reached past Kara to knock on the front door, and she grabbed his arm, knowing with sudden certainty that Taff was dead and that if they stepped into this house there would be no turning back, and the loss of her brother would become a real thing, a forever thing. But it was too late. The door opened, and Jacob Lamb stepped onto the porch. Three days' stubble roughened his cheeks, and he stank of moondrink. The wart beneath his eye leaked a thick, clear fluid.

He held a hatchet in his grimy hands.

"Come to gloat, witch?" he asked, his words a drunken slur. "You come to celebrate? We're done for. All of us."

"Where's my father?" Kara asked.

Jacob leaned closer. His breath was warm and rank.

"Maybe *she* sent you. You're one and the same. Evil

through and through." He gazed blankly at a point just to the left of Kara's eyes. "We should have roasted you along with your mother when we had the—"

Suddenly Jacob stiffened. His throat emitted a low, rumbling sound.

"Drop the hatchet," Lucas said, holding the fen'de's dagger against Jacob's neck. "Grace is our enemy. We have to work together, not fight with each other."

Kara tensed, waiting for Jacob to do something. Lash out with the hatchet. Spit in her face. Grab the dagger from Lucas's hand.

The last thing she expected him to do was cry.

"It ain't fair," he said, his eyes welling up. The hatchet slipped from his hands and clattered to the wood below. "Why did it have to be her? She never hurt anyone her whole life."

A numbing cold sunk through Kara.

"Constance?" she asked.

Jacob winced at the mention of his wife's name. "She

ran. But she wasn't fast enough, not for something like that." He turned to Lucas. "Why didn't it go after me, boy? I ain't walked the Path like she did. Why didn't it go after me instead?"

Lucas lowered his dagger. Kara stepped forward, intending to offer some words of consolation, but Jacob turned from her.

"I called her Connie, when we was alone," Jacob said. Despite the tears a bright smile filled his face. "Even at the end, I was the only one she ever let call her that."

He stumbled off the porch and into the bleak afternoon. They watched him for a few moments and then entered the dead woman's house.

Father lay on the floor of the master bedroom, deeply asleep with no blanket to cover him. His breathing was light and rapid. Kara stepped over him and looked down at the small form in the bed. "Taff," she whispered. Several quilts were tucked carefully beneath his chin, and a small washbowl filled with murky water sat on the table next to him. Even standing an arm's length away Kara could feel the heat radiating off his body. The bandage around his head had been freshly changed, yet it did little to contain the black stench of infection that spoiled the air.

"You're here," Father said, joints cracking as he pushed himself into a sitting position. Though he seemed genuinely relieved, he looked too exhausted to embrace her. "I wanted to get you myself, but I couldn't leave him."

Kara studied her brother. There seemed less of him somehow. She was glad the windows had been boarded up. She feared the slightest breeze might blow him away.

"Taff is more important," Kara said. "You did the right thing."

"We should let him sleep. It's the one comfort we can offer him right now."

"I'll wait here. Lucas is out back. He can tell you what happened."

"We need to talk. There are decisions to be made."

Father tried to take her by the arm, but Kara shook him off, so he sat on the edge of the bed and cupped her cheek with his hand. Kara's tears ran freely between his fingers.

"It's not your fault," he said.

"I need to be here when he wakes up."

"He's not going to wake up, Moonbeam."

It was the name—the name he hadn't called her since before Mother died—that convinced her. She allowed him to guide her downstairs into the kitchen. He lit a small fire and heated a pot filled with thick gruel. Kara watched the flames sputter and crackle. She thought, *Taff is going to die.* Time passed. She looked down and saw a steaming bowl in front of her. Kara had no desire to eat, but her stomach grumbled rebelliously, responding to the smell.

Father sat across the table from her. His eyes were red and swollen but filled with a clarity she hadn't seen in years, as though this latest sorrow had awoken him at last.

"He hasn't spoken for two days," he said. "I change his bandage, make sure he's clean. Cover him with quilts when he's cold. Pry open a few planks when he's warm. I don't know what else to do."

"There are weeds in the Fringe that can cool his temperature," Kara said. "That's the most important thing. We have to control his fever to give his body a chance to fight the infection. I can leave now, be back with what we need before nightfall."

Father shook his head.

"I don't pretend to know as much about healing as you do. But I know when an infection has made its home for good."

"Wendsdil might help too. Hard to find this time of year, but not—"

"It's a fool's errand."

"I'm not giving up!"

Father looked at her, his eyes hard. "I'm not either. We're leaving the island first thing tomorrow. Six families in total, plus a few children with nowhere else to go." He spoke the words slowly, for even now the thought of leaving De'Noran was difficult for him. "If we follow the shore and avoid the village, we should be fine. We aim to steal the ferry and take our chances in the World. I've heard there are medicines there that can cure anything."

"It's a three-day journey, Father. What if he doesn't make it?"

"We have to try."

"We can heal him first and then go." Kara's voice grew quiet. "There's a spell."

Father absentmindedly stroked his chin. Usually there was stubble there, but he was clean-shaven today. "So it's true," he said. "What they say about you."

"No! I mean, I can do magic—that part's right—but I never meant to hurt anyone! I was trying to protect Taff. I'm not bad, not like they say! You believe me, Father, don't you? Please tell me you believe me!"

Kara's father did not reply. Instead he gathered her

into his arms, and Kara let herself sob freely. It had been years since he'd held her, and it felt so good to feel safe and protected. To be a little girl again.

When Kara returned to her seat, she was suddenly starving. "Grace knows a spell that can cure Taff," she said between mouthfuls of gruel. "I have to convince her to help me somehow. Or maybe I can steal the grimoire and—"

"No," said Father.

"No?"

"That's right. No." He removed a notebook from his back pocket. Kara half expected him to pull out a quill and start writing the usual words, but instead he just twisted the book in his hands. "I realize I haven't been the best parent since your mother died, but you are still a twelve-year-old girl, and I am still your father. And I am telling you no."

"You can't—"

"You've been locked up in a cell. You have no idea

how Grace Stone has changed. That girl has *killed* people, Kara. You can't just waltz into the village and expect her to listen to reason."

"What other choice do I have?"

"Heal Taff yourself."

Kara slammed her hands against the table in frustration.

"You're not listening to me! Even if I wanted to use magic again, even if I knew what spell to cast, Grace has the grimoire!"

Father shook his head. "Grace has *Abigail's* grimoire." He slid the battered notebook across the table. "You have your mother's."

Kara stared at the book. Dumbfounded.

"Father?" She spoke slowly and softly, as she did whenever he had an episode. "That's just a schoolbook. There's nothing magic about it. You can buy one at the general store for three browns."

"One of your mother's more clever ideas, actually. From what she told me, most witches' grimoires are bulky, ornate tomes—a bit of an ego thing, apparently. What better way to hide it than as a simple notebook?"

"But you've written in hundreds of these. I've seen you!"

"You assumed there was more than one book, because that's the reasonable thing to think. But magic isn't a thing of reason."

He opened the book and folded it back to the most recent entry of *FORGIVE ME* sliced into the page. Kara watched as a single *E* bubbled to the surface and cascaded down the page, vanishing before it hit the kitchen table.

"Every day I fill this book," Father said. "And by morning it's blank again. Every day. For seven years."

He held out the book to her, his hands trembling. Kara looked into his eyes and saw the pleading there: *Please take it. Please rid me of this curse.*

Kara took it.

She knew the moment she touched the book that it

was indeed her mother's. *This is right*, it seemed to be saying. *You have found your path at last.*

Kara opened the book.

Her father's words had vanished, replaced by the same liquid-black leaves she had seen in Grace's grimoire. Kara placed her finger into one of them and sent concentric ripples to the four corners of the page.

My mother used this page to cast a spell, she thought. *But it's closed to me.*

Kara turned to the next two pages. Both black. She flipped frantically through the book, trying to control her rising panic. Black, black, black. *Is this some sort of joke? Why would Mother leave me a useless spellbook?* She flipped the book over and started from the back. The last page was torn and yellowed with age, but blank. *Except that one doesn't count*, Kara thought, remembering Abigail's horrifying final screams. *I can't cast it.* She flipped to the previous page and sighed with relief: At least she could use this one.

Kara worked her way backward, counting castable

pages. It did not take long.

"Five spells," she said. "That's all she left me. Not counting the Last Spell, which is—"

"—not an option. Ever."

Father's quick response surprised her. "You sound like you know a lot about it," Kara said.

Father shrugged wearily. "Just enough," he said. "Helena explained it to me one night and never spoke of it again, which was fine by me—I could overlook the fact that she was a witch because I couldn't imagine a life without her, but I never got comfortable listening to the details. She said that a grimoire, like a lantern, needs fuel to power it—except instead of kerosene it burns the life force of witches foolish enough to have used it. When such a witch is all used up—when the grimoire has sapped her completely dry—she just fades from existence. This process might take decades. Or centuries. But according to your mother—and I have no reason to doubt her—the pain is so excruciating that you would be driven mad within the

first hour." Father looked at her with a curious expression. "But all it takes is one spell to heal Taff. As far as I can tell, you have more magic than you need."

Kara leaned over and kissed him on the forehead. There was no longer any need to confront Grace at all. The spell Kara needed to save her brother's life was right in her hands.

Once she figured out how to cast it.

Kara filled the washing basin and splashed some water onto her face, then tied her hair back so it wouldn't get in her eyes. The candle next to Taff's bed had been reduced to a misshapen stub, so she worked with the last vestiges of daylight filtering through the wooden beams.

She placed the grimoire on the bed and smoothed the first blank leaf with a trembling hand.

This is going to work. The other grimoire only let me conjure creatures, but this is different. This is Mother's—and Mother was a healer.

Taff's breathing had become even weaker since she had last seen him. There was a fresh spot of blood on his pillow, where he had turned and coughed in his sleep. Thin blue veins pressed against his skin.

He already looked more dead than alive.

She laid her hand over the notebook. Unlike Aunt Abby's grimoire, this one did not call to her; there were no seductive promises of power. On the one hand, this was encouraging. Maybe a grimoire could be good or evil, and if so this one was definitely good. That meant it would be more likely to grant her a healing spell.

On the other hand, some kind of sign would have been nice. When Kara touched the page of the grimoire, she felt *nothing*. Summoning animals had become second nature to Kara, and although she had not used magic in over a week, she had little doubt she could still do it with ease. Casting a healing spell was not the same thing. Conjuring was a language she spoke. Healing wasn't.

With no idea what to do, Kara wished for Taff to be well again.

Nothing happened.

She commanded him to be well, and when that didn't work, she said it out loud. "Taff Westfall, let your wounds heal and your body be whole again!"

For a moment she thought the page might have moved slightly, but she decided that it was just a wisp of breeze playing a trick on her.

Kara strained harder, visualizing a Taff shed of his illness. His cheeks no longer wan but rosy with health. His laugh, bursting with life. Kara bent forward until her forehead pressed against the notebook. She reached out and took Taff's cold hand in her own, willing him to health with feverish intensity until her clothes were soaked with sweat and the room's last remaining candle burned away.

Taff's hand remained motionless.

Kara picked up her chair and hurled it across the room. "Why isn't this working?" she screamed. "Am I a witch or not?" There was a concerned knock at the door, but Kara ignored it and eventually it stopped. "What do I do? Will someone please tell me what to do?" She touched her locket for strength, then climbed into bed and cradled Taff in her arms. It was like holding fire—except flames, at least, flickered with life. The only sign that Taff remained in this world was a vague flutter in his chest.

Nothing so fragile could ever survive the journey to the World. Her magic had been his last, desperate hope.

If Kara could have taken his illness as her own, she would have done so without hesitation. However, there was no spell for such an act of redemption, so she simply held Taff close, allowing guilt to envelop her like a black cocoon. *None of this would have happened if I had followed the Path and listened to the lessons of my people.* They had been right the entire time: Magic was a corrupting force, an evil temptation that could lead only to darkness and death. She had been a fool, and her brother had paid the price.

The night grew dark and quiet. Eventually the heat of Taff's body against her own became so unbearable that she slid a little to her right, and in doing so felt something unusual beneath the blankets. A book. At first Kara thought it was the useless spellbook, but no—this new book had fewer pages, not all the same size. Kara turned to the first page and, squinting through the darkness, was able to make out a child's drawing. There was a boy and, judging from the length of hair, a girl. . . .

With a thrill of recognition, Kara realized that it was the book she and Taff had created together. Father said that Taff had still been able to speak earlier in the week—he must have insisted that they bring it here. Kara wondered if Father had actually read it to him. A mere week ago, he would have burned the book after the first mention of magic, but she supposed that in this new world a small bit of comfort was worth far more than superstition.

But had it just been for comfort? Or is Taff trying to send me a message?

An idea burst to life, a swarm of glow-wings in her head.

"That's insane," Kara said. "That can't possibly work."

And yet . . . would it hurt to try?

Resting the grimoire on her lap, Kara closed her eyes. Without a live example to work from, she was forced to envision the Jabenhook in her mind, in much the same way she had pictured a healthy Taff. The results, at first, were dishearteningly similar. But then she felt something. A vague sensation of *pulling*, as though the spell were a lost memory just out of reach but right there, right within her grasp, if only she could find the clues to lead her there.

And so Kara told the story.

"Long before the remembrance of the oldest man on earth, there was a boy called Samuel. He and his sister liked to play with tadpoles and climb tall trees and dance to the music of the river, until one day Samuel was visited by a dread sickness and could not play any longer."

The words, so often repeated, came easily. As is always the case with the best stories, the mere telling of it was a comfort, and by the time Samuel and his sister spoke to the Spider Lady, Kara's mind had been primed to embrace the impossible. Her fingertips drifted toward the open grimoire, and strange new sigils rose to the surface. Golden light, brighter than the sun, speared the cracks between window boards.

"As Samuel lay in bed shivering, the Jabenhook drifted across the room. . . ."

Kara opened her eyes. There was no need to finish the story.

The Jabenhook had arrived.

It was different than she'd imagined it. Kara had no idea how this was possible—the creature was, after all, a figment of *her* imagination—but so it was. Its wings were the same golden hue she had pictured in her head, but their span was so much greater, even greater than the room itself, the wing tips (flecked with green, another new detail) forced to bend against the walls, giving the impression that, instead of hovering above Taff, the Jabenhook was holding itself up. Its eyes—a gentle amber that spoke of sleepy summer days and long naps in the shade—gazed down at Taff like a new mother.

"Thank you," Kara said. If it happened the same way it did in the story, it was going to be fast, and she wanted to make sure she had a chance to say it.

In this most important aspect, at least, the story proved true. Opening its fleshy beak, the Jabenhook cawed, the sound monstrously loud in such a confined area. Taff's bedpan clattered to the floor, and the walls shook in response, jarring loose what little glass remained in the window frames. Kara heard pounding at the door, but the Jabenhook's left wing held it firmly shut.

From Taff's mouth something was rising.

It was black and viscous and alive, a shapeless lump of cruelty and hopelessness. The cough that comes with a wet morning and never leaves. The mad crush of stone and earth. A baby's cry, cut off in the middle of the night.

It was death itself, cold and calculating and implacable.

The Jabenhook ate it.

If Kara had blinked, she would have missed the feeding entirely. The Jabenhook was fast, impossibly fast, snatching her brother's Death from the air as easily as a bird plucking a worm. There were no sounds of swallowing; its beak clacked shut, and that was all. For a brief moment, the Jabenhook regarded her with what might have been bemusement, then blinked out of existence. In the story it had left Samuel a feather, but here the only proof of the Jabenhook's visit was the faint smells of pinecones and honeysuckle.

The door crashed open. Father and Lucas burst into the room.

"Are you all right?" Lucas asked. "We heard strange

noises, but no matter how hard we tried, we couldn't break down . . ."

Lucas's words trailed off when he saw Taff sitting on the edge of his bed, swinging his legs back and forth.

"Is it dinnertime yet?" Taff asked.

TWENTY-TWO

Once Taff had eaten his fill of sodden potatoes and barley soup, he fell back asleep. At first Kara refused to leave his side, fearing that the cure was a temporary one and that another visit from the Jabenhook might be required. But after an hour of listening to his steady breathing, Kara finally felt comfortable enough to make her way downstairs.

The Lamb house was packed with people. Father, figuring there was safety in numbers, had decided they should gather together now so they could leave for the ferry at the crack of dawn. Many had already laid claim to a section of floor space, making it difficult for Kara to navigate her way to the front door without stepping on an outstretched hand or a curled-up child. They watched Kara as she passed, and there was something different in their eyes. Not fear or hatred—though there was still a little of that to go around as well—but something . . . different. Kara avoided looking at them as she made a twisting passage toward the front door.

An old woman blocked her path.

She wore the brown vest of a tanner and had hazel eyes, a rarity in their village. The woman's frame was slight and wizened, but her arms were sinewy with earned muscle. When she spoke it was with the certainty of one who demands respect.

"We heard what you did, Witch Girl. How you called forth a creature of smoke and shadows to heal your brother. Magic can bring only misfortune, we all know that. And yet . . . to heal is to walk the Path. This complicates things."

The woman picked at the skin of her hand, dyed a permanent brown from her work. Her next words were spoken hesitantly.

"My grandson has been missing for two days," she said. "He lives just outside the village, in the barracks. He was training to be a graycloak, though I never encouraged such foolishness, training for a war that may never come. Perhaps there is pride in such a calling, but not for Ethan. His disposition is far too gentle."

The woman cleared her throat and looked straight into Kara's eyes.

"It would please me to see him again," she said.

As though the old woman's words had opened some sort of floodgate, the silent room erupted into a deluge of shouts and entreaties.

"My daughter! She's only five . . ."

"My family holed up in the schoolhouse, and we got separated. . . ."

"Save my husband. . . ."

". . . wife . . ."

". . . father . . ."

". . . son . . ."

"We don't deserve this!"

They began to touch her, then, their hands clawing at her dress, her arms, her legs, forcing her to bear witness to their demands. Kara tried to push her way to the front door, but there were so many of them, all shouting now, fighting to be heard. Unable to keep her balance against a sea of swirling faces, Kara pushed her way in what she hoped was the right direction.

"Help us! Help us! Help us!"

She made it through the front door and onto the porch, past their outstretched hands. Kara backed away, expecting the villagers to pursue her. Instead one brave hand reached out and shut the door.

Their need for her might have been great, but they wouldn't go outside at night. Not anymore.

A thousand stars stared down at her like bright, impassive eyes. She made her way around the back of the farmhouse, where she found Father loading a wagon with supplies. His shirt, soaked with sweat, was rolled up at the sleeves. He looked happy for the first time in years.

"Have you seen Lucas?" Kara asked.

"He set out with a lantern some time ago," replied her father. "Said he had a small errand to attend to before we left."

"By himself?"

Father nodded. "I told him it wasn't a good idea, but he was persistent. I wouldn't worry none though. He said he'd be back shortly, and I get the sense that boy can take care of himself."

"He can," Kara replied, but worry gnawed at her regardless.

"Taff asleep?"

"Yes. I suspect he'll need a lot of rest in the coming days."

"He'll have it. Once we're out at sea."

"You still think that's the best plan?"

"I do."

"It's just—the people still in the village. What's going to happen to them?"

Father hefted a barrel onto the wagon. "I'm not sure that bears thinking about. It's a hard thing, but we need to take care of our own right now."

Kara nodded. He was right, of course. There was nothing she could do, and it was foolish to think otherwise. *Besides, if the situations were reversed, they wouldn't spare a moment's thought for me.*

"There's something I have to tell you," Kara said. "About Mother."

Father stiffened, but instead of saying it wasn't the right time, he leaned against the wagon and waited. In that moment Kara began to love him anew.

"When I was in the Well, I saw the past. I know what happened that night. Abigail Smythe was a witch, but she lost control."

"Yes," Father said. If he thought it strange that she had seen these things in a vision, he did not say so. "I warned your mother from the beginning that Abby was not to be trusted, but she didn't listen. It was going to be your time to learn magic soon, and I think Helena was nervous." He gave a small smile. "Though of course she wouldn't admit it. It seems cruel, but Abigail was just practice, a way to hone her teaching skills. Her first choice was Constance, a far better—"

"—but Constance didn't possess the talent."

"Right."

"Why didn't Constance tell me the truth?"

"Because then you would have known that Helena was not evil at all. Instead of being frightened by magic, you would have thought, '*If my mother can control her powers, then I can too!*' And you would not have been so cautious when you used the grimoire." Father picked up a small crate, eager to continue with his work. "Now what was it you wanted to tell me?"

Kara placed a hand gently on his arm. "Stop, Father. Listen."

He lowered the crate to the ground and met her eyes.

"Mother gave me a message for you."

"Kara. Don't."

"*Shh*. Mother said, 'It's not your fault, William. You were a true husband to the end. You don't need to beg for my forgiveness, because there is nothing to forgive. Just honor my memory by living your life.'"

Father did not cry or sob, but Kara folded him into her arms anyway. As they held each other, Kara Westfall, the Witch Girl, thought about Constance's words: *These are not bad people, Kara. They may do bad things out of fear or foolishness, but most of them want to live simple lives with their families. They are no different from anyone else, even you.* She thought of her mother, who risked everything to save her friend. And finally she thought of the mysterious looks in the villagers' eyes and understood, at last, the responsibility her magic conveyed.

Within an hour everyone had fallen asleep. Kara did not blame them. The trek to the ferry was not a short one, and they would need their rest. Before leaving she took one last look at her family. Taff had kicked off the blankets and lay sideways, nestled into the crook of his father's arm. Both slept soundly. On Father's face was the slightest hint of a smile.

As far as parting memories were concerned, she could do worse.

Kara took what she needed from the supply wagon: a lantern to light her way until morning, a canteen of fresh water, a black cloak to keep her warm. These would make her journey more convenient, but in the end they were unimportant. All she really needed was the tattered notebook in her pocket and its five (*four!*) blank pages.

By foot, the village was almost an hour's trek from here.

Kara did not intend to walk.

The stable doors creaked as she pulled them apart. Most stalls were empty, but the few horses that remained shied away from the sudden starlight. The floor had not been swept or mopped in weeks, and the smell of feces and mold was overpowering.

She made her way to the last stall.

"Good evening, Shadowdancer," Kara said.

The mare looked thinner, as did they all, but the true hunger in her eyes was for freedom. The moment Kara reached for the latch, Shadowdancer bucked, her powerful hind legs slapping against the wood behind her.

"Are you sure that's a good idea?" a familiar voice asked. Kara twisted around to find Lucas peeking over the wall of the next stall. His eyes were sunken but alert.

"You're back!" Kara exclaimed. Despite her father's reassuring words, she had been very worried about him.

"Floor space was hard to come by, so I found an empty stall." He gave her an impish grin. "Or maybe I've just become more comfortable sleeping in stables."

"I've always suspected you were part horse," Kara teased.

"Maybe that's why you like me so much."

The words were just playthings, their usual banter. Nonetheless Kara found herself looking away. There was a heaviness in the air tonight.

"I have something for you," Lucas said. "I planned to give it to you on the ship, but now's as good a time as ever." He dipped down beneath the wall. "I'm sorry I didn't have a chance to wash it first."

He handed her a carefully folded bundle tied neatly together with straw. Her mother's dress.

"You went back and got this?" Kara asked. "For me?"

"I saw it in the maze that night, and I knew you might want it. We're never coming back to this place, so . . ."

Kara traced one of the golden swirls with her finger. She remembered her mother sitting by the fireplace, sewing these very lines into the fine red cloth. It had taken her many months.

"Thank you," Kara said. "This is the kindest thing anyone has ever done for me."

She led Shadowdancer out of the stable, and Lucas fell into step beside her.

"There's another reason I'm out here," he said, swatting at a few persistent mosquitoes. "I suspected you might do something foolish. Like you're doing. Right now."

"They need my help," she said. The words sounded strange on her lips.

"Of course they do," replied Lucas. "But that doesn't mean they deserve it. Taff is alive, Kara. You did exactly what you set out to do. Tomorrow morning this will all be over. We're safe."

"But we're leaving so many of them behind."

"So be it." Kara had never heard such coldness in her friend's voice. "What if you were the one trapped in the village? Would a single one of *them* even think of helping? Of course not! All they care about are themselves. That's the way it is. The way it's always been."

"We're abandoning the Clearers too," Kara said. "Your people. Don't they deserve our help?"

Lucas stiffened.

"You can't fight her," he said. "She'll kill you."

There was nothing to say after that. With the mare between them, Kara and Lucas crossed the field to the white fence that marked the property's border. A dirt path lined with weatherworn stones wound deeper inland. Here, Kara would pick up the main road—which they simply called the Way—and, beneath a sheltering sky of hornbeam trees, make haste to the village.

She swung open the gate. Blurred fingers of light blotted out the stars. In the distance the tall trees of the Thickety swayed and creaked, a beckoning song.

It really was a beautiful island, this place. Her home.

"Everything that happened is my responsibility," Kara said. Shadowdancer jerked impatiently at her bit, eager to get started. Kara stroked her face tenderly. "Not only what happened to De'Noran, but what's going to happen to Grace if she falls into the grimoire's trap."

"She has spun her own web, Kara."

"So she should be doomed to an eternity of suffering? No one deserves that fate, no matter what evil they've done. I have to save her. I have to make things right."

"If you're that sure," he said, "then let me come with you."

Kara shook her head.

"You can't do this alone," he said. "You know that—I can see it in your eyes. Let me help you."

"No."

Lucas's expression hardened. "Too bad. There's nothing you can do to stop me. I'm coming."

"Are you sure about that?" Kara asked. "There's nothing I can do to dissuade you?"

"Nothing," he said.

She wanted him to come with her—that was the worst part. She didn't want to do this alone. But instead she fingered the grimoire in her pocket and spoke the right words, and Lucas tumbled forward into her arms. Kara laid him gently on the ground. His breathing remained steady, but he would sleep for at least a few hours.

A shadowy shape fluttered into the sky, leaving behind a small red mark on the back of Lucas's neck and the scent of bedside candles. It was the first story Kara could remember, her mother leaning close and telling her about a special butterfly from the land of dreams whose kiss sent restless children off to a peaceful sleep.

Kara opened the grimoire, and there it was: a perfect sketch. It would be easier to call next time, if she needed it.

A bird and a dreamfly. Against a girl who can bend nature to her will and command the minds of men. Grace will surely be terrified.

It probably wasn't the wisest plan, using one of her precious spells on such a gentle conjuration. But there was no other way to get Lucas to stay behind, and she couldn't let him risk his life. No one else would suffer for her mistakes. Especially him.

Kara brushed the hair back from his face.

"No matter what happens," she said, "I'm glad I cast it."

She kissed him, soft, on the cheek. If this had been one of Mother's stories, perhaps he would have stirred, awakened by the magic of her caress. But this was no story, and she was no princess.

She was a witch.

Sliding the grimoire carefully into her pocket, Kara swung open the gate and took her first step toward the village.

TWENTY-THREE

By early afternoon, with the village almost within sight, Kara decided to find out if she could inscribe animals from memory.

She could.

She chose the first creature because it could protect her. The second one was its complement, capable of dealing great harm. And the third . . . she wasn't sure exactly. It was an odd decision, but it felt right.

It was a comfort knowing her creatures lay nestled between the pages of the notebook, ready to be called.

She hoped she had chosen wisely, but since she had no idea what spells Grace would cast, it was all a guessing game anyway.

Before closing the book, Kara spent some time staring at the last page, blank and terrible.

She prayed she would not need it.

The village stretched out before her. At first glance little had changed. The same one-story buildings lined the main road, painted the same eggshell white. General Store. Blacksmith. Tack Shop.

None of the buildings had signs. People knew what they were.

A light rain began to fall, spotting the dirt coffee-brown, and Kara pulled her cloak tightly around her. Her mother's dress fit perfectly, but it did little to shield her against the cold. Above the door of the cobbler's shop, a wooden chime danced in the wind, adding gentle music to the patter of raindrops. The chime was in the shape of an owl—Timoth Clen's favorite animal—and meant to ward off magic. Kara had always found that ironic.

She dismounted Shadowdancer and ran a hand along her mane.

"Go on," she said. "This isn't your battle. You're free."

Shadowdancer stood stone still. She regarded Kara with suspicion, as though this were some kind of trick.

"I can't protect you," Kara said. "You need to get away from here! She'll hurt you." Kara leaned forward and whispered in her ear, "Thank you for helping me. Now go!"

Turning quickly before she lost her resolve, Kara took a few steps deeper into the village.

Don't look back, she told herself. *It'll be easier if you don't look back.*

She looked back. Shadowdancer remained rooted to her spot.

"Go!" Kara said as loudly as she dared. *"Please."*

Her eyes found Shadowdancer's. Holding Kara's gaze,

the mare bent her graceful neck forward and low to the ground.

A bow.

And then Shadowdancer was off, a black blur racing toward a stableless existence of open plains and freedom. Kara watched the horse until she was just a dot on the horizon. It was hard to look away from such unadulterated bliss.

When she turned around, the village was filled with people.

A visitor watching the crowd from afar would have thought everything was all right. More than all right: Here was a bustling community of merchants and farmers, fishermen and teachers, Elders and children. Each inhabitant was living proof that the Children of the Fold were a prosperous, civilized people. Bethany James haggled over the price of a sack of flour. The Whitney sisters, their heads pressed together as they strolled along the road, gossiped about some rumor they had overheard at

school. A wizened old man swept the porch of the general store.

It could have been any day in De'Noran. Kara wondered—just for a moment—if this had all been some sort of bad dream.

Then she looked closer.

The man was not sweeping the dust to the street, where it belonged, but to the other side of the porch. There, a second worker, standing only a few feet away, swept the dust back again, like some bizarre game of catch. Judging by their gnarled hands and stooped shoulders, they had been at this for a long, long time.

Perhaps the Whitney sisters were indeed gossiping, but the words came out as soft, desperate bleats.

As Shopkeeper Wilkins held out the bag of flour to Bethany James, they haggled in the same bleat language as the Whitney sisters. Neither woman noticed the maggots that had spilled forth from the sack and found new homes on their arms and legs and faces.

Stifling a scream, Kara moved onward. She saw more of the same: a corrupted version of the village's daily routine. No one seemed to notice her presence.

Is Grace punishing them? Kara wondered. And then a second, even more horrifying possibility: *Or is this the way she sees the world?*

Kara found the rest of the villagers sitting around the Fenroot tree, hands folded neatly on their laps. Black half rings swelled beneath their sunken eyes. Their lips were cracked with thirst.

How many days have they been sitting there?

Not a leaf of the Fenroot tree remained, and its trunk, usually the rich brown of fertile soil, was as black and smooth as obsidian. Its branches sagged down at impossible angles, as though the tree itself had given up. The top of the tree, however, was where the greatest change had taken place. Here the limbs gathered together into a base, behind which a hundred sharpened branches pointed toward the heavens like the claw of an infernal beast.

In the cradle of this unnatural throne sat Grace Stone. She had changed as well.

Grace had always been beautiful, but this beauty had become a fierce and terrible thing. Her hair, ash blond and sumptuous, gathered around her ankles like a cloak. She wore a white dress cut short at the knees, revealing two legs that were whole and perfect.

Only her eyes remained the same: a startling turquoise that swirled with the cold fire of madness.

"Nice dress," Grace said. "It suits you."

From below, Kara could just make out the black shape in Grace's lap.

The grimoire.

"Ah," said Grace, following Kara's eyes. She placed a hand on the open book. "You came for this. I'm disappointed. I still hoped, despite everything, that we might be friends. But no. You want to steal what's mine."

She doesn't know I have my own grimoire. I have to pick the right moment. Surprise is my best weapon.

"I have no desire for the book," Kara said. She stared up at the tree throne with what she hoped was a determined expression. "I came to save you!"

Grace laughed, dulcet tones beautiful enough to draw sailors to a rocky shore. Jerking on their stone seats like hideous marionettes, the congregation joined in. Their laughs were not so beautiful.

"Save me? From what, Kara Westfall?"

"The grimoire. It's tricking you."

"And how is that, exactly? By letting me do anything I wish?"

"There is a price for such power. Each time you cast a spell, you get closer to the end of the book, and when that happens——"

"Then I'll be able to cast spells without using the book at all. The grimoire told me all about it, Kara."

"It lied."

"My book obeys me. Not the other way around."

She was too far away to tell for sure, but Kara thought

she might have seen a flicker of doubt cross Grace's face. The congregation, unsettled by this disturbance in their universe, keened softly.

"How many pages are left?" Kara asked. "How many pages until the Last Spell? Because, unless you listen to me, that's exactly how long you have to . . ."

Grace stepped off the throne. She plummeted though the air at frightening speed, her hair trailing behind her like a reverse waterfall. Just before hitting the ground, Grace vanished—and reappeared right in front of Kara.

"You've tried to trick me before," Grace said. "Remember? You told me the grimoire wouldn't let me hurt people." She smiled. "Well, you were wrong about that, Kara Westfall. Let me show you all the different ways."

Grace stroked the black book clasped in her hands and spit out a stream of words. Kara had just enough time to note Grace's place in the grimoire—*just a few pages left*—and then she was airborne. She landed squarely on her back, the impact sending a puff of dirt into the sky along with the oxygen in her lungs.

The congregation, as one, clapped gently.

Before Kara could stand, a cold force squeezed her neck. Kara clawed at the invisible noose, but all she did was scratch bloody rivulets into her own skin. She gasped for breath, and the noose tightened, lifting her into the air. Just as the world was becoming a darkness from which Kara would never return, the spell released its hold. She fell to earth and lay in the dirt, gasping desperately for air.

The congregation moaned their disappointment.

When Kara looked up, Grace was standing before her. The expression on her face might have been mistaken for pity.

"Surely you didn't think you could fight me," she said. "Even when you had the grimoire, your power did not compare to mine. And now." She shook her head. "Now you're no better than one of them. Perhaps you should just join my followers and be done with it."

"You need . . . to stop," Kara said. Each word was a struggle, more air than her body was willing to impart. "The book . . . using you. It will make . . . you . . . suffer. Don't—"

Grace spoke a single word and set Kara on fire. Flames licked the skin between her fingers. Eyeballs boiled in sockets. Kara would have thought it impossible, but somewhere, deep within her lungs, she found the air to scream.

And then the pain ended. In astonishment Kara held her hand in front of her. The skin was whole, without so much as a sunburn.

"I want to say this will eventually get boring," Grace said, "but, unlike you, I refuse to lie to another witch." She held the grimoire open and flipped to the next page. Almost the entire weight of the book, nearly two hundred pages, rested in her left hand. She continued. "I don't even pick the spells. The grimoire does it for me. But it's always the *right* spell." With a mocking grin, she showed Kara the next page. "Take this one right here. You can't see it, of course, but that's probably for the best. It's vicious. Much different than the others. That's the book's way of telling me it's time to stop playing games and put an end to this." Grace looked at her. "And I agree."

Before Grace could open her mouth again, Kara touched the grimoire in her pocket and mumbled the necessary words.

"What was that?" Grace asked. Her voice was bubbly with amusement. "Did you just try to cast a spell? Without a grimoire? Oh dear. Don't you understand anything about magic at—"

The gra'dak plowed into Grace just below the knees, tossing her over its squat body. She hit the ground hard but quickly rose to her feet, more stunned than hurt. Kara sent the gra'dak again, faster this time. It leaped at the last moment, its tusks knocking the grimoire from Grace's hands.

The book landed with a *thud* at Kara's feet.

"No!" Grace screamed, crawling toward her. "Give it to me! It's mine!"

The gra'dak nipped Grace's calf with its human mouth. Then it circled the girl, its five mouths quivering eagerly, longing to finish what they had started. Exercising all her will, Kara managed to calm its violent nature, freezing it in place.

She picked up Grace's grimoire.

Instantly Kara was flooded by a desire to use it that was far more powerful than before. *KILL HERKILLTHEMPOWERPOWERPOWER.* Before she even realized what she was doing, the grimoire was open in her shaking hands, a spell inscribing itself before her eyes. *ANYTHINGYOUWANT. REVENGE. MOTHERALIVE. ALLYOURS.*

The sketch, nearly finished now, showed an achingly beautiful woman with the long, graceful neck of a swan. Kara knew the drawing's power: the ability to grant any wish. All she had to do was speak her desire and it would be hers.

Don't listen. This is a thing of evil.

"You are not my mother's book," Kara said, and slammed the grimoire shut.

A dark blossom of pain spread throughout her chest. Her entire torso felt slick with blood, but she knew that it was an illusion. She recognized this pain. Looking up she saw Grace kneeling over the gra'dak, a dagger in her hands. Though there was no need, she plunged it into the dying creature one more time. Then another. Each strike of the dagger sent a sharp lance through Kara.

I'm sorry, Kara thought as she felt the gra'dak's spirit weaken and waver. In order to save Grace, she had taken away its power to move, and it had been unable to defend itself. *I'm so sorry. I'm so . . .*

It was gone.

Slowly the pain began to recede, but not before Grace yanked the grimoire from her hands. Kara was too weak to stop her.

440

Unmindful of the gore, Grace slipped the dagger back into her boot.

"How did you do that?" she asked. "It's impossible to cast a spell without a grimoire. Unless . . ." Grace's eyes brightened. "There's a second grimoire, isn't there? Yes! I can see it in your eyes!" Grace clapped her hands. "Well, why didn't you tell me that, Witch Girl? That makes everything *much* more fun."

Grace opened the grimoire and read the spell before her with unconcealed delight. It was a long one. Still too weak to stand, Kara crawled away on her elbows. She heard gentle tinkling sounds to either side of her, up and down the street. A small crack split the center of the window in the general store. The crack grew larger, heading off in every direction, inching its way along the glass like a snake.

All at once every window in the village shattered.

Kara shouted out her own spell, but the thunderous sound of breaking glass was so deafening that she could not hear the words. Covering her ears she watched the glass gather together in a mini-tornado, hovering just in front of Grace's outstretched hands. It spun and twisted in the air, the sun glinting off its jagged edges in an oddly beautiful paroxysm of light.

Grace pursed her lips and blew. The glass shot forward.

Kara shielded her face with her hands and curled into a ball, trying to make herself as small as possible. She waited for the glass to slice her skin into a thousand pieces. It never did. Instead she heard a series of clinking sounds, like tiny icicles falling off a tree and shattering on the rocks below. The sound was peaceful, with a certain music to it.

Kara opened her eyes.

She was surrounded by a squirming darkness. Holding out a hand, Kara felt the silverworms she had summoned. There were hundreds of them—maybe thousands—moving close enough together that not even light could pass. A little one nipped her finger playfully as it darted by. The underside of the creature—the part facing Kara—was soft and tender to the touch. Its back and wings, however, were made of an armor as hard as steel. Down by the stream, she had once seen them form a similar phalanx to protect their young from a larger predator. Kara felt honored that they would treat her with the same devotion.

The clinking slowed and then stopped altogether as the storm of glass ended. Before Grace could retaliate, Kara set the silverworms free. She felt responsible for the creatures and wanted to keep them safe.

Shielding her eyes against the harsh sunlight, Kara scanned the empty street.

Grace was nowhere to be seen.

She stepped over a ring of broken glass as high as her knees. It was more difficult than it should have been. Kara's neck throbbed with pain, and countless scrapes and abrasions weakened her body. These physical injuries, however, were minor in comparison to the mental strain of casting one spell after another. Her head felt foggy, out of sorts. She looked over at the Fenroot tree and saw that the people of De'Noran had risen. This seemed important for some reason, though Kara couldn't figure out why. She continued to stare. There was something she wasn't *seeing*, something that would have been obvious had her mind been clear.

It snapped into place, then. And as it did, panic cleared Kara's mind of any lingering fog.

The sitting stones are missing!

By the time the first stone thudded into the earth just a few steps to her left, Kara was already running. Two more followed, landing where she had just been standing. *Thunk!* Another one fell directly in front of her, not just embedding itself in the dirt but *plummeting* through it, leaving a crater in its wake. She risked a quick look at the sky and saw gray dots in the distance, some hovering above her and others already on a downward trajectory, growing into their real size before her eyes.

A dozen rocks crashed through the roof of the general store. At first Kara thought Grace had missed, but she knew better. This was a message: *If they can do that to solid wood, imagine what they're going to do to you.*

Kara ran for the schoolhouse.

Its roof had been fortified to provide safe shelter for the entire village during a storm. Kara wasn't sure if it was strong enough to withstand something like *this*, but it seemed the best option.

All she had to do was make it there alive.

Physical ailments forgotten, Kara found the will to sprint, zigzagging along the road in what she hoped was an unpredictable pattern. Rocks fell around her in a deadly hail, their impact sending giant clouds of dirt into the air. Soon it was difficult to see, and Kara had to slow down to avoid the new holes in the ground. A fragment of rock passed close, the angry *whiz* of its descent buzzing along her ear. Two inches to the right and she would have been dead.

I won't make it this way, Kara thought. *She's toying with me, but as soon as she gets bored her aim will improve. She'll never let me reach safety.*

Kara touched the battered notebook in her pocket. The spell she wanted, inscribed on the penultimate page, was far more complicated than the others. Even if her mind was fresh—and she was not trying to dodge instant death at every turn—it would be a difficult spell. She searched her thoughts for the words, finding a trail of them and then losing it again when she realized it was the middle of the spell, not the beginning. She began anew, from the right place this time, but just as she neared the end, she inhaled a mouthful of dust and the unfinished spell broke into pieces.

Kara rounded a bend and saw the schoolhouse in the distance, sheltered by a copse of evergreens. The trees were small and pretty, their purpose to provide rest and shade, not protection from falling rocks.

She thought of Father. She thought of Taff.

Would Grace really allow them to escape the island unharmed?

In one long breath, the spell spilled from her mouth. Kara knew she had said the words correctly, because she instantly felt dazed and wobbly, like someone had peeled her head open and removed a week of sleep.

She ran into the copse.

The rock storm was louder beneath the trees, accentuated by snapping branches and wailing wind. A tree crashed to the ground, blocking her path. Kara leaped over it just before a stone split it in two.

Her left foot landed in a hole, twisting in an unfortunate direction.

There was no pain—not yet—but a quick-setting numbness promised plenty of that in the near future. Kara tried to lift her leg, but it wouldn't budge. Looking closer she saw that her ankle was wedged between a stone and packed dirt. Bracing her right leg firmly against the ground, she pushed forward, succeeding only in driving a fresh splinter of pain into her calf.

All at once the sky grew darker.

Directly overhead a gray blur was falling, far larger than any simple rock. At first Kara thought Grace had enlisted one of the boulders closer to shore, but then she recognized the singular shape of the falling object, the sharp rise at the top she had seen at every Service since birth.

The Speaking Stone.

Kara pulled at her left foot once again, hoping for a miracle. It wouldn't budge. There was no time to do anything else. She watched the Speaking Stone fall, spinning slightly, until it was so close she could make out the first words of the Path etched into its base.

At the last moment, on pure reflex, she raised her hands over her head.

The stone stopped in midair.

Kara stared at her hands in wonderment. *What kind of magic is this?* she thought. But then she looked again and saw the purplish strands of web wound about four nearby trees, holding the boulder like a hammock. From the branches above, a webspinner chittered a greeting, its boneless arms flapping up and down with what might have been a wave. It wasn't the only one. There were at least a dozen more of the creatures, playfully crawling up and down the unfamiliar trees on their spiderlike legs.

They came! she thought. *The spell worked!*

Just as Kara allowed herself a sigh of relief, the Speaking Stone started to fall again: slowly this time but still quite sufficiently to crush her. With a loud groaning sound, the four trees bent forward, unable to sustain this new weight. Kara dug her fingers into the hole, frantically searching for some kind of purchase around the rock, some way to shift it just enough. No luck. The first tree snapped, and the Speaking Stone, unbalanced, swayed back and forth, so close that Kara could have reached out and touched it. Instead she unlaced her boot, sliding her left foot free and crawling backward, just before the telltale *snap* of the remaining trees. The Speaking Stone crashed to the ground, missing her by inches.

The webspinners, clearly entertained, chittered their appreciation.

Kara limped toward the schoolhouse. Above her a deluge of stones rained down from the sky in an attempt to keep her from shelter. She couldn't dodge them all, so she simply moved in a straight line, trusting the webspinners in the trees above her to catch the rocks in time. Soon the copse was filled with web baskets, each hanging low with a rock that could have killed her. Kara continued, pausing only when she heard a high-pitched squeal and, at the same moment, felt a stabbing pain in her side. One of the webspinners had perished trying to save her. She would grieve for it later. Right now there was only the door of the schoolhouse, so close, right within her grasp. . . .

Made it!

Kara immediately slammed the door shut. She waited for the sitting stones to hit the roof above her—surely

Grace would test the fortifications—but it never happened. Possibly she had run out of stones. Or maybe, like Kara, she was too tired to use magic anymore.

For now Kara was safe.

In the sudden silence, she heard a different noise: the click-clacking of chalk against blackboard. Its familiarity should have been comforting, a reminder of less dangerous times, but instead it sent a chill through her body.

Kara turned around.

No light shone through the windows. She could *see* the sunlight just outside the school; it was simply prohibited from entering the room. Instead a single candle sat in the center of each desk, which were arranged in perfect rows.

She knew I was coming here. She prepared this for me.

Master Blackwood stood at the front of the room, writing on the blackboard. His hand was a blur of violent motion, nothing like his usual precise penmanship. The same three words filled the entire blackboard:

MAGIC IS GOOD. MAGIC IS GOOD. MAGIC IS GOOD.

Master Blackwood's wrinkled face was caked with chalk dust and dried tears.

"Class is so much better now," Grace said. "Wouldn't you agree?"

Kara turned to find Grace sitting in her usual seat near the front of the room. Grace slid her hand playfully through the candle flame as she spoke.

"There's someone waiting for you," she said, pointing toward a dark corner of the room that seemed immune to candlelight. "Over there. A surprise."

"I think I've had enough surprises."

"But this one is *so good*. I used my next-to-last spell on it." There was a hint of regret in her tone. "They get more powerful as you near the end. Or maybe I'm getting stronger. I think, with my Last Spell, I'm going to destroy De'Noran and everyone in it." Grace squeezed the flame between two fingers. "Yes. I think that's something I'd like to do."

"Why?" Kara asked.

Grace tilted her head to one side, deeply confused by

the question. Then her eyes brightened as she saw something behind Kara. "Oh look! He grew tired of waiting for you."

Kara did not have time to turn around. The smell of decay hit her first, and then she was picked up by two impossibly cold hands and hurled across the room. She collided with a desk, overturning it. Ignoring the fresh blood running down her temple, Kara scrambled to her feet and faced her attacker.

"No," Kara said.

Simon Loder had not been improved by death. His muscular frame was encased in a thick layer of mud and grass. Only the vague impression of facial features poked through, like an unfinished sculpture.

"How could you do this?" Kara asked Grace. "He was your friend."

Grace shrugged. "You're the one who killed him. I gave him *life*."

Simon took a step toward her. Kara slid to the right, toward the exit, but although Simon's eyes were obscured by mud, he managed to block her path anyway. Kara tried the other direction with the same result. It didn't matter how quietly she moved; somehow Simon could sense her.

So she ran instead.

Simon pursued her, wooden desks slamming into the walls as he tossed them out of his way. One by one each candle was extinguished, plunging the room into a preternatural darkness. Grace watched from her seat, smirking with amusement.

Kara had her hand on the doorknob when Simon pulled her back and pinned her to the floor, his eyes seeing her and yet also somewhere else, somewhere distant. His dirt-encrusted hand wrapped around her neck and squeezed. Kara knew she should feel horror and revulsion, but all she felt was pity. This was her fault. Grace might have cast the unthinkable spell that brought him back, but she had killed him in the first place. She was the one who had turned him into a monster.

I'm sorry, Simon.

She summoned the Jabenhook with more energy than her exhausted body was capable of producing, unleashing a river of ice deep through her veins. The creature came quickly this time, filling the dark schoolhouse with its golden light. All she had to do was call it to her. It could restore her to perfect health, give her the strength she needed to fight again.

She sent it to Simon instead.

The Jabenhook took him in its great talons and started its work. Simon struggled, but even he was tiny in comparison to the magnificent bird, and it wasn't long before a dark cloud hovered between them. Simon's Death was older than Taff's, a miasma of corruption that twisted and screamed in the air. Upon leaving Simon's body, it immediately darted toward Kara, looking for a new body to occupy: This Death had no respect for the rules. Before it could reach her, however, the Jabenhook snapped its beak and removed it from the world.

And then vanished.

Kara tried to get up, but her body wouldn't cooperate. The skin of her right hand was numb and blue. With each spell it felt like a little more life was being pressed out of her. *I have to stop. Another spell like that will kill me.* She heard Grace slide out of her seat. Kara concentrated hard, willing her feet to move. Nothing. She watched Grace's footsteps come closer, saw her kick all that remained of Simon's body: a pathetic mound of dirt.

"That was a magnificent spell!" she exclaimed. "Stole the life right from him."

Kara spoke through numb, unmoving lips. "It healed him. From his suffering. From what we did."

"Oh," said Grace. "That's not nearly as impressive." She poked Kara's stomach with her foot. "Get up."

"I can't."

Another kick. Harder this time.

"Get. Up. We're not done yet."

Kara felt her eyes closing. Sleep—wonderful, blissful sleep—pulled her toward its warm embrace. "I'm not

like you," she mumbled as she fell. "The magic makes me weak."

"Just one more." Grace leaned forward, positively beaming. "The Last Spell. I want to see what *happens*."

Kara opened her eyes. Wide.

"You can't, Grace. It's not worth the price."

"Are you still trying to save me, Kara Westfall?" Grace leaned forward and whispered in Kara's ear. "Let me tell you a secret. I don't want to be saved."

She kissed Kara tenderly.

"My graycloaks found your family," Grace said. "They're outside waiting for you."

Kara pushed her away. The sudden movement almost made her vomit.

"Look at that," Grace said. "Are we feeling a little more mobile all of a sudden?"

"If you hurt them, I'll kill you!"

"Yes, Kara! Yes! Kill me! Or at least try."

Though her right side felt as though it were encased

in ice and even the slightest movement made her want to scream, Kara got to her feet. As soon as she stepped forward, however, the room tipped to one side. Grace caught her before she could fall and began walking her to the door. "It's going to be like a story from the Path," Grace said. "A witches' duel! Maybe they'll talk about us in years to come. Wouldn't that be something? Wouldn't that make it all worthwhile in the end?"

Kara was too tired to respond, and Grace finally stopped talking. The only sound as they exited the building was the clack of Master Blackwood's chalk as he continued to write his message.

MAGIC IS GOOD. MAGIC IS GOOD. MAGIC IS GOOD.

The Shadow Festival had come again. Everyone Kara had ever known—all those who remained alive, at least—lined the main road of the village, waiting patiently for the entertainment to begin. She was the Leaf Girl. Grace was the Forest Demon. Or perhaps it was the other way around. Kara saw Father and Taff standing in the front row, spines straight and shoulder to shoulder, faces devoid of expression.

She did not see Lucas. She thought it might be better that way.

Grace remained where she was as Kara, a bit steadier on her feet now, walked slowly to the other end of the road. The eyes of the villagers followed her as she passed. Other than that, there was no movement. No whispers, muffled coughs, baby cries. The silence was so absolute that Kara could hear her footsteps in the dirt. This was Grace's moment, and she would not permit any interruptions.

When she reached the end of the line, Kara turned around. Knowing that there was no more use for pretense, she removed the grimoire and held it in two hands. Grace had already done the same.

What will it be like? Kara wondered. *To suffer for all eternity. After the first few years, will I even remember who I am anymore? Will I even be capable of thought? Or will I know only pain?*

"Children of De'Noran," Grace announced, "all your lives you've been told that magic is wrong. Evil. Ungodly. But this evening, I am going to give you the greatest of all gifts. Enlightenment."

Kara looked down at the blank page before her. Her hands trembled.

I don't want to do this. Why does it have to be me?

"You are going to witness the true power of magic. You are going to learn that everything you've been taught in your pathetic little lives has been a lie. And then you're going to die." Grace shrugged. "Sorry."

Mother! Why didn't you warn me? Why didn't you tell me this would happen?

Grace faced Kara and curtsied.

"We cast on three," she said.

Kara looked past Grace to her brother, his eyes blank but somehow *seeing* her as he always did. He would remember. He would know the sacrifice she made.

And, most important: He would live.

"One," Grace said, but Kara had already summoned what she needed. She smiled with relief as its likeness appeared in the grimoire. It had been a long time, and she feared the memory wouldn't be strong enough.

Grace spoke the second word distantly: "Two." Her mouth trembled, eager to say the words forming in the book . . . but then she jerked up her head, sensing something.

Kara's grimoire burst into flames.

She tossed it away, but not before its heat singed her fingers and turned the palms of her hands an angry crimson. The fire swirled high, a cone of blinding light that split the sky and scattered the neat lines of villagers. In it crackled words just beyond Kara's understanding.

Is this how it works? Will I burn forever?

The flames made no attempt to envelop her. Not yet. She heard screams, shouts for help. Kara tore her eyes away for just a moment and saw that Grace's enchantment had been broken. Confused villagers were fleeing this nightmare as quickly as they could. The crazed mob pushed past Grace, knocking her to the ground.

Only one figure was actually moving toward the flames.

"Kara!" shouted Lucas. He held a hand to his eyes, shielding them from the light. "Run!"

"I can't!" Kara said. *It hasn't taken me yet.* "Get my family out of here!"

They faced each other, the spiraling flames between them. Lucas took a step toward her.

"Please, Lucas," she said.

"I'm not going to leave you!"

I don't want Taff to see this.

"There's nothing you can do. Just keep them safe."

"Kara."

"Please. For me."

Lucas took another step. Then he nodded once and

ran off in the opposite direction. He passed Grace, who was stumbling through the chaotic crowd, screaming: "Where is it? Where is it?"

Something brushed past Kara's face.

She watched it vanish into the distance: a bird made of flames. But that wasn't exactly right. It *was* a bird, but its body lacked the fluidity of flesh; it was rigid, almost mechanical.

A page from the grimoire, folded into a winged creature.

As though inspired by Kara's epiphany, a dozen page-birds burst from the flames and sailed into the night. Another dozen. Fifty. They did not travel together but shot off in all directions, leaving trails of light in their wake. With the passage of each bird, the tunnel of flame shrank. Finally it was only the size of a campfire—and then, four birds later, a flame so small, it could barely light a candle. From this a tiny glowworm emerged and burrowed into the ground.

And then there was nothing. Her mother's grimoire was gone.

Kara remained.

What just happened? She ran her hands over her body, amazed at its wholeness. *I cast the Last Spell—why didn't the grimoire take me like Constance said it would? Could she have been wrong?* Kara stared at the charred ground.

How am I still alive?

She didn't even feel particularly weak. If anything, she felt . . . restored.

"It didn't even let you cast your Last Spell, did it?" Grace asked. "You weren't worthy. Pathetic." She opened her grimoire. "Let me show you the power of a true witch."

Grace's eyes widened as a spell filled the page before her. "Yes," she said. "This is the one. This will be *forever*." Grace read the first word, and a thimbleful of blood spilled from her lips. She paused for a moment and continued anyway, louder this time. Beneath Kara's feet the

464

earth moaned, as though beasts dormant for thousands of years were awakening from their slumber.

Suddenly, Grace stopped.

A feeble-looking creature sat before her, its fur matted with age and filth. It tottered forward on bent-back paws, emitting a short, piteous moan with each agonizing step.

Grace burst out laughing.

"*This* is what you summoned?" she asked. "A dog? For what purpose? Did you think I might play nicer if I had a pet?"

"It's not a dog."

The creature looked up at Grace with violet eyes that were quite beautiful in their way and growled deep in its throat. With a sharp series of cracking noises, its paws unfolded and straightened. Just before the creature leaped, Grace was blessed with a moment of recognition, but by then it was too late; she was pinned beneath the nightseeker's now muscular frame, unable to move.

"I don't blame you for not remembering," Kara said.

"You're not the one who saw your mother murdered before your eyes. If you had, perhaps you would have remembered the pet your father brought from the World—and its very peculiar talent."

A long, translucent needle extended from the night-seeker's paw. Grace screamed and then screamed louder as the needle was plunged into her forearm with brisk efficiency. She jerked in pain, and the grimoire slid from her fingers, landing open on the ground. Grace reached out, screeching. She clawed at the last page, trying to pull the book closer, but before she could the nightseeker swept its paw across the grimoire and slammed it shut on her hand. Grace screamed again, and it wasn't the scream of a powerful witch but the terrified plea of a thirteen-year-old girl. Kara turned away. She had thought that revenge might bring her some satisfaction, but there was no pleasure in this.

The nightseeker inserted the needle into its nostril and inhaled deeply. Years ago—when Kara had been in Grace's position—there had been a long hesitation. On this day, however, judgment came instantaneously. Keeping its quarry in place with one paw, the nightseeker lined its needle claw with Grace's right eye.

"*No!*" she shouted. "*Kara! Please!*"

The fearsome creature rose up on its haunches. Kara could feel its fury surge through her own blood. It wasn't just going to blind the witch. It was going to kill her.

Before it could, Kara sent it away.

Grace lay there shivering, unwilling to open her eyes. "It's over," Kara said. She stepped quickly to her side and kicked the grimoire away with her bootless foot. Grace's hand, clenched in a bloody fist, fell to the ground.

"You saved me," Grace mumbled.

"Yes."

"Why?"

"I don't want anyone else to die."

"Not even me."

"No."

Grace chuckled. "A good witch. Can there be such a thing?"

Kara sat on the ground next to Grace. Evening was starting to settle in, and the colors of the setting sun were their own kind of magic.

"You won't be able to save me from the villagers. When they return they're going to kill me."

"Maybe both of us."

"No. They know the truth. You saved them."

"With magic. The greatest sin."

"They will speak of your great deeds for years to come. They will throw flowers at your feet and trade hard-earned seeds for your wisdom. They will worship you and dream of your attention. Just like him." Her eyes sought out the swaying treetops of the Thickety, and she tilted her head to one side, as though listening. "After all I've done to prove myself, it is still you he covets. The world is not a fair place, Kara Westfall. And not even magic can change that."

Grace mumbled three words—only three—but Kara recognized a spell when she heard one.

"What did you do?" Kara asked.

Grace turned her head. Her beautiful eyes focused on something unseen.

"I gave him what he wanted," she said.

Blond leeched from Grace's hair as it turned its original shade of white. With a grotesque *snap*, the bones of her leg twisted into their familiar crippled form.

"No! That's impossible!" Kara shouted. "You couldn't have cast a spell! I have the grimoire!"

Grace smirked, a little of the old arrogance returning—*Won't you ever learn?*—before opening her bloodied hand. A piece of torn, crumpled paper rolled out.

Cold dread nestled in Kara's stomach. *She really did it. She cast her Last Spell.* With no grimoire of her own, Kara was helpless to defend herself—to defend anyone. She had failed.

She scanned the skies, listening carefully for the sound

of an approaching apocalypse. All was quiet.

"What did you do?" she asked again.

"You'll thank me," Grace replied. "In the end. Once you learn to accept the true nature of his love."

Grace's grimoire was torn from Kara's hands by an invisible force. It sailed high in the air before landing on the ground between them. Kara stepped back, expecting it to burst into flames. Instead the pages flipped to the precise center of the book, where there were no longer spells but a gaping hole that led into absolute darkness.

"That's new," Grace said.

A woman's arm shot out of the hole and grabbed Grace's ankle. By the time Grace tried to pry off the fingers, they had melted into her flesh like wax and there was nothing to disengage. The second arm, this one thinner—the arm of a child—grasped Grace's other leg and became part of it, and it yanked her toward the hole, which by this point had expanded well past the confines of the grimoire. Another hand rose from the darkness,

this one wearing a familiar wedding band (*Abby! That's Abby!*), and Grace managed to slap it away, but then there were three more, four, half a dozen—all eager to do their part. Kara held Grace's hands and pulled as hard as she could, but it was no use; it was one against many, and they were legion. From below—deep within the impossible recesses of the grimoire—she heard cackling, screams of pain, the singsong chant of the damned:

One of us! One of us! One of us!

Kara fell backward as Grace's fingers slipped from her hands. The white-haired girl slid into darkness, brilliant blue eyes watching Kara until the very end.

Satisfied at last, the grimoire slammed shut.

EPILOGUE

It was Kara's first time on a ship, and she feared that the swaying motion would make her ill. Lucas did not share that problem. As he stared out at the great blue horizon his expression was peaceful, like a young man who had found his home at last.

"This far enough?" he asked.

"Yes," Kara said. Even if it wasn't, it was as far as she was willing to go. The island was still visible in the distance, but it was fading fast, and the idea of no land in sight—of being swallowed whole by all this vastness—terrified her.

From her satchel she withdrew Grace's grimoire.

Although its pages were once again white and pristine, it did not call to her as it once did. Kara liked to think that it had given up.

"Is she in there, do you think?" Lucas asked.

"Maybe. But I don't know if that . . . place . . . is in the book itself, or if the book just provided the passageway."

"Either one is impossible. So it's impossible to know which is true."

Kara nodded and watched the water pass. In one quick motion, she dropped the grimoire. It hovered on the surface for a few moments and then vanished beneath the waves.

"It wasn't your fault," Lucas said. "She made her own decision."

"I just don't understand why I was spared the same fate."

"Maybe the grimoire can sense intentions. You used magic to try to help people. So you didn't need to be punished."

Kara nodded, but she knew that wasn't the right

answer. What happened to Grace had been payment, not punishment. Just like Aunt Abby, the grimoire had granted her unearthly powers—but when the time came, it demanded a steep price in return. Kara should have been relieved that her Last Spell produced a completely different result, but this apparent exemption made her nervous. No power came without sacrifice, and her time would come. She was sure of it.

Maybe when you finally discover what Grace's Last Spell was . . .

This was a happy day, however, and Kara refused to get distracted by such dark thoughts. She pulled at Lucas's new sailor's cap.

"This suits you," she said.

"I'm glad you think so," Lucas said. "All it does is make my head itch."

Lucas wore tan trousers and a fitted knit shirt. That morning he had gone to the Burning Place—along with the other Clearers making the journey to the World—and set his old clothes aflame.

"Are you surprised that so many Clearers are staying behind?" Kara asked.

"This is all they've known," Lucas said. "It's a scary thing, to give that up for a strange world they've been cautioned about their entire lives."

"How about you? Are you scared?"

Lucas shook his head. "I feel like my life is finally beginning."

They walked in silence to the other side of the deck, where a rope ladder led to a small boat bobbing cheerfully in the waves. Kara turned to Lucas but did not look into his eyes. It had taken her two weeks to convince him to go. If he saw how much she wanted him to stay, he might still change his mind.

This is best for him. This is what he needs.

"Kara . . . ," he started, but one of his shipmates called his name, and although Lucas held one finger up—*Give me a moment*—Kara waited until his back was turned and then climbed down the ladder and into the boat. By the time Lucas returned, Kara had already halved the distance to shore. He waved to her, and Kara waved back, glad he was too far away to see her tears. Lucas had promised to return next season, but Kara couldn't help thinking that she would never see him again.

The people of De'Noran had worked quickly to repair their ruined village. Windows had been replaced. Roofs patched. Debris collected. And perhaps most impressive, almost all the sitting stones had been located and moved back to their original positions. Only those caught by webbing remained where they were, as neither steel nor fire could free them. The Elders had discussed cutting down the trees that held them suspended, but Father refused. He thought the hanging stones would serve as a reminder to future generations, of how magic—and people—could both save and destroy.

Kara was the last to arrive at the Fenroot tree. Heads

turned to note her appearance, and a hush fell over the crowd. As usual most people stared down at their laps as she passed, refusing to meet her eyes. Father assured her this was no longer due to fear, however. It was reverence. Maybe even love.

Kara felt a blush warm her face. She wasn't sure if she was ever going to get used to this.

Taff had saved her a stone in the first row. His cheeks were bright and healthy and covered with crumbs.

"Widow Miller made us a whole tray of apple fritters! I meant to save you one, but you were late, and I got hungry."

Laughing, Kara wiped away the crumbs. Widow Miller had been spending a lot of time at their house lately. Kara heard her and Father talking out on the porch when they thought she was asleep, the sounds of their laughter. She liked *Rachel*—as Widow Miller insisted she call her—but she wasn't sure how she felt about this new development. Her real father had only recently been returned to her, and she wasn't quite ready to share him yet.

"I'm going to miss Lucas," Taff said. "But he promised he'd bring me some new tools from the World, tools I've never even seen before. And he said when I'm older, I can come with him and see—" He stopped, noticing the way she was trying to smile but failing.

"Oh," he said. "You're *really* going to miss him."

"I'll be fine," Kara said. "As long as I have you."

Sudden applause filled the air as Father made his way through the crowd, wearing a crisp white shirt that Kara had starched herself. The Elders had wanted him to don the crimson robes, but Father refused. He would be their fen'de but under his conditions.

"Work hard. Want nothing," Father said.

"Stay vigilant," the congregation replied.

Kara smiled, remembering him in the days after the battle. How he had taken charge so effortlessly: organizing search parties and healing stations, delegating the various tasks of rebuilding. He barely slept that week, leading with a firm kindness that bound villagers and Clearers together. Years ago the people of De'Noran had loved him; they fell in love with him again. By the end of the week, children stopped their play when he passed. A coterie of followers trailed him about the village, awaiting orders. When it was time to choose a new fen'de, no other names entered the discussion.

"I've never been much of a good talker," Father said. "And I don't seem to be getting any better with age. But I can accept that. Words can be pretty things, but they can't hoe a field or patch a roof in the thick of winter. They can't make everything better again. Only people can do that."

He shifted his feet uncomfortably, tucked his hands into his pockets. The congregation watched him, lingering on every word, every pause. Hypnotized.

"You'll notice that, since the tragedy, things have been good for us. Everyone getting along like we're supposed to. That's because we've had a common goal. A desire to fix our home, make things right again. There's nothing that bonds people together more than the same dream."

Kara thought it was a nice speech, but she was anxious for it to be over so things could return to normal. Since that night in the stable, she had barely spoken to Father. He had been so *busy*, and even when he came home there were the visitors, knocking on the door at all hours, asking his advice or sometimes just wanting the touch of his hand on their forehead. She had woken one night to find a pregnant young farm woman in their kitchen *kneeling* before Father. Kara had thought it strange, but Father laughed it off, saying the woman was simply overenthusiastic and worried about the health of her child.

"But now that our village is once again whole," Father continued, "I do not want to fall back into the old ways. We have to remain united. We have to remain true to our original dream—the one true dream. The complete and utter absolution of magic."

What? What did he say?

"Every life lost—mother, father, son, daughter—can be traced back to magic. Recent events have only proven what the Fold has known for hundreds of years: There can be no good through witchcraft, only evil and death. Now, it would be easy, even tempting, to absolve Grace Stone of her actions. She was just a simple girl, as much a victim of magic as anyone else standing here this fine morning. But as Children of the Fold, we know better, don't we? Anyone who uses magic is not one of us. Anyone who uses magic does not deserve to live.

"Which brings us, unfortunately, to my daughter."

Kara looked around the congregation, but their faces were blank with acceptance. Only Taff had begun to look nervous and confused.

"Rise, Kara Westfall. Face your judgment."

Why is he saying these things? This can't be happening.

She got to her feet.

"Are you a witch?" he asked.

"I'm your daughter."

"That wasn't the question."

"Why are you doing this?"

"A simple yes or no will suffice."

"You know the answer."

"Yes. Or no."

"Yes!" she exclaimed. "I'm a witch! Just like my mother!"

A rumble of hatred flowed through the crowd. It was hard to make out the specific words, but occasionally a few broke through: *evil . . . heathen . . . witch . . . fault . . . die!* Taff stood on his stone seat and screamed back at them: "What's wrong with you! She saved your lives!" He was just a boy, however, and his words were easily ignored.

Father held one hand aloft, and silence filled the air. It was unnatural, how instantly and completely the villagers obeyed him, and Kara noticed, for the first time, that his eyes were a slightly different hue than before, a wet-sand shade of brown. As she gazed into his eyes she felt her

desire to resist fade away. . . .

And then, with shocking clarity, Kara realized the truth: This was Grace's Last Spell.

"You're not my father," Kara said.

The thing in her father's body nodded. "I am Timoth Clen, destroyer of Witches, Voice of the One True Way, returned to all of you in your time of direst need."

She expected the crowd to laugh this claim away. But she saw only smiles and tiny nods, as though this was only confirmation of something they had known for some time.

Timoth Clen folded his arms across his chest. "Do your duty, my Children."

The first stone hit her in the back of the neck. It was small, not much more than a pebble, but it stung. The second stone was much larger and missed her entirely, skipping off the bark of the Fenroot tree. Kara risked a glance behind her and saw that the congregation had come prepared this morning. They were withdrawing rocks from aprons, pockets, drawstring bags. Everyone had known except for her.

"Taff?" Kara asked.

He slipped his hand into hers.

Instead of heading back through the congregation, Kara pulled Taff toward their father (*No, that's not him, not anymore*), knowing that the villagers would not risk hitting the holy man with an errant throw. Timoth Clen watched them pass with a cold, bemused expression that her real father could have never replicated.

They ran.

Rocks filled the air, whizzing past them, over them. Finding their mark. Trails of blood ran down Kara's calves. Taff let out a high-pitched yelp as a stone clipped his elbow. The important thing, Kara knew, was to remain standing. If either one of them fell, the villagers would be upon them. She ran faster, but Taff couldn't keep up, so she slowed down. A rock hit her in the back of the shoulder, and her arm went numb. She heard a whoop

of delight, applause. It was a game now. Taff began to cry. "This isn't fair," he said, and of course he was right, but she told him to save his breath. They crested the rise that led out of town, and the graycloaks were waiting for them at the bottom of the hill. They were human again, but their faces were devoid of all compassion. They sat on their tall horses, ball-staffs held at the ready.

"Kara?" Taff asked.

There was desperation in his voice and, even worse, a hint of hope. He trusted that she would know what to do. It broke her heart.

"Kara?" he asked again.

The graycloaks strode slowly up the hill. There was no need to hurry. The villagers held on to their rocks and stones and spread themselves out, blocking all avenues of escape.

She looked up at the sky. Blue and clear. A beautiful day.

"Kara?"

To the west stood a large, leafless tree. Though there

was no wind, its branches scratched together, and Kara heard a familiar voice in her head. *Your power cannot be bound in a book. You are special. Don't let them hurt you. Don't let them hurt the boy.* Images fluttered through Kara's head: a nightmarish beast with a mouth of claws sweeping out of the sky and yanking the Widow Miller away; flesh tearing as two creatures fought over a screaming man; the Clen-Father impaled on the Speaking Stone, a golden tusk through his throat. *You can have this,* Sordyr continued. *You can make this so.* Kara knew he was right. She could feel the words on her lips, begging to be used. *You are not like the others, Kara Westfall. Become the witch you were meant to be.* The head graycloak was only a few yards away now. He withdrew his ball-staff and raised it over his head.

Kara spoke. But it was not the words in her head.

"Shadowdancer," she whispered.

The mare appeared out of nothingness, and the graycloak's mount bucked in surprise, throwing its rider to the ground. Shadowdancer turned to Kara and snorted—*What have you gotten me into now?*—but bent forward so she could lift Taff onto her back. By this time the rocks had started again, but Kara pulled herself onto Shadowdancer and they were off, leaving the villagers behind in a blur of speed.

The graycloaks set off in pursuit.

Shadowdancer was faster, but these horses were ridden by trained men and had spent countless hours canvassing the trails of De'Noran. They knew the terrain. Eventually they would catch up. *Besides*, Kara told herself. *It's an island. There's nowhere to hide.*

Except for one place.

Once the other riders saw her change direction, they drove their mounts harder, intending to cut her off. Shadowdancer grunted with determination and pulled ahead. They dashed across the island in a blur of motion, but by the time they reached the Fringe, Shadowdancer had begun to stumble with exhaustion. A graycloak pulled to their side and raised his ball-staff, intending to knock Kara from her seat. *We're not going to make it*, she thought, but then she heard a sharp *crack* and a whinny of pain, followed by the solid impact of a body hitting the earth. Kara glanced behind her and saw weeds shoot out of the ground and trip up forelegs, low-slung branches grab riders as they passed.

The Fringe was helping them escape.

In front of her, the trees of the Thickety peeled open, revealing a space just large enough for a single horse and two riders. Shadowdancer hesitated, but Kara screamed, "Go!" and the mare galloped through the hole. Taff buried his face in Kara's arm and murmured something soft. "It's going to be all right," Kara said, but she didn't really believe it. She was suddenly struck by the suspicion that her entire life had led to this point, that everything— her mother's death, Grace, the grimoire—had been an elaborate web to trap her in this place.

What have I done? she thought, and then the branches closed behind them and all was dark.

Read on for a sneak peek of

ONE

Though she was only twelve years old, Kara Westfall had known many kinds of darkness. The smothering darkness of a potato sack as it knotted tightly over her head. Watery darkness so absolute she could lose herself in it. The darkness of temptation, blotting her mind with promises of power and revenge. All these darknesses, in their own specific ways, had left their imprint on her soul. They were all different. They were all the same.

She had never known darkness like this before.

After the branches closed behind them, Kara and Taff

were set adrift on an ocean of starless night. All was silent save the muted sound of horse's hooves against the soft surface of the Thickety.

Kara clung tightly to Shadowdancer's mane and closed her eyes, trusting the mare to guide them. She could do little else.

"They tried to kill us," Taff whispered in her ear. His breath was warm and came in quick, needy gasps; the air here was thin and strange. "Why didn't Father stop them?"

"That *thing* is not our father."

Kara felt his body tremble against her back.

"Our father is gone," she continued. "Grace used her Last Spell to change him. He is Timoth Clen now."

"*The* Timoth Clen? From the stories?"

Growing up they had been taught the legends. The Mighty Clen. Vanquisher of witches. Creator of the One True Path.

"Yes," Kara said.

"But that doesn't make any sense."

"*Magic* doesn't make any sense."

"Not that part. The part about Timoth Clen. Even if he was Father—even if he was *anyone*—he would never hurt us. He's *good*!"

"Maybe to some," she acknowledged. "Not to witches."

Kara thought she heard a sound in the darkness but it was only Taff shifting into a better position on Shadowdancer's back.

"Is Father dead? Dead forever? Or just gone?"

"I don't know."

"You'll bring him back."

"Taff."

"I've seen what you can do. You're a witch. A *good* witch. You'll cast a spell and fix this."

The hope in his voice was a dagger driven deep in her heart.

"My spellbook is gone," Kara said. "And even if I had it, I couldn't use it. It's not safe. You saw what happened to Grace."

"You're different."

"Not different enough."

"But there has to be something we can—"

"I'm not a witch anymore."

"But—"

"Shh," Kara said. "Let's just ride for a while."

Taff linked his hands around her waist and rested his head between her shoulder blades. "I hate magic," he murmured.

They journeyed deeper into the darkness of the Thickety. Kara wondered if they would ever see the light of day again.

When Taff began to snore, Kara smiled at her brother's ability to fall asleep and stroked the back of his hand, the skin as soft as chicken feathers. Although she would wish the boy to safety if she could, Kara was grateful for his presence.

The Thickety was no place to be alone.

Looking to either side she tried to distinguish any kind

of outline against the utter blackness. Some landmark, some hint of shape or form. Some . . . *something*. But in every direction stretched nothing but absolute darkness.

If this were the other part of the Thickety, she thought, remembering her first visit, *the webspinners might light a path to guide us. I could call them here, if I could still use magic.* But she couldn't, not anymore, and she felt its absence as keenly as a lost friend.

A light mist began to fall, tingling her cheeks. At least she wasn't cold. Though it was nearly winter in De'Noran, the temperature here was more like the sticky warmth of summer just after a thunderstorm. Sweat rolled down Kara's forehead and matted her clothes to her back.

The warmth, and Shadowdancer's steady cadence, allowed her mind to drift to the events preceding their flight to the Thickety. *Grace, dragged down into the impossible abyss of the grimoire. Lucas's face growing smaller as his ship disappeared into the distance. Rocks and pebbles buzzing past her head, the savage hatred of the villagers she had saved.*

And over it all, words spoken in her mind with the timbre of rustling leaves: *Your power cannot be bound in a book. You are not like the others, Kara Westfall.*

She awoke.

For a single, terrifying moment she was certain that Taff had fallen from the horse. Then the fog of sleep dissipated and Kara felt his comforting weight against her back.

This relief was short-lived, however, once she realized how difficult it was to breathe.

Kara's chest burned as she tried to suck stubborn air into her lungs, but she was limited to short, meager breaths, as though she were pulling air not from the outside world but the tiny opening of a reed whistle. Taff, who had been the picture of health since the Jabenhook rescued him from the brink of death, sounded even worse.

"Taff," Kara whispered, and even this tiny exhalation of air was difficult for her oxygen-deprived body. "Taff," she repeated. "You need . . . Wake up."

"I'm hungry," her brother muttered, still drowsy. But then he jolted upright in panic. "Can't . . . breathe."

"Shh," Kara said. "Shh. Don't talk. Save."

Although she couldn't see Taff nod in the darkness, Kara knew he understood. His heart, which had been pounding like a drum, settled into a less frantic rhythm.

"Air," Kara said. "Wrong."

On Kara's first journey into the Thickety, the air had been fine—better than De'Noran, actually. *But that was two hours south of here. Maybe the air is different in this part of the Thickety. Maybe it's not meant for people.* If that were the case, what should they do? She had no idea how many hours they had traveled. At the rate they were losing oxygen, turning back might be futile. Besides, even if she *wanted* to go back, she didn't know which way to turn. The darkness devoured all sense of direction.

She heard a sickly rumble and realized it was Shadowdancer's heaving chest, desperate for air. *How far has she carried us like this?* Kara thought, patting the mare's flank, longing to speak reassuring words but unwilling to spare the oxygen. Instead she slid off Shadowdancer's back to lighten her load.

The moment Kara's feet touched the surface, she knew that this section of the Thickety was even stranger than she thought.

The ground was moving.

This slow, steady motion had been easily masked when they were riding Shadowdancer, but there was no doubt about it now. Kara felt the ground and found that it was not dirt at all but something ridged and slippery and as smooth as skin. It tickled her fingertips as it passed, like a lily pad floating along a rolling stream.

Impenetrable darkness. Moving ground. Mist.

Kara remembered what Mother had taught her about certain Fringe weeds, and in her mind an impossible thought began to form—though surely she would have to reconsider the meaning of the word "impossible" in a forest capable of blotting out the sun.

If we're even in the forest at all.

She pulled Taff off the horse, her chest aching with the effort.

"Come," she said. "Hold hands. Don't . . . let go." She guided him through the darkness, Shadowdancer close behind.

"The ground," Taff said. "Do you feel—"

"Yes."

"What is this place?"

Kara longed to explain, but there wasn't enough time.

"Trap," she said.

The ground pulled them in a certain direction—she couldn't have even guessed which one—but Kara led Taff perpendicular to the moving surface. Each step was exhausting, like walking through water. No matter how deeply she inhaled, only a trickle of air wisped through her lips.

But when their progress was impeded by a wall-like structure, Kara's spirits lifted. *I was right!* she thought, and then chided herself for such overconfidence. They weren't out of this yet.

She put her ear to the wall's slippery surface and heard the muffled patter of raindrops outside.

"Help," Kara told Taff. She took him by the hands and guided them over the fleshy wall. "Feel . . . gap. Dig . . . fingers into it."

Taff squeezed his sister's hand to acknowledge that he understood.

They traced the wall with their fingertips, inspecting the slightly moist surface for openings. The search would have been more efficient if they parted ways, but Kara wouldn't risk sending Taff off on his own. Besides, she wasn't even sure this was going to work. *Just because I saw Mother do it in the Fringe doesn't mean anything here.* Kara ran her fingers across a particularly smooth patch and found her hand continuing to travel downward. It took a few moments for her to realize that she had fallen to the ground. She lay there, her breathing raspy and quiet, wondering why she wasn't getting to her feet. All she could do was listen to Taff's footsteps vanish into the darkness.

He thinks I'm still beside him, but he's all alone.

The world spun.

Taff screamed something in the distance, but though she heard the words Kara could not make out their meaning. She tried to take a breath so she could call out his name, but her lungs had finally closed up completely and the first wave of true panic hit her.

And then the ground dropped and Kara was sliding backward down a sudden slope. Cold rain pounded her face, and air, sweet air, filled her lungs. She heard Taff scream with exuberance. Turning her head she watched him tumble down what appeared to be a shiny green mountain, his hands held aloft as though this were some sort of festival ride.

A few moments later Kara was rolling across the soft soil of the Thickety. It was black and granular and nothing like the fertile soil of De'Noran, but it was still dirt and she had never been happier to feel it. Her breathing came free and easy.

High above, black treetops coiled together and swallowed the vast majority of late-afternoon sunlight, but errant beams speared the forest floor, providing Kara with just enough light to observe her surroundings.

Their former prison hung overhead, suspended by ocher vines. It resembled the type of Fringe weed Mother called a *tulinet*, except you could hold those in your hand and this was large enough to hold hundreds of people, its massive weight distributed among a perfect circle of trees. Black petals fitted together at its center, giving it a dome-like appearance similar to the frame-skirts some girls favored during Shadow Festival. The petal that had provided their escape route retracted into place like a giant tongue.

"What is it?" Taff asked. He stroked Shadowdancer, who looked quite put off by her sudden tumble but was otherwise uninjured.

"A gritchenlock, of course," said a female voice behind them.

Kara and Taff turned to face her.

The woman was as tall as Kara, which was very tall indeed, and wore a tattered cloak that had been patched together from different sources. Her hair was cut as short as a man's and stuck out in jagged clumps. Based on her dry, wrinkled skin and slightly stooped back, Kara put her at just north of seventy, but there was an ageless quality to her flinty eyes that spoke of lost kingdoms and forgotten lands.

Over her left shoulder drooped a simple rawhide sack. Whenever the woman moved, it rattled mysteriously, as though filled with marbles or shards of broken glass.

"Drink," the woman said, nodding to a nearby creek.

"Is it safe?" Kara asked.

The woman's eyes narrowed with amusement.

"As safe as it gets here," she said.

Before Kara could stop him, Taff was ankle-deep in the stream. He plunged his face beneath the water.

"It's delicious!" he shouted, coming up for air. He bent down to drink more, but Kara held him back.

"The water's *fine*, Kara," he insisted.

"You don't know that."

Cupping her hands, Kara took a hesitant sip, then a longer one. The water, cold and refreshing, soothed her parched throat. Though her body yearned for more, Kara stopped herself; she would give it time to settle first and see how her stomach reacted.

"How long have you been watching us?" Kara asked warily, leading Shadowdancer to the stream.

"Since the gritchenlock first snatched you up. I was waiting to see if you would live or die." She shrugged. "It passed the time."

"You could have helped us!" Taff exclaimed.

The woman shook her head. "Today is not a day for tree-climbing, I'm afraid. If you had caught me yesterday—well, that would have been a different story."

Taff put his hands on his hips. "That doesn't make any sense."

"And yet it's true," replied the woman. "Rather like a gritchenlock."

"That's nothing like a gritchenlock."

"Also true. How did you know you were inside one? Most just walk around in circles, all oblivious-like, until their air runs out and the digestive process begins. The spinning, you see. Makes the prey think it's still moving, when really it has not moved at all." The woman clucked with appreciation. "Rather clever."

"It's terrible," said Kara.

"No," said the woman. "Not terrible at all. Most of the gritchenlock's victims die in their sleep. In the Thickety, that passes for kindness."